The flashing blue lights  her bones. From here, it looked ███ Her only driver's license was for R███████, who was now a fugitive. It was too late to turn around without being seen, and already, three more cars had lined up behind her.

Ruth's knee bounced uncontrollably as she inched forward and saw with relief that the commotion wasn't a checkpoint after all. Apparently, it was just a minor accident of some sort, because there were yellow lights from a wrecker on the other side of the road. As she drew closer, she followed the patrolman's direction to keep right, finally seeing what all the activity was about. Two uniformed officers were guiding a red motorcycle down the embankment. Parked behind the wrecker was a black sedan with government plates.

So they found Spencer's bike.

With a sick feeling in the pit of her stomach, Ruth realized that the woman she had dropped off was at this very moment walking right into the hands of her pursuers, as a man wearing a suit and a dark-colored raincoat was starting up the bank toward the woods. He had been standing in front of the government car when she approached, and it suddenly occurred to her that this might even be one of the men who Spencer said wanted her dead. But surely the Manassas police were all over the scene and they would keep her safe, and Spencer could explain what happened.

But what if everything that Spencer had said was true? She might never have a chance to tell her story. She might be whisked away in the black sedan and killed in their custody. They would just say she tried to escape or something. It's not like it hadn't ever happened before. Suddenly Ruth felt as though she held the woman's fate in her hands.

Visit

Bella Books

at

BellaBooks.com

or call our toll-free number

1-800-729-4992

MALICIOUS PURSUIT

KG MacGregor

Bella
BOOKS

2007

Bella Books, Inc.
P.O. Box 10543
Tallahassee, FL 32302

First Printing Cavalier Press 2004
Second Printing Bookends Press 2005
First Bella Books Edition 2007

Printed in the United States of America on acid-free paper
First Edition

Editor: Kay Porter
Cover designer: Stephanie Solomon-Lopez

ISBN-10: 1-59493-118-6
ISBN-13: 978-1-59493-118-5

This book I dedicate to Tami, whose steadfast excitement
about my stories has made writing a joy.

Acknowledgments

There is a great deal of technical information in this book about which I know very little in a practical sense. Thank goodness for all my smart friends: Tami, AK, and T. Novan. They saved me from myself with their guidance about computers, programming and police protocols.

Thanks also to Kay Porter, my editor. I vote we change the phrase "the patience of Job" to "the patience of Kay."

About the Author

Growing up in the mountains of North Carolina, KG MacGregor dreaded the summer influx of snowbirds escaping the Florida heat. The lines were longer, the traffic snarled and the prices higher. Now that she's older and slightly more patient, she divides her time between Miami and Blowing Rock. A former teacher, KG earned her PhD in mass communication and her writing stripes preparing market research reports for commercial clients in the publishing, television and travel industries. In 2002, she tried her hand at lesbian fiction and discovered her bliss. When she isn't writing, you'll probably find her on a hiking trail.

Chapter 1

"Five . . . ten . . . fifteen . . . twenty . . ." Ruth Ferguson mumbled to herself as she counted the nickels from her drawer. With a quick tap to the calculator, she scooped the change into its tube and continued with the pennies. If there were twenty-six, her drawer balanced for the forty-third day in a row. "Twenty-four . . . twenty-five . . . bang!"

"Again?" Arlene Jones was envious of her coworker's streak, though she was seldom off in her own drawer. "How do you do that?"

"How does anyone explain perfection?" Ruth teased. She had always been meticulous when it came to her cash drawer, but she had been extra careful today. It was Friday—and her weekend to have custody of her daughter—so she wasn't interested in hanging around the bank to reconcile her balance sheet.

"Congratulations! And the grand prize is you get to keep your job another week," Sharon Petrie joked. She supervised the tellers at the Bank of Madison and loved the fact that Ruth kept the pressure on all of them.

"Lucky me," the blond woman answered with playful cynicism, shouldering her purse as she readied to leave.

"You got Jessie this weekend?" Arlene asked.

"Yeah, I'm headed to pick her up right now."

"Any big plans?"

"No, we'll probably just hang out at the house and play. This rain's supposed to be around all weekend."

"Well, you two have fun."

"Thanks. Good night." Ruth stopped at the door and took one last look back. She liked working here. The work was fun because her customers were so nice and some of the people she worked with had shown themselves to be true friends throughout her ordeal of the past year. Arlene especially had come through for her, lending a shoulder or an ear and often including Ruth in her weekend plans when Jessie was with her father. "Arlene?"

"Yeah?" The teller looked up at her friend.

"I hope you have a good weekend too."

Arlene smiled. "Thanks, hon."

Ruth tightened the sash on her raincoat while the security guard unlocked the back door. "Goodnight, Roger."

The November wind had torn the last of the leaves from the trees. Now it was serving final notice that the cold Maine winter was ahead. Ruth hurried across the parking lot in the drizzle, pulling up her collar to ward off the chill. The days were getting shorter now and it was dark already by five thirty. A tap on the keyfob inside her pocket unlocked the door and caused the lights to flash on her black Saturn coupe. Shivering, she got into the car and started the engine. By the clock on the dashboard, she would be early.

As usual, Skip would be late.

"A kid's meal, please. With an orange drink and a . . . chicken sandwich with a cup of coffee." Ruth placed her order at the busy fast food restaurant, her regular dining establishment every other Friday when she met Skip Drummond to pick up their four-year-old daughter. Her ex-husband was better behaved in public places, so the restaurant was mandated in the court order to host the exchange.

Ruth hated it when her ex-husband came to her house and she had managed to get this one small concession by pressing the social worker who monitored her visits. *Monitored her visits.* That thought caused the young mother to shake her head in disbelief. It was beyond Ruth's comprehension that things had fallen this way. But she had her daughter for two full weekends a month, and she wasn't going to look that gift horse in the mouth.

The pickup truck pulled onto the lot at six twenty. She knew it was Skip by the obnoxious fog lights positioned on top of the cab. Knowing him, he had driven by the place at five till six on the off chance of getting there before she did so he could raise hell about her being late. But Skip and his bullying demeanor wouldn't matter to her in about two minutes once he delivered their precious little girl. Then he could go fuck himself.

"Mommy!"

"Jessie!" Ruth knelt down to catch the running child in a fierce welcome that made her eyes sting with tears. She steeled herself against the image of the tall booted man who followed carrying a colorful backpack. At six-foot-six, Skip Drummond cut a handsome figure in his faded jeans and white shirt. Though he was only twenty-nine, his sandy hair was thinning already, but it was nothing a Red Sox cap couldn't hide.

"Well, she's your headache for the next forty-eight hours," he muttered low so no one around them would hear.

Ruth ignored him. "How are you, sweetie?"

"Fine." Jessie was the spitting image of her mother: blond hair, slightly built and with expressive green eyes. Eyeing the kid's meal already spread out for her, she climbed eagerly into the booth and began to munch on a fry.

"Jessie, what happened to your arm?" Ruth felt her blood run cold when she saw the bruise on her daughter's forearm as she pulled off her coat. Angrily, she glared at her ex-husband in accusation.

"Tell her."

"I fell."

Ruth didn't believe it for a minute. Skip knew it and didn't care. "She's got one on her butt, too. She's pretty clumsy." He dropped the backpack with a thump as he turned to walk out. "See you on Sunday. Don't be late," he taunted.

That son of a bitch! How could he hurt his own daughter like that?

Ruth took three or four breaths before sitting down with her child. It was important never to cloud their time together with the specter of Skip Drummond, and in ten seconds he would no longer exist in her mind.

"So, what did you bring in your backpack, honey?"

"Just a shirt . . . and pants . . . and socks."

"Who packed it for you?"

"Grandma."

That was good to hear. When Skip packed, he usually "forgot" things that he knew Ruth would have to go purchase on her meager salary. As it was, Jessie already had nightclothes, a toothbrush, underwear, and several changes of clothing at her mother's small house. At least she was wearing her heaviest coat, Ruth noted with relief.

"Where's Lisa?" Lisa was Jessie's favorite doll, a lifelike infant in a diaper and terry sleeper.

"Grandma said I had to leave her there 'cause she'd get dirty at your house," the child answered innocently.

Ruth took another calming breath as she processed this tidbit.

4

Barbara Drummond, her former mother-in-law, was a sour woman—which sure explained what made Skip a genuine son of a bitch. From the day she and Skip were wed, Barbara had never missed an opportunity to put down her daughter-in-law. Why she had ever agreed to keep Jessie during the day was a mystery, since she resented the child's very existence.

"Do you want ketchup?" Jessie had stopped eating her fries.

"Uh-huh," the little girl nodded vigorously. "Can we go out to the slide when I get finished?"

"Not tonight. It's raining a little and we really need to get home soon."

"Why?"

"Somebody's coming to see me. He'll only be there for a minute, but I need to be sure we're home when he comes."

"Who is it?"

"His name's Dennis. I don't think you know him."

"Why is he coming?"

Jessie was world class in the question-asking department. Ruth tried very hard to be patient with her because she knew that Skip probably never answered anything.

"He's coming to pick up something."

"What?"

"You'll see. Eat some more of your cheeseburger." Ruth forced herself to take another bite of the chicken sandwich. She had lost her appetite after the encounter with Skip but knew she needed to eat. It was going to be a long night.

Ruth pulled into the driveway of her small rented house, suddenly anxious about the impending visitor. Guiding her child up the back steps, she fumbled with the key and pushed open the back door.

"It looks different," Jessie announced, looking from one side of the room to the other. "I know. You took my pictures down!"

She pointed to the refrigerator where Ruth had proudly displayed Jessie's art work, not only as a reward to her daughter, but as a bright reminder of all that was good in Ruth's life.

"I put them in a box, sweetie. I've put all of our important things in a box."

That sent Jessie running to the closet in the hallway where she always kept her toys and games. They were gone. "Where's the box?"

"I'll show it to you later, honey. I need to change my clothes before Dennis gets here. You want to come into the bedroom?" On their weekends together, they barely spent a moment apart.

Jessie came in to bounce on the bed and chatter as she watched her mom change. Earlier, Ruth had laid out jeans, a pullover, socks and tennis shoes, so she dressed very quickly. When she was finished, she hung her dress on a hanger, draped it across the bed and rolled her shoes and stockings inside her slip.

A sharp knock on the front door interrupted Jessie's story of what her Lisa doll had done that day.

"That's probably Dennis, honey. I need to go outside with him for a few minutes. Can you stay in here? Please?"

The four-year-old didn't want to do that and she shook her head no.

"Jessie, please? When I'm finished, we're going to put our coats back on and go somewhere. Okay?"

"Where?"

"You'll see." Ruth had used that answer already and didn't want to put her daughter off any more than she had to, but there wasn't time now for explanations. "Just please stay in here."

Flipping on the front porch light, she swung the door open wide to find a young man in pressed slacks and a fleece pullover. "Are you Ruth Ferguson?"

"Yes. Are you Dennis?"

"That's me! I thought for a minute I had the wrong house."

He turned to wave to the driver who had dropped him off. In response, the driver turned off the car's engine and headlights.

"I'm sorry. I just got home a few minutes ago. I should have turned the light on for you."

Dennis held out an envelope. "Mr. Huggins said for me to give you this." Dick Huggins owned a used car dealership in Farmington about twenty miles away. Ruth had stopped in on Wednesday night to see what they would give her in a cash deal for the four-year-old coupe.

"Thank you." Ruth quickly opened it and counted out sixty-five one hundred dollar bills. "Yes, that's right. It's right out here." She grabbed her keys from the table and clicked the fob to turn on the interior lights of the Saturn as they walked outside. "I have a screwdriver in the glove compartment. The title's there too, if you want to fill out the mileage. I just need to sign it."

"Why don't you fill all that out while I take the tags off?" he offered, holding up his dealer tag. In just a few moments, Dennis was trading the plates for two sets of keys. "Thank you very much, ma'am. You buying a new car?"

"Yeah, I'll go looking with a friend tomorrow."

"Good luck finding what you need."

"Thank you, and thanks for coming to pick it up." Her plan was now irrevocably in motion.

"No problem."

Ruth stood and watched the two cars back out, glancing across the street and to either side to see if the activity had drawn anyone's attention. This continuing drizzle was a nice cover for her clandestine moves tonight. No lights had come on outside, and no one appeared to be coming or going at any of the houses, so she had every reason to believe that this part of her plan had gone off unnoticed.

"Jessie?" Ruth returned to the bedroom to find her daughter looking in the empty closet.

"Where's your clothes, Mommy?"

"Jessie, listen. You know how I always try hard to answer your questions so you'll understand things?"

The little girl nodded.

"Tonight, I need for you just to trust me. I won't be able to answer a lot of your questions right now, but I will soon. I promise. Can you trust me tonight and try not to ask so many questions right now?"

Jessie agreed hurriedly. She didn't want to see her mother get mad the way her father did when she asked too many questions.

"Okay, I need you to go put your coat back on. We're going to take a short walk to where I parked our new car." Ruth slid the license plates and screwdriver into her daughter's backpack along with her rolled-up slip and shoes.

"We have a new car?" Jessie asked with excitement.

"Yes, we do."

"What color is it?"

"Sweetie, remember what I asked you to do. No more questions right now, okay?"

"Okay." But Jessie couldn't help herself. "Are my toys in the car?"

"Yes, honey. It has all of our stuff in it already, as much as I could fit. I got all of your toys and games, and all of your clothes." As she was talking, she helped Jessie zip the pink coat that she had bought just a little large a few weeks ago. "Can you carry this?" She handed her daughter the booster seat from the Saturn.

Jessie nodded and hugged the lightweight cushion to her chest.

"Now when we go out, I need you to be very quiet, okay?"

"Okay." The four-year-old made a motion of buttoning her lip.

"That's right. Until we get in our new car, I don't want you to say anything, starting right . . . now!" Ruth picked up the dress from the bed, the child's backpack, and her own purse and raincoat. Leaving the light on in the kitchen, they walked out onto the back porch where Ruth turned to lock the door.

Juggling her load, she dropped one hand to grasp the hand of her daughter and they walked soundlessly across their own back yard, and then through that of the neighbor behind them. Stopping by the thick shrubbery next to the house, Ruth scouted the street for traffic or for people out walking in the persistent drizzle. Seeing neither, she led Jessie into the front yard and onto the sidewalk, where they turned and walked half a block toward a line of parked cars. Reaching the third, a dark red Taurus station wagon, she unlocked the door and positioned the booster cushion on the passenger side of the front seat. She helped the small child into the car, leaning across to fasten the safety belt as she shoved the things she was carrying into the cargo area behind Jessie. Quietly, she closed the door and hurried to the street side, where she slipped in and slid the key into the ignition.

"You okay, honey?"

"Is this our new car?"

"Yes, it is."

"I like red."

In minutes, Ruth was headed toward the outskirts of town, where she pulled into a strip mall and parked next to the large blue box for outgoing mail.

"What are we going here for?"

"We're not, honey. I just need to stop for a minute. I have to do a couple of things, but I'll leave the heater on so you won't be cold," she explained.

Ruth got out with her screwdriver and fastened the plates to the front and back mounts, wadding up the "Lost Tag" sign she had made for the Taurus. Next, she grabbed a small bundle of envelopes from her purse, including one that wasn't yet sealed.

She dropped her house key into that one, inside a folded thank-you note she had written last night. In her apology for the late notice, she gave her landlord permission to keep the two hundred dollar security deposit for the furnished house and wished him luck finding a new renter.

The other letters were mostly bills, each containing just a little extra to cover any additional charges since her last statement and a note with instructions to close her account. Only one note was personal, the one to the bank where she had worked for most of the last seven years.

The mail from the drop box wouldn't be picked up until Saturday afternoon, meaning the local letters wouldn't be delivered until sometime on Monday. By then, most people would already know that she was gone. This would confirm that she had planned it that way, and that she had not met with any sort of foul play. She hoped her friends wouldn't worry and she couldn't care less how Skip took the news.

Chapter 2

"I think you ought to call her." Spencer Rollins scooted across the small office in her swivel chair, a move that intimidated the man almost more than the thought of making a date.

"And I think you're insane."

"Aw, come on! How are you going to get a date if you don't ever ask anyone out?"

Henry scoffed at his coworker, though he appreciated her encouragement more than he could ever say. Spencer was quite simply the best friend he had ever had.

"You like her, don't you?" Spencer continued to prod him.

"Yes," he answered meekly.

"And she waved you over to her table at lunch. I'm telling you, Henry, she likes you too."

On the surface, Henry agreed with his friend's assessment. Kim from payroll had been very nice and it seemed that she was going out of her way to be friendly. But the young man's confidence fell short when it came to personal relationships. At twenty-six years old, he could count on one hand the total number of dates he had ever had.

"Maybe just a movie or something, you know, something casual," Spencer encouraged. Guys as nice as Henry Estes were rare, she thought, but few women were willing to see past the snow-white hair, red eyes, and chalky skin. In the spirit of political correctness, he called himself "pigment challenged." But Henry was her kind of guy—smart, funny and decent—except that guys weren't her thing.

She and Henry had worked together as programming partners for six years, the last four at Margadon Industries, where they had applied as a team when their former company went under. Headquartered amidst several industry giants in Rockville, Maryland, Margadon was a leading manufacturer of pharmaceuticals.

"Here comes another one. Only three to go." Henry logged the report and sent it to the queue for processing.

Each Friday between five and six o'clock Eastern Time, product managers from the Margadon plants submitted final inventory figures for the week. The complex system that Spencer and Henry had designed tracked not only production, but also materials, thereby automating the inventory control and accountability. Tracking inventory was a continuous process, as each new unit of materials was earmarked to a specific product and to a unique lot number. Should quality control issues arise, line producers could easily isolate the affected shipment. Another benefit of their system was that supplies and materials were automatically reordered as they were consumed, assuring uninterrupted production.

The product managers at each of the Margadon plants, which were scattered throughout the country and abroad, were required to constantly monitor the inventory for their line of pharmaceuticals. But senior managers in Rockville couldn't absorb that level of detail, so the Friday reports formed the basis for the executive summary that was sent to management each week. Spencer and Henry had even automated the production of the summary report so that it would be processed over the weekend and available first thing Monday morning.

"What are we missing?"

"Let's see . . . we're missing the Dolicaine . . . the Kryfex . . . and the—wait. Here comes the Dolicaine now. And the Topectol. So it's just the Kryfex."

Kryfex was Margadon's new wonder drug for the Dawa virus, an autoimmune disease that was prevalent throughout eastern Africa. Last spring the company had won a massive government contract to distribute the drug through diplomatic and humanitarian channels in Ethiopia. In return, the United States military was given permission to locate a permanent air base in the northeastern part of that African country, an area essential to operations in the Middle East.

The Kryfex account was by far Margadon's largest and most profitable contract. The terms guaranteed payment for a minimum of ten years, even if the virus was defeated.

"Come on, guys! Find your butts and get them in gear." Spencer was growing impatient at having to wait for the final report. She had a party on tap tonight and had promised Elena she would try to get there early to help set up.

"Why don't you go on? I'll wait," Henry offered.

"Nah, then I'd owe you, and you'd ask to borrow my bike."

Henry chuckled. "Fat chance." He had no interest at all in borrowing the big Kawasaki. It was all he could do to get on behind Spencer just to go to lunch.

Twisting in their chairs, they chatted another ten minutes as they waited for the last report from the plant outside of Little Rock. "I think I'll give 'em a call," Henry finally said.

As if on cue, the phone rang and Spencer lunged to grab it

first. "Margadon, Spencer Rollins . . . Oh, no wonder." Holding the phone aside, she explained the holdup to Henry. "It's Tim Wall in Little Rock. He said somebody dropped the barcode reader and they didn't have another one that worked. They had to do it all by hand."

"Do they have the numbers?"

"Yeah, he's going to read them off. I'll pull up the screen." With a few short keystrokes, Spencer accessed the Kryfex form. "Okay, Tim. Go ahead."

One by one, Spencer entered the numbers into the corresponding fields, watching as the "Cost" columns filled automatically. That was the beauty of a well-written program, she thought, mentally congratulating herself and her partner. The final report would show the week's production of Kryfex, its expenditure of resources, and its corresponding cost and net for the company. Only a handful of people at Margadon got to see these production figures and it was rare that Spencer or Henry did. When the data were uploaded from the barcode readers, the reports generated automatically and went directly to their boss, James Thayer, the company's controller. He would then route them for distribution to company executives.

Spencer and Henry figured out when they were writing and testing the code that they could just about deduce the chemical formulas for nearly every product on Margadon's shelf using only the gross quantities of ingredients and the size of shipments. As the dock manager read off the figures, Spencer found herself playing the game in her head, trying to guess the number in advance, knowing approximately how much of each component would be used for the week's total. She was close on each part until they got to the cytokines, which were the active proteins used in Kryfex. By the quantities already listed in the report, she expected a larger number than the one Tim supplied.

"Wait a minute. Let me have the cytokines again." She backspaced to clear the field and waited for Tim to find his place again on his sheet.

He repeated the number and she verified it. "Does that sound right to you, Tim?"

He had no idea, he said. Clearly, Tim didn't play these formula games in his head. His job was to get the shipments in one door and out the other.

"Okay, go ahead." Spencer tabbed to the next field and the most amazing thing happened.

"What the fuck? Sorry, Tim . . . Hold on." Spencer backed up again to the cytokines field and hit the delete key. "Something's wrong here. Give it to me one more time." She jotted the number on a yellow legal pad and read it back.

Her obvious confusion got Henry's attention and he quickly came to stand behind his partner. He watched as she entered the number and tabbed to the next field. Both were shocked to see the number change.

"Did you guys switch suppliers on the cytokines? Or did they change the packaging or something?"

No, nothing had changed as far as he knew. He finished his list and Spencer finally let him go.

"Something's fucked here, Henry."

"Cool! I was looking for something to do this weekend," he joked.

"I mean really fucked. If this is doing what I think it's doing, we may be looking for new jobs next week."

Spencer re-entered the numbers and watched as both the quantity and cost columns for the cytokines inflated when she moved to the next field. "That's how many I think there should be, but that's not what he said they used. Either way, somebody had to write something in our code to get that number to change all by itself." With that thought, she was pissed. It wasn't cool to patch someone else's program when the original programmer was still available to do it.

"Pull up the code," Henry suggested, wheeling his chair close to hers.

She did and they pored over what would be gibberish to most but to them was a source of immense pride. Line by line, they studied the program. Nothing in their code explained the adjustment on the data sheet.

"Look at Alvadin. It's set up the same way," she said.

Henry slid back to his terminal, called up the weekly report for Margadon's protease inhibitor, and studied the field calculations. "This one's okay. See the cytokines?" He deleted the field and re-entered. "They stay the same."

"So what the fuck's going on with Kryfex?" Spencer scrolled down to the bottom of the program to see if any comments were written to denote changes, though she didn't expect to find any.

"You sure are saying 'fuck' a lot." It was an observation, not a criticism.

"That's because I'm pissed."

"Okay, I don't know what's doing that. We didn't write it. Unless . . ."

"Unless it's calling a different module." Modules were application programs—lines and lines of syntax that caused a program to do what it was supposed to do.

"Exactly."

Henry opened the global file, the one they applied to all of the uploaded data in order to generate the weekly reports. Without this master program of macros and loops, they would have to repeat procedures for each product manufactured by Margadon. Using the global file, they could execute all the reports with a single command. "It's calling the right module."

"Then where the hell is the new number coming from?" Spencer used the calculator on her partner's desk to compute the number change for the cytokines in Kryfex. The altered figure was one-fourth higher than the one she had entered. "Okay, watch this."

She entered 80 and hit the tab. The number changed to 100,

and its cost increased by the same percentage. Then she entered 100. It changed to 125. "Somebody's fucked with it."

"Tell you what," Henry offered, "why don't you let me look at this? You're going to be late for your party."

"I can't just leave you with this mess." Spencer knew it could take hours, maybe even days, to track down a problem like this and fix it. On the other hand, Henry was the smartest programmer she knew—though she wasn't about to give her friend the satisfaction of knowing that—so he might find the glitch and have it fixed in no time.

"I don't mind. It'll be fun. Besides, if you're late, Elena will think it's my fault and kick my ass."

"I don't know why you're so afraid of her. She's only this high." Spencer stood up and held out her hand shoulder high, gradually moving it upward until it passed her own five-foot, ten-inch frame.

"Yeah, and not only is she taller than you, she carries a gun."

"That's just to pick up chicks."

Henry laughed. "Go on. I'll work on this and park whatever I find on the server so you can look at it over the weekend."

The two had set up their own server years ago in Vienna when they took on a small contract for after-hours. Last year, when Margadon implemented a new policy restricting file access to the local area network, they had gotten into the habit of parking bits of code on their server so they could work on things from home. The company would have a fit if they ever found out, but no one at Margadon knew of the server except Henry and Spencer. Besides, programmers were notorious rule breakers.

She looked over his shoulder at the code. "If somebody did this on purpose, it's really going to piss me off, Henry!"

"Fuggedabouddit! Go have fun. If it's really that bad, it'll still be here on Monday."

Spencer picked up the black helmet beside her desk and

grabbed her leather jacket and gloves. "Okay, but call me if you need me."

"I will. Tell Elena I said hi."

"Thanks, pal. I'll tell her."

Spencer bounded down the steps of the fire escape and exited through the back door to the employee lot. Most of the staff had gone home already, and her red Kawasaki 650 stood alone in a corner space where it usually sat alongside two Harleys. On occasion she would arrive or leave at the same time as the others and would have to endure their ridicule over her ride. But Spencer liked the feel of the Kawasaki, and the brand would always be her sentimental favorite because it was the kind of bike her father had ridden. It was also the first one he had bought for her.

She had taken up motorcycles at twelve when her father began taking her to dirt trails where youngsters could ride. When she was old enough to get her license, she got a bigger bike, and they took trips to the mountains and coast, detouring off the roadways whenever they could for a more rugged ride.

With rain and a cold snap in the forecast for tomorrow, tonight would probably be Spencer's last ride before parking the beast on the patio of her garden apartment and covering it for the winter. Next week, she would be sitting in a long line of commuters in the car she had picked up several years ago as her "basic transportation." The jibes she got for the Kawasaki were nothing compared to those for her Chevy Cavalier.

Spencer's best bet for getting to Alexandria in rush hour traffic was to hop on the George Washington Memorial Parkway, as most of the commuters would be pushing their way out of the city in the opposite direction. In just under an hour, she was squeezing the bike between two cars parked in front of her friend's townhouse.

"Agent Diaz?" she called playfully, letting herself into the foyer.

"Thank God you're here," a woman's voice called from the kitchen. "I've got six bags of ice melting in the trunk of my car. Will you bring them in and take them out to the back porch? The keys are by the door."

Without taking another step forward, Spencer dropped her helmet and gloves in the coat closet, grabbed the car keys and headed back out and down the steps. Making oneself at home had a whole new connotation at Elena's house. Clutching a ten-pound bag of ice in each hand, she made the first of three trips up the stairs and through the kitchen, stopping to greet her former lover with a quick kiss on the lips.

Women and men alike admired the beauty and charms of Elena Diaz, an IRS criminal investigator whose wide brown eyes could slay from across the room. Spencer knew from experience what it felt like to have those eyes on her, and for a very brief time, she thought that she might be just the one to tame this beautiful creature. But it wasn't to be.

"You only invited me for the heavy lifting, didn't you?"

"Don't be ridiculous. You're here in case I get dumped by my date."

"*Serpiente.*" Even before they became lovers, Spencer learned of Elena's love 'em and leave 'em reputation, and dubbed her The Snake. The IRS agent had insisted that the Spanish word was much more exotic, so it became her moniker.

Spencer tossed the two bags into the large cooler and returned to the kitchen, this time wrapping her arms around the taller woman from behind. Elena was one of her favorite people in the universe, someone Spencer trusted with her life and limb, but not with her heart. The word "monogamous" just wasn't in the Latin woman's vocabulary.

"Kelly asked a few of her friends over," the agent said. Kelly was Elena's Woman of the Month.

19

"You mean there'll be people here you haven't slept with already?"

"There are always a few, Spencer."

With a snort, Spencer bounded out the front door again for a second load, then a third, finally stopping in the kitchen to await her next orders.

Elena stopped her preparations to address her friend. "I was just thinking that if one of Kelly's friends turned out to be cute, you might be able to turn on that charm of yours and get lucky tonight."

"God, it's been so long since I've been lucky, I wouldn't know which end to fuck."

"Now that's exactly the charm I'm talking about!" Despite herself, Elena laughed at the crude remark. "Just keep talking like that and you won't have anything to worry about."

In the deep recesses of her heart, Elena knew that one day she would regret not accepting the simple gift of love that Spencer had offered her seven years ago. Like all of the other relationships in her life, she and Spencer had started out as passionate lovers, getting to know each other as more of an afterthought to their sexual adventures. But the more they talked about their lives, their interests and their values, the closer they drew—until one day when Spencer had uttered the words that gave a name to what they had together.

"I love you."

"You shouldn't say that, you know."

"I can't help it." Twisting in the bed, Spencer rolled on top of her naked lover and pinned her in place. "And I don't want to share you anymore."

Elena reached up and pulled her down, tucking her dark head to the side so she wouldn't have to look into the insistent blue eyes. "You know I'm no good at that kind of stuff, Spence."

Elena could give her heart easily to the likes of Spencer, but she knew herself well enough to know that sooner or later, another pretty lady would turn her head. She wouldn't risk hurting someone she loved by making promises she couldn't keep.

With the realization that they couldn't go forward, Spencer had taken the painful step to end what they had. She wanted more out of love than Elena could offer and she couldn't ask Elena to be someone she wasn't. In the end, they had forged an unbreakable bond of friendship and trust, finally getting past the lustful pull.

It was hard, though, for each woman not to wonder what would happen if the door between them were to open again.

Chapter 3

REDUCED SPEED AHEAD.

It seemed like every time Ruth started to gather speed on the outskirts of a small town, another sign would appear to announce the next wide spot in the road. She would make much better time on the interstate, but the back roads were necessary for staying out of sight. Practically all of the major highways running through New England were toll roads, and that meant stopping, being seen and—worst of all—being caught on a surveillance camera. Once the authorities realized she was gone, that was probably the first place they would look. If her face were recognized on one of the toll booth tapes, they would know what kind of car to look for, and then it would be only a matter of time before she was caught.

The child beside her was asleep, her head on a soft pillow and a light blanket pulled up to her chin. They had laughed and sung until almost ten o'clock, when Ruth could hear the tired lilt in Jessie's voice. Even with the back seat folded down to make room for all of their things, the passenger seat reclined a little, and leaning it back had been the impetus for the little girl to finally fall asleep.

The way Ruth looked at it, she and Jessie probably had a two-day head start. With the rainy weather keeping everyone indoors back in Madison, no one was going to miss them until Sunday night at six, when she was due back at the restaurant to turn her daughter back over to Skip. Two days was enough to get away.

Welcome to Sturbridge, Massachusetts!

At last, Ruth could pull onto an interstate without worrying about tolls. From what she could tell from the map, I-84 would take her across Connecticut and the corner of New York into Pennsylvania, where she could pick up something going south. She hadn't quite worked out where they were headed, assuming that if she didn't know, no one else would be able to figure it out either.

All Ruth knew for sure was that she wanted to start a new life far away from Madison, Maine. She wanted her daughter to have a happy childhood and to be safe from her father's bouts of rage. Ruth tossed her head in disgust at that thought. Skip had always been angry when things didn't go exactly his way. It was as if no one could please him.

But Ruth couldn't lay all the blame for this mess at her ex-husband's feet. No, she had to own up to her own mistakes, of which she had made plenty.

Her parents, Roy and Mildred Ferguson, were not well off by anyone's standards, but the family had always gotten by. Roy had worked his whole life at the paper mill, bringing home a check just big enough to cover their bills but not to provide many extras. Still, her mother had been resourceful, making many of their clothes at home and finding ways to save for coats and shoes or something new for the house.

They were a close-knit family, something her father had insisted on. Ruth, named for the faithful Biblical figure, was expected to spend most of her free time at home, even when her high school friends begged her to come along to football games or parties. Roy and Mildred were strict, guarding Ruth's virtue by refusing her permission to go out with boys until she reached the age of seventeen. Even then, the young men who took her out were scrutinized and given a set of rigid rules.

Her parents were angry and dismayed when, soon after Ruth graduated high school, she moved out into her own small apartment, taking a clerical job at the Bank of Madison. The division deepened when it became obvious that she had abandoned the lessons of her upbringing by going out to dance clubs and bars in Augusta with her new friends and coworkers.

Skip was her only real boyfriend of any duration. After just a few dates, they "went all the way," Ruth's first time. That seemed to solidify their relationship, and Ruth began to think of them as a couple, as did their friends. Skip's family owned the area's biggest home appliance and electronics store, thus his future was carved out in retail before he was even born. Four years ahead of Ruth in school, the twenty-four-year-old was considered quite a catch in the small town. He was good-looking and popular. He played in all the sports leagues at the recreation center. He also liked to go out and have a good time.

They had been dating for about six months when Ruth made her first real mistake. She got pregnant. Though she had been faithful with her diaphragm, the doctor had told her it would be more effective if her partner used condoms as well, but Skip wasn't about to do that. After all, he had argued, he wasn't the one at risk of getting knocked up.

So there she was, ten weeks along with a boyfriend who was furious and parents who were inconsolable. But Ruth wanted to have this baby and raise it, no matter what anybody said or thought. The only other person who seemed to like the idea was

Skip's father, Roland Drummond, Sr., for whom Skip was named. It was time, Roland thought, for Skip to settle down if he was to be entrusted with more responsibility at the store. A wife and a child on the way might do that, he thought, so he encouraged the couple to get married. To sweeten the pot, he offered his son a raise and a manager's post at the store, both conditional on his becoming a family man.

Accepting a marriage proposal that had been coerced in the first place was what Ruth considered her second mistake. Even as she and Skip sat in the car after they agreed to go through with it, there was no joy, no anticipation, nor even resolve. Instead, there was just a shared sense of resignation that they had both lost control of their lives. Looking back, she should have just—

The little girl shifted in the seat beside her, bringing Ruth back to the present. Almost an hour had passed since she had pulled onto the interstate, and she was making pretty good time. There wasn't much traffic, as the steady rain kept people off the roads. She couldn't resist reaching over to caress Jessie's cheek. Despite the seriousness of running away with her daughter, she felt almost giddy about the freedom that lay ahead. Tonight, they were leaving behind not only Skip and his cold, overbearing parents, but Ruth's parents as well. All she and Jessie needed was each other.

Living with Skip had been difficult right from the beginning. There was hardly a day that went by that he didn't make known his resentment about the trap his father had laid for his life. But everything that bothered Ruth about her new role as Skip's wife vanished when Jessie Riane Drummond was born. Becoming a mother was simply the greatest thing she had ever done. For the first time in her life, Ruth really liked herself. She was proud of the way she took care of her daughter, and excited about spending time with other young mothers and learning the best ways to do things. Best of all, she was starting to feel like the events of the last year and a half—getting pregnant and getting married—

weren't at all the trap she thought they would be. Skip liked showing Jessie off to his family and friends, carrying her proudly everywhere they went. He didn't help much with taking care of their daughter at home, but Ruth wrote that off to Skip being the typical husband her friends had described.

It wasn't until Jessie started teething that Ruth really started to understand how Skip felt about their daughter.

"Will you shut her the fuck up!"

Ruth practically leapt out of bed to go see about Jessie in the night. Picking up the child from her crib, she shushed her to calm her down. It always comforted the baby to be held, even though her mouth still hurt.

Skip was growing increasingly agitated by Jessie's everyday behavior, none of which was out of the ordinary for a ten-month-old. He complained about her crying and hated having baby things in every room. He even ridiculed her in her high chair for having baby food on her chin and hands. Not that Jessie could understand his cruel words, but it hurt Ruth badly to hear her husband speak to their daughter that way, and she asked him to stop.

"Fine! I don't have to talk to her at all, do I?"

"She can't help the things she does any more than you could when you were a year old. Why can't you get it through your head that she's just a baby?" Ruth always jumped to her daughter's defense, but the yelling obviously upset the child, and she started to cry. That made her husband shout even louder.

"Because I never wanted a baby, and I've got news for you, Ruth. I never wanted you either."

"Then why did you get married, Skip? Why didn't you just let me have Jessie all by myself? You think I needed you? I've got news for you too. I didn't, and I still don't." Ruth was past hurt. She was hopping mad. "And neither does Jessie!"

That was the first time she had seriously threatened to leave her husband, and looking back, Ruth wished she had just done it that night. Jessie was less than a year old, too much trouble for a single father to deal with, especially one with little or no interest in the welfare of his child. It would have been an easy parting, and not walking then was what Ruth thought of as her third big mistake.

Instead, she hung around for another year, taking the insults and watching her husband go out alone at night. She didn't care if he wanted to go screw somebody else. She was long past wanting to have sex with him. It wasn't like she was going to miss something she dreaded most of the time anyway.

Then one night, everything changed forever when Ruth ran into the kitchen to find Skip towering over a screaming Jessie, his hand raised high and coming down hard on her backside. Ruth screamed too and lunged to wedge herself between them to take the angry blows.

That night she locked herself and Jessie in the child's room. The next day she packed up everything that wasn't Skip's and returned to her parents' home with her daughter. They were none too thrilled to see her and blamed her headstrong ways for bringing this on herself. The way Roy and Mildred saw it, Skip wouldn't feel the need to lash out like that if she were stricter with Jessie and if she didn't provoke her husband with her sassy mouth.

Ruth stayed two weeks with her parents, quickly growing tired of the constant berating. When she found a small, furnished house for rent, she called the landlord and arranged to move in right away. She and Jessie lived there for almost a year. It was the happiest time Ruth had ever known.

But she underestimated the impact her leaving Skip would have on the community gossipmongers and the subsequent reflection on Drummond Appliances. Roland Drummond was not going to have his son's standing in the community harmed by the vicious lies Ruth was telling about how Skip had beaten them both in a fit of rage. Skip had told his father a completely differ-ent story, so Roland was insistent that his son do something to squelch these rumors.

Ruth filed for divorce, seeking permanent custody of Jessie and asking the court to allow visitation for Skip only under close supervision. She doubted he would ever want to see Jessie at all, but she insisted on the minimum recommended amount of child support so that her daughter would have some of the things growing up that she had been denied.

Her biggest mistake of all was thinking that her storefront lawyer could handle the divorce transaction. She had expected her ex-husband's objections to be about the financial settlement, so she was prepared to make concessions to end this miserable stage of her life. She was totally blindsided when he stood to ask for full custody of their daughter, attacking her fitness as a parent.

"She's got problems of her own, Your Honor. Serious problems."

"What kind of problems?"

"Well, sometimes I'd come home from work at night, and poor little Jessie hadn't had a bite to eat all day. She'd be wearing dirty diapers and still be in her pajamas. I'd bathe her and put her in fresh clothes. I was worried she'd get sick being dirty and soiled all the time. It got better after Ruth went back to work, because she had to clean her up to take her to day care. She wanted people to think she was such a great mother, but it wasn't like that at all at home."

"That's not true!" Ruth was incredulous at the pack of lies pouring out of Skip's mouth.

"You will control yourself, young lady, or I will hold you in contempt of this court. You've already had your chance to speak," Judge Howard admonished from the bench.

The biggest blow, though, came when Roy Ferguson stood and told the judge that he believed Jessie would be better off in her father's care. Ruth had always been uncontrollable, he said, and if the child stayed with her, he feared that his granddaughter would be neglected or allowed to run wild.

Her father's testimony had sealed her fate. Reminding Ruth that she had already been given an opportunity to testify—and without even asking her to answer Skip's charges—Judge Howard granted the divorce and awarded full custody of Jessie to a father who couldn't stand her. Ruth was allowed two hours of visitation every other weekend, but only in the presence of a social worker.

When three-year-old Jessie was ripped screaming from her that day, Ruth felt as though her heart had been cut out. The triumphant look on Skip's face boiled her blood. In that moment, she understood completely why some women simply killed their husbands in their sleep.

In no time at all, the social worker assigned to oversee their visits saw the truth about Jessie Drummond and her mom. She petitioned the court on Ruth's behalf to have visitation extended to two full weekends a month, with the restrictions loosened to "monitored" rather than "supervised." Skip was glad to have his freedom for a change, and those weekends with Jessie had become Ruth's lifeline.

From one of Skip's cousins, Ruth learned a little about her daughter's life with the Drummonds. Jessie spent most days with her stern paternal grandmother, who resented having to care for a small child all day. From what Ruth could gather, the little girl was confined to a single room for most of the day, rarely allowed to play outside. In the evenings, she usually played alone in her room while her father watched television. Skip hated having to stay home so much, but his dad convinced him that it would look bad for him to be out when people around town knew that his little girl depended on him so much.

What a crock!

Ruth pushed the thoughts of Skip out of her head again. He

wasn't going to be part of their lives anymore. Tonight she had taken the biggest risk of her life, kidnapping her own daughter and running away with no intention of setting foot in Madison, Maine, ever again. And so far, everything was coming together just as she had planned it.

Last Monday, she drove to Augusta after work to have a look at the Taurus, a 1989 model that she had seen in the *Auto Trader* as for sale by owner. She took out the $3,400 from her savings account, and managed to buy the car for only $2,000 on the stipulation that she could pick it up on Thursday. Then last night, she took a bus back to Augusta, then a cab to the man's house to pick up the car. She got home late and packed the new car with practically everything she owned before parking it around the corner from her house.

After settling her bills and selling the Saturn, Ruth now had about $7,500 in cash. That would have to last her and Jessie until she found a job and got back on her feet.

The weary driver turned her attentions back to the road signs. It was almost midnight and she was sixty miles from Waterford, Connecticut. She needed to start looking for a gas station, and a cup of coffee would really hit the spot.

Chapter 4

"So who's your new girlfriend?" Elena teased as her ex-lover came into the kitchen to pour another soda. Spencer wasn't much of a drinker.

"Her name is Kaitlyn."

"Kaitlyn! That sounds so . . . young."

"She says she's twenty-one. What do you think?" Spencer had locked eyes with the young woman as soon as she walked in the door. The smile she got in return was all the encouragement she needed to proceed. Hanging out mostly in the kitchen, she was on hand when Kaitlyn came in for her first drink, and she introduced herself. Throughout the evening, Spencer circulated, helping to keep things picked up so Elena wouldn't have a mess the next morning. But after each pass through the house, she would return to the pretty, brown-eyed blonde for more flirting.

"I'd check her ID if I were you," Elena joked. "Hell, even if she is that old, thirteen years is a pretty big age difference."

"Well, if I was looking to get married or something, I'd be inclined to agree."

"Oh, I see. So you have something a little more frivolous in mind?"

Spencer grinned mischievously. "Maybe."

"Think you'll need any technical advice?" That jibe was in reference to Spencer's earlier remark.

"No, I think it'll come back to me," she smirked, sauntering out of the room with exaggerated cockiness.

Fifteen minutes later, Spencer retrieved her gear from the floor of the hall closet. Bidding her host goodnight with a knowing grin and a peck on the lips, she walked out to find the young woman waiting at the foot of the steps.

"Should I just follow you?" Kaitlyn had her keys out already. "I really don't want to leave my car here overnight."

"Sure. My bike's right here. I'll pull out and wait." Spencer leaned forward for their second kiss. The first one had come on the back porch when they had gone out to get some air and had clearly signaled where the rest of their evening was headed.

As she watched the pretty blonde disappear down the sidewalk, Spencer pulled her hair into a ponytail and tucked it beneath her collar. Her cell phone jingled in the inside pocket of her jacket, bringing an immediate smile to her lips. It was probably Elena calling to tell her not to do anything she wouldn't do, which meant she could do anything she wanted.

But it was Henry.

"Hey, what's up?" She hadn't given Margadon a second thought since she had left.

"Spence, you're not going to believe this!" he said excitedly. "You've got to come look."

"No way! I'm about to get laid." She had no secrets from her longtime friend. "What'd you find?"

"Somebody's fucked with it, all right, just like you said. It's backing out the cytokines."

"What do you mean backing out? How?" She had never heard Henry this agitated.

"It's in the global. It bumps the number for the report, but then it takes it back out in a hidden field. And the cost, too."

"You're not making any sense, pal. We looked at the global. There wasn't anything wrong with it."

"It's not calling ours, though! It's a whole different one, Spence."

"Whoa, that can't be right. How would it do that?"

"Look, you have to come see it. I already called James. He's on the way in."

"You called James?" It had to be serious for Henry to actually call their boss. James himself had admitted to having only a basic understanding of writing code, and he was content to give them free rein when it came to running the programming department. As a result, they usually had very little interaction with the controller.

"This is a big fucking deal! Somebody's fucking with the formula for Kryfex, and it looks like they're skimming the books."

Just then, a set of headlights pulled up behind the motorcycle and stopped. Spencer looked at her watch. It was almost midnight. So much for servicing her libido, she thought miserably. She might be able to make another date with Kaitlyn, but an actual date wasn't exactly what she had in mind with the young blonde.

"Okay, I'll be there in about an hour. Prop the back door open, will ya?"

Spencer doubted seriously that Margadon would appreciate her sacrifice tonight, but as Henry had said, it sounded like a pretty big fucking deal, and she and her coding partner were right in the middle of it. Forty-five minutes after the call, she swiped her card across the eye at the automatic security gate at the company's headquarters, and the gate screeched open to allow her to enter. She rode through the parking lot and jumped the curb to park the big bike on the sidewalk by the fire escape. As promised, Henry had slid a piece of paper between the door latch and the cutout so she wouldn't have to walk all the way around to the main entrance. Employees had gotten no fewer than a half dozen notices warning them against this practice, but everyone thought it was silly. Even with the fire escape open, the building was still secure, since a key card was needed to access each floor.

When she exited the stairwell onto the third floor, the programmer stopped in confusion. Except for the floor-level emergency lighting and red exit signs, the entire floor was dark, including the glassed-in office on the other side that she shared with Henry. Spencer walked around the hallway that surrounded the cubicles in the center of the large room. Over the top of the cubicle walls, she could see two people in her office, but couldn't imagine why they were standing there talking to each other in such hushed tones. *And why didn't they turn on the lights?*

She was seconds from calling out to them when she realized that neither was Henry. One was their boss, James, but the other man was a stranger. Stopping in her tracks, she listened to what sounded like a frantic conversation.

"Can't you just delete it?"

"This is our version of the code that he found, the one we changed," James explained. "We need this for things to work. But I have to move it off his doc list."

"Well, do it!" the stranger ordered impatiently.

Spencer stepped closer to the office and peered through the window to see what they were doing. Henry was lying on his side at their feet. Even in the dim light, she could see that his red eyes were open in a blank stare, a power cord knotted around his neck. A wave of nausea gripped her as the reality of the awful scene sank in. Henry was dead.

Shaking violently, Spencer stepped back from the window, tiptoeing backward down the hall toward the fire escape.

"We need to get this cleaned up," the stranger's voice said.

She rounded the corner and ducked below the level of the cubicles, narrowly missing being seen by the mysterious man as he stepped out into the center area.

"I'll have this terminal fixed in a minute," James said. "What are we going to do with him?" As he asked the question, the controller turned to face his accomplice, just in time to see the door to the fire escape open and close behind him. "Somebody's here!"

When she reached the stairwell, Spencer picked up her pace, still careful not to make any noise. Halfway down, she heard the door above her open.

"Hold it right there!"

No fucking way! No longer concerned about the noise, she raced down the final flight, flinging open the door as she pulled her helmet into place. In mere seconds, she had the bike in gear, tearing toward the guard gate to escape her pursuer.

As she reached the lot, a black sedan came out of nowhere to block her exit, blue lights flashing from the grill.

Her headlight shone on a U.S. Government license plate on the front of the car. She didn't stop to think why someone might have called the feds instead of the Rockville police, but Spencer automatically relaxed at thinking she would greet a friendly face—the authorities . . . someone who would take charge and arrest the people who had killed her friend. She started to remove her helmet when she saw the figure from the fire escape emerge and continue purposefully toward where she sat on her bike.

Something wasn't right. The man from upstairs was undaunted by the presence of this federal vehicle. Was he some kind of federal agent also? Had James called the feds when he found Henry dead? From the way the two men were acting upstairs, she had assumed they were the killers. *It doesn't make sense*.

Spencer looked nervously from the car to the man walking toward her, and then glanced back at the car. No, this wasn't right at all. *Why would anyone call the feds?* Suddenly terrified, she gunned her engine and squealed around the car and across the parking lot, jumping another curb to tear across an open field to the gated entry. But the gate was closed, and the only way to open it was to swipe her card and wait. There wouldn't be time for that, as the black sedan had turned and was closing in from behind.

A fence, six feet high with a row of barbed wire at the top, surrounded the Margadon property. Spencer whipped back through the lot over the curb, tearing up the wet autumn grass as she searched for a way out. The driver cut off her exit, while the man on foot was running diagonally toward the back of the property to corral her. Swerving left, she raced behind the building, realizing too late that a sliding gate secured the loading dock and sealed off her outlet to the other side. Now she found herself cornered by the two men, who angled toward her on foot from only fifty yards away.

Out of choices, she turned the bike in their direction and watched them slowly approach. Behind them, in the far right corner of the property, the ground sloped to a ravine where the fence dipped out of sight. This was the view from her office, the picture she saw every day. The top of the fence was downhill, lower than the ground level before the property started to slope. But Spencer couldn't envision the distance between the hilltop and the fence. If the hill was steep, the fence might be close enough that she could clear it on the fly. And if it wasn't . . . well, crashing into a chain-link fence at eighty miles an hour was probably preferable to Henry's fate, she concluded.

The clock in her head ticked loudly as the men cautiously

approached. She couldn't let them get close enough to grab her, but if she bolted too soon, they would close the gap and cut her off. Patience . . . patience . . .

Now!

Gunning the engine again, Spencer charged between her pursuers, one of whom whirled to chase her on foot as the other dashed back to the car. As she neared the corner of the lot, she leaned forward on the racing bike, searching for the top of the fence. *Please be close . . . please be close.* The instant she saw the top line of barbed wire, she jerked the front wheel off the ground and went airborne, clearing the fence by scant inches.

It was Hollywood perfect—almost.

The bike landed at an angle, and Spencer was thrown end over end, barely missing a tree trunk that might have killed her. On her first impact with the ground, her left elbow jammed against her ribs and her hip hit something hard. When she finally stopped rolling, a protruding stick pierced her shoulder where her leather jacket had opened.

Dazed and wounded, she realized with growing fear that her ordeal wasn't over. From beneath the bushes where she lay, she could see one of the men now climbing the fence.

"I'll drive around and come through the woods," the other shouted.

In the dark, she rose and stumbled to her fallen bike, pulled it upright, and climbed back aboard. The key wouldn't fire the ignition, so she dropped the kick starter.

Three pumps.

Four pumps.

The man had reached the top of the fence. For a split second, she weighed her chances of starting the bike versus dropping it to run like hell.

Five pumps.

He cleared it, vaulting to the ground on a dead run toward her, his gun now drawn.

Frantically, she jumped high in the air and came down hard on the lever. With a sudden roar, the bike came to life again.

Lurching forward, Spencer rode recklessly through the dark woods, praying at each popping sound that she wouldn't find out what it felt like to be shot. Just as she reached the highway, the black car emerged from the gate and quickly closed the distance between them, threatening to bump her from behind. On the open road, she lost the advantage of maneuverability and rapid acceleration.

Keeping her head low, she gunned the engine, swerving from one lane to the other on the deserted road to keep her distance from her pursuer. The Beltway loomed ahead. She spun the throttle, climbing the onramp and scooting rapidly to the far left lane. With a top speed of only ninety, she would have to use the other traffic as a shield in order to outrun the faster car.

Jockeying for position, the sedan fell back a bit, encumbered by slow-moving traffic and cars that changed lanes as the drivers became aware of the flashing blue lights. The pursuit was relentless, and at every opening, the driver of the black car would swerve and surge forward.

Spencer pulled up behind two cars driving side by side, shooting between them on the dotted line to increase her lead. Up ahead, she saw the exit for the Georgetown Pike and held her position in the far left lane, mentally mapping where each car on the highway would be when they reached that point. At the last possible second, she veered across three lanes to the exit, too late for the sedan to react without risking a pileup.

As she coasted down the ramp, Spencer blew out a breath of relief, realizing as she finally relaxed that her left shoulder and side felt as though they had been crushed and mangled. All she wanted was to stop and rest.

Instead, she saw the commotion ahead, where the government car had pulled off onto the shoulder and was now creeping down the embankment to the entrance ramp. *The fucker isn't giving up!*

And neither could Spencer.

She turned left onto the Georgetown Pike in plain sight of her pursuer, but when she dipped beneath the overpass out of his view, she skipped over the median into the westbound lane, still heading east. Hugging the yellow line to avoid oncoming traffic, she pushed the Kawasaki again to top speeds, this time putting real distance between herself and her pursuer. When she reached a long gap in the traffic, she turned off her headlamp and slowed, executing a U-turn that sealed her escape. Riding west now with her lights off, Spencer watched as the black sedan flew past her in the opposite direction.

Out of danger for the moment, she drove underneath the overpass for the Beltway and turned right onto a two-lane road that took her out of traffic, entering the only haven she could find—a public park. A paved bike path wound into the woods, and she followed it until she came upon a small service shed. At last, she killed the engine and coasted to a stop, taking off her helmet to listen for any sound of traffic coming into the park. Satisfied that she was alone, the tall rider dismounted, her legs shaking so badly that she could hardly walk. With her last measure of strength, Spencer pulled the heavy bike behind the structure and out of sight.

Exhausted, sore and bleeding, she collapsed in a heap to assess her injuries. Merely touching her left arm sent fire all the way to her fingertips. She wrenched free of the leather jacket to find a small stick protruding from her shoulder just beneath her collarbone. Grasping the end, she tugged, seeing stars as it twisted deep inside. Finally it snapped, leaving a part still inside—*the part that hurts so goddamned much.*

"Elena . . ." she murmured, searching her inside pocket for her cell phone. It was gone, probably lost when she crashed over the fence. *Fuck!*

Spencer scooted up to lean against the edge of the shed, completely spent. She needed to make sense of what had happened, but all she could think about right now was Henry Estes.

"This is Akers."

"I lost him, Cal. He was headed east on the Georgetown Pike." FBI Agent Mike Pollard knew that his partner, the senior agent, would be pissed. They couldn't afford a breach like this.

Akers sighed in disgust. "You lost a her, not a him. Thayer says it was Spencer Rollins. She's one of the programmers. There was a call to her on the dead guy's logs, so he probably already told her what he found." This was a problem, a big problem. They had planned just to clean up the computer mess and dump the programmer's body where it would never be found. But there was no way to cover up what had happened with the biker on the loose. No, they needed another story now. And they needed Rollins out of the picture. "Okay, get on back here and pick me up. I found her cell phone in the woods. We'll start there."

"So did you and Thayer finish things?"

"Yeah. He says he got rid of all the evidence, and we changed the log on the gate so it looks like Rollins was the only one here. Thayer's all to hell about this dead guy, though. Guess he wasn't expecting that."

"You think he's going to be a problem?"

"Nah, he's up to his balls in this. He'll have his story straight. If he fucks up, he's toast." Akers shook his head in disgust. *This is a big fucking mess.* "Oh, and Mike? Stay clear of the cameras. We already reset 'em. I'll meet you by the woods on the main road."

Chapter 5

Jessie stirred in the front seat and began to fidget, her eyes still closed as she fought against waking. From the dashboard glow, Ruth could see the marks on her child's forehead from where she had leaned against the door.

"Hey, sweetie." She reached over and softly stroked her daughter's thigh.

Jessie made a face—her grouchy face, Ruth noted—and struggled against the seat belt to sit up.

"You okay?" The dashboard clock read 4:14. They had been on the road for almost nine hours and had just crossed the Pennsylvania state line. Ruth had been watching for a rest area, as she was long overdue for a break.

"Where are we going?" the four-year-old whined.

Ruth was too tired to talk about things right at that moment, but she felt bad about putting the girl off again. "I know this is hard for you, honey. I'm going to pull over soon, and we'll go to the bathroom and rest for a little while. Will you be okay for a few more minutes?"

Jessie didn't answer. At least, she didn't answer verbally. But her body language gave away her mood as she slumped against the seat in frustration.

As promised, Ruth pulled into a rest area and parked alongside several other cars. Quietly, they went to the restroom together, and then got back into the car. Ruth leaned her seat back and fixed the small pillow so that it covered the console. That let Jessie stretch out with her head in her mother's lap, and soon, they were both asleep.

Only three hours later the sound of slamming car doors roused the pair from their slumber. The restroom was busy with travelers, and Ruth was careful not to call attention to herself, squeezing into a small stall with Jessie instead of waiting for the handicapped one to open. Afterward, the two walked around a bit to stretch their legs, but the steady cold drizzle made the car's interior more inviting. Once they got settled in their seats, they were underway again.

"Where are we going?" Jessie asked again, this time with more curiosity than impatience.

"We're looking for a new place to live, sweetie, just you and me."

"Why?"

Why indeed? "Honey, you remember a long time ago when you asked me if you could stay with me and not go back to your daddy?"

Jessie nodded. It made her nervous to talk about her daddy because he was always telling her she had better not say anything to her mother, or else.

"Do you still want to stay with me and not have to go back to

42

the other house?"

"Yes," the child answered, not hesitating at all.

"It means you won't see your daddy anymore, not even on the weekends." Ruth glanced at her daughter's face to see the response. "Does that make you sad?"

Jessie thought only a second before shaking her head no.

"And you won't get to go back to your room and play with your toys anymore." With that bit of news, she saw the anxious look on her daughter's face. "Not the toys at your daddy's house, anyway. I brought all of the toys from our house. We can get some new toys and some new things to wear, but we'll have everything we need and never have to go back there."

"What about Lisa?"

"That Lisa will have to stay with your grandmother. We'll get another one," she assured. "Jessie, if you stay with me, it means that no one will ever hurt you again. I promise." As she said the words, she felt the rage inside from what her ex-husband had done to their child. "But you have to help me. Can you do that?"

The little girl nodded eagerly. If she had her mommy and Lisa, she didn't need anything else.

"You remember that game we play sometimes, hide and seek?"

"Yeah!"

"Well, honey, that's what we're doing. We're hiding from your daddy. That's why we had to drive a long way, so he won't find us."

"Is Daddy going to look for us?"

"I think he will. But if we both keep a secret, I don't think he'll ever find us. Do you think you can keep a secret?"

She nodded again. Even at four years old, Jessie was an old pro at this secret stuff.

"We can't tell anybody about Daddy or that we're hiding. We can't tell your new friends or my new friends. Not anyone. Can you promise me that?"

Jessie was confused about the secret part. "But if we don't tell them it's a secret, they might tell Daddy where we are."

Clever child, Ruth thought. "No, this is the kind of secret that's so secret, we can't tell anyone. In fact, it's so secret that we can't even tell anyone that we have a secret."

The child looked bewildered.

"Honey, if people know we're hiding, they might tell somebody else, and maybe that person would tell Daddy. So it's best if nobody knows. We want them to think that it's just you and me . . . no daddy."

"Where will we live?"

"I don't know yet, honey. But we'll find a place that's nice and we'll be happy. Just you and me."

"And I don't have to go to Grandma's anymore either?"

"No. We're hiding from your grandma too, both of your grandmas, and your grandpas. We can't tell anybody, Jessie. It's very important." Ruth wanted to spell out what would happen if someone found out, but she knew her daughter had been threatened with horror stories before. Why else would the girl keep saying that she fell when asked about her bruises? "There's something else, honey . . . something we need to do to help us hide. Are you listening?"

Jessie had turned away to look out the window, but her mother's question brought her back. "Yes."

"Your daddy is going to ask people if they've seen a little girl named Jessie and a mommy named . . ."

"Ruth!"

"That's right! So to keep him from finding Jessie and Ruth, we need to change our names. Okay?"

"Can I be Brittany?"

Ruth groaned inwardly. Brittany Schaefer was Jessie's best friend from pre-school. "No, Brittany is a very nice name, but I've picked out something a little different. I want your new name to be Megan. I think it's very pretty," she coaxed. "Do you like that?"

Jessie thought it over. She didn't know anyone named Megan, but that was okay, she finally decided. "Yeah."

"Okay, honey, and I'm going to change my name to Karen. You can still call me Mommy, but I'm going to tell people that my name is Karen Oliver and you are my little girl, Megan Oliver."

Changing identities was the most critical element of Ruth's elaborate preparations for dropping out of sight. She had worked for days to make convincing copies of their real birth certificates with the new names. She had to hope that the sluggish bureaucracy of the IRS would allow her to go unnoticed as she got a new job, set up a house, and applied for credit.

The sadness in Edward Melnick's eyes brought tears to her own. From the story in last week's newspaper, Ruth knew why the old gentleman had come to the bank today. Quietly, respectfully, she walked him through the closure of the two savings accounts he had started a few years ago, cutting a cashier's check for the total made out to the Children's Home Society. Ed Melnick had tragically lost both of his beautiful granddaughters, Karen and Megan Oliver, when they had drowned in a boating accident at Great Pond.

Ruth vacillated between shame and honor at commandeering the names and social security numbers of the two lost children. In her heart, she hoped that Edward Melnick would understand and accept that she needed to do this to save her daughter from danger.

"You and me will have the same last name," Jessie realized.

"That's right. Megan"—she pointed first to her daughter, then to herself—"and Karen Oliver. Starting right . . . now!" Ruth smiled at Jessie's obvious delight. "Okay, little girl, what's your name?"

"Megan."

"Megan who?

"Megan Allber," she answered.

"Megan Oliver. Say it with me. *O-li-ver.*"

"Oliver!"

"Good, let's try again. What's your name?"

"Megan Oliver!"

"You're so smart. Karen and Megan Oliver have a secret that no one will ever know. Right?"

"Right."

"So tell me little girl, do you have a secret?"

"Uh-huh. Me and my mommy—"

"Un-unh! Do you have a secret?"

"No!"

Ruth laughed aloud at her daughter's enthusiasm. It would take a few days to instill the importance of hiding who they really were, but over time, she knew that her daughter would forget much of what had been her early life. That could only be a good thing.

At the next exit, they pulled off to get gas. Inside the food mart, Ruth gathered sweet rolls, orange juice and coffee for breakfast, and they set out again beneath dreary skies.

"Where's our new house going to be?"

"I haven't decided yet, sweetie. If we see a nice town, maybe we'll stop there and find a place to live."

Chapter 6

Talking . . . the rhythmic scuffing of feet as they lightly touched the asphalt . . . soft noises growing louder, people getting closer. The sounds seeped into Spencer's consciousness as she stirred. She opened her eyes as two men jogged past without seeing the woman who lay crumpled behind the shed.

Spencer rolled over on the hard ground, adding injury to insult when her knee collided with the cinderblock wall. With a whispered yelp, the battered woman awoke, momentarily confused about her surroundings until the fire-like pains in her shoulder and arm brought the events of the night before rushing back. And as if lying on the ground in agony wasn't enough, it had started to rain.

Using her good arm, Spencer pushed herself up and scooted under the meager overhang of the shed, her back to the wall. There was a rain suit in one of her saddlebags, but she just didn't have the energy to get up.

Clearing her head as she stared into the empty woods, tears suddenly rushed to her eyes as she allowed herself to fathom all that had happened. Her friend was dead, apparently murdered by their boss and a man who she was beginning to think was a government agent. Whatever Henry had found in the code last night had gotten him killed.

Now the killers were after her, presumably because she had seen them standing over Henry's dead body, or maybe because they knew he had called her to tell her about the code. On the phone, her partner had said something about a different global, one that "backed out the cytokines," whatever that meant. Henry was right—it really was a big fucking deal, and calling James about it had sealed his fate.

But why were the feds involved in this? What the hell did they have to do with Margadon? And with James?

As she had last night, Spencer reached into her jacket pocket for her cell phone, now remembering that she had lost it during the chase. She needed to tell Elena what had happened. The IRS agent had many friends in law enforcement, so she might be able to find out what was going on. At the very least, Elena could help Spencer figure out what to do next.

Still weary and now hurting a lot more than she had last night, Spencer gingerly pushed herself onto her feet. Her injuries seemed to be only on her left side. Her ribs ached with every breath, but it was her shoulder and arm that hurt most, the wound oozing blood through her shirt and into the lining of her jacket. Staggering a bit, she walked to the bike and yanked the strap on the saddlebag, from which she extracted a one-piece black and white nylon rain suit. Leaning against the building, she stepped into it, wincing in agony as she pushed her arm through the sleeve.

Shivering against the damp chilly air, she pulled on her helmet and climbed back onto the Kawasaki, cranking the engine with a turn of the key. Sitting for a moment as the big bike idled, it occurred to Spencer that she didn't have a clue about where to go. Obviously, she couldn't go home now. Thanks to James, these fuckers knew who she was and they would be waiting for her.

First things first, though. Spencer needed gas. She had been buying gas a little at a time, not wanting to leave much in the tank over the winter. It was a miracle she hadn't run out last night.

Now creeping down the bike path toward the park entrance, she alertly scanned the parking lot for a dark-colored sedan, hoping against hope that she had seen the last of the sinister tail. Only a couple of cars were there, both of them economy compacts. *The joggers.* When she reached the main road, she headed back toward the Georgetown Pike, turning east toward the District, this time in the proper lane. On a corner up ahead was a gas station with a food mart. Spencer was relieved that she still had her wallet, though it held only about sixty bucks.

She parked her bike by the pump and removed her helmet. Her whole side hurt like hell when she snaked her good arm through the snaps of her rain suit to pull her wallet from her back pocket.

Spencer waved to the clerk, but he motioned her in. According to the sign, payment was required in advance. "I'm going to fill up," she said, handing him a twenty dollar bill.

Ten-fifty filled the six-gallon tank. When she finished, Spencer pulled to the side of the building by the pay phone and went back inside to get her change. "Can I have change for a dollar?"

Without even looking up, the clerk pulled back one of the bills in his hand and replaced it with four quarters.

"You got a restroom?" She followed the nod of his head to a smelly, grimy room where she took care of her business as quickly as possible.

Back outside, Spencer dropped two quarters into the slot and dialed the number for her friend. Elena wasn't going to believe any of this.

As she stood in the rain waiting for the agent to answer, she set the heavy helmet at her feet and gently tugged the brown leather jacket away from her throbbing shoulder. Getting this *goddamned spear* out of her body was a top priority.

"Hello?" The groggy woman would need many more hours of sleep to recover from the night before.

"Elena, it's me, Spence."

"Wha—? This is way too early, bitch. Didn't you get laid?"

"Elena, listen to me. I'm in trouble. Henry was murdered last night. I got called in to work when I left your house and I think I saw the guys who did it. They chased me, but I got away. I need your help. I don't know where to go."

Spencer waited for the inevitable barrage of questions, but it didn't happen.

"Elena?" *Fuck!* "Elena?"

"If you'd like to make a call, please hang up and try again . . ."

Angrily, she slammed the phone down and dug into her pocket for more quarters. This time, she called her friend's cell phone.

"All circuits are busy." It cost her fifty cents to find that out.

"Fuck! Goddamn it!" Spencer screamed in frustration as she threw in her last two quarters and dialed the home number again. It didn't even ring. Nor did it return her coins.

Who else could she call? Henry and Elena were her only real friends, so she would have to keep trying until she reached her ex-lover again.

She needed more quarters, but this time the clerk inside wasn't in the mood to make change. Grudgingly, she tossed a sweet roll onto the counter. "How much?"

"A dollar nine."

"Perfect." After pocketing the change, she grabbed another

roll and threw two ones on the counter.

"You got a dime?" he asked. Dense.

"No."

"But I just—"

"I lost it. May I have my change, please?"

The light bulb finally went on and the young man sighed and shook his head.

Armed with six quarters, Spencer decided to try the cell phone one more time. Again, she set her helmet on the ground by her feet, cradling the phone to her ear as she dialed with her working hand. This time, the call went right to voicemail. Elena had call waiting, so she must have turned it off, probably to avoid being disturbed again. *Fuck!*

Out of options for the moment, the injured woman pulled one of the sweet rolls from her pocket and ripped open the cellophane. She needed to find a dry place to wait out the day, a place near a phone.

Turning toward her bike, Spencer caught sight of a police cruiser slowing as it headed toward the store. A coffee run, probably . . . she hoped. *Relax . . . be cautious, but relax.* She had done nothing to warrant the attention of the police. Gripping her bruised side as she swung a leg over the wet saddle, she shoved the remains of the roll back into her pocket and prepared to ride out.

It was at that moment that she saw the second black and white, creeping around the corner from behind the building. Spencer tried to calm her rising paranoia, starting the bike and gripping her helmet.

"Stay where you are and put your hands on your head!" the officer barked through the loudspeaker as he pulled onto the lot.

What the fuck! Surely this wasn't about telling the clerk that she had lost her dime, so it could only be about one other thing.

There wasn't time to weigh options. Spencer's instincts were screaming at her to get the hell out of there, and that's exactly what she did, dropping her helmet to the ground as she shot past the incoming cruiser. Crossing three lanes of traffic on the nimble bike, she skipped over the curb at the median and sped off, this time heading west back toward the Beltway. Over her shoulder, she saw one of the police cars already in pursuit, lights flashing and sirens blaring. The other was hung up on the median. She never saw the third car that joined the chase, a black sedan with U.S. Government plates.

Accelerating wildly, Spencer felt the sting of the cold rain on her unprotected face and hands. She had gotten a good jump this time—better than last night—but with the commotion behind her, it was only a matter of time before her pursuers caught up. She had to lose them.

Once on the Beltway, she picked up even more speed, crouching low behind the small windshield as her speedometer topped out at ninety miles per hour. A cyclist couldn't afford a lapse in concentration at this speed. Nor could she spare a glance over her shoulder. The sirens had faded, but she doubted they would give up the chase this soon.

At the junction with I-66, Spencer peeled off at the last second toward Fairfax, unknowingly missing the patrolman who was lying in wait at the underpass up ahead. When the lookout radioed that she never passed, all three cars giving chase abandoned the Beltway, two turning east on I-66 toward Arlington, the third following the interstate west to Fairfax.

In the left lane ahead, Spencer spotted yet another law enforcement vehicle, this one a Fairfax County sheriff's deputy. She hung back near the exit lane, trying not to call attention to herself riding in this rain without a helmet. Too late, she heard the siren behind her as the deputy drifted to the right to seal off her advance.

Cold, wet, bleeding and now completely demoralized, Spencer slowed and pulled over to the shoulder, coasting to a stop as the deputy pulled over in front and got out of his car to walk back toward where she waited. If this was about last night, she was ready to talk. She would just tell him exactly what she saw at Margadon, and surely they would get to the bottom of it. Spencer knew she wasn't guilty of anything and she had nothing to hide.

Her knees still shaking from the adrenalin rush, she sat idling on the bike as the car behind her came to a stop. With her thumb, she wiped the rain from the tiny rear view mirror.

The sight nearly stopped her heart.

In disbelief, Spencer turned to see the black sedan that had chased her from Margadon, prominently sporting its U.S. Government plate. A suited agent in an open trench coat walked abruptly toward her, his steely eyes daring her to move. The sudden shiver that ran up her spine had nothing to do with the cold or rain. This was the man who had been in Henry's office with James last night. Her instincts told her that he was the one who had killed her friend, and now he wanted her dead as well.

Not waiting for an introduction, she spun the throttle and popped the clutch, rocketing forward as the deputy scrambled back to his car. Without her helmet, she was able to hear the unmistakable sound of gunfire from the man in the trench coat.

"Come back to bed," Kelly groaned, incredulous that her lover would be up and about so early after the party that had raged until almost three a.m.

Instead, the IRS agent pulled on her jeans and slipped a rumpled sweater over her head. "Something's wrong with Spence."

"What is it?"

"I'm not sure. She said she was in trouble and then the line went dead. I can't call out, not even on my cell phone." Elena grabbed her socks next, then her ankle boots. "I'm going to head over to her place and see if she's okay. Go back to sleep."

The naked woman stretched . . . and then did as she was told.

Chapter 7

Watching out for a new home piqued Jessie's interest for an hour or so as they moved south on I-81 through eastern Pennsylvania. But eventually, the child returned to dreamland, worn out by her night on the road.

In Harrisburg, Ruth drifted over to I-83 toward Baltimore, imagining what it might be like to live in a place like that. But as she approached the outskirts of Maryland's largest city, she knew that she wasn't cut out to live in that kind of hubbub, no matter how much she wanted to leave the small town behind.

She had never lived in a big city, but from what she had heard from her friend Arlene, it meant that even though people lived close to you, you never got to know them. Workers came home, went inside their houses, closed their doors, and retreated to their fenced-in back yards. There was more traffic and longer lines, and people were more anonymous. Being anonymous had its advantages, for sure—especially if you wanted to blend in—but Arlene had lived in Boston and she said it gave people permission to be flaming assholes, since the chances were pretty low you would ever see them again.

No, Ruth didn't want that kind of stress or aggravation. She wanted a place a little more out of the way, but large enough to afford at least a modicum of anonymity. Small towns like Madison guaranteed that everyone knew your business. It wouldn't do for people in a new place to start asking questions of the newcomer and to start comparing notes.

Traffic picked up considerably as she got closer to Washington, D.C. No way did Ruth want to live in a place that crowded, but she had to admit it would be nice to live close enough to be able to visit all the monuments and museums.

Were they far enough from Skip? If she drove another day, they could get to northern Florida. Or if she headed west, she may get as far as Kentucky or Missouri. Skip wouldn't look there. Of course, he wouldn't know where to look no matter where she stopped. It wasn't like Ruth was going to a place she had always dreamed of and talked about. And it wasn't like she had friends or relatives that she wanted to be close to. The fact was she could stop anywhere. It made no difference if it was Maryland, Texas or Minnesota. As long as she was away from the people she knew in Madison, she and Jessie should be safe.

Were they far enough from Skip? She asked herself again, knowing that she was looking for justification to stop. She was exhausted from driving all night, and had gotten very little sleep during the nights leading up to their escape. If she and Jessie could get settled somewhere today, she wouldn't be out on the highway tomorrow—a mother and daughter in a car with Maine plates. Ruth had every reason to think that come six o'clock tomorrow night, policemen everywhere would be looking for her.

Skirting the maze of interstates and parkways, the young

mother continued south into Virginia on a state highway. A series of turns landed the old Taurus wagon on the outskirts of the town of Manassas. It was sort of a bustling town, with lots of shoppers out on Saturday, even in this rain. The stops and starts at the busy intersections woke Jessie and she sat up to look around.

"I'm hungry." The girl's whiny voice gave away her grumpy mood. Jessie's usually pleasant personality always got displaced for those first few minutes after waking up.

"Me too, honey. We'll stop as soon as we find a good place, okay?" What Ruth wanted was a diner where she could sit in a booth and drink a bottomless cup of coffee. Instead, to her daughter's delight, she pulled into a fast food restaurant that boasted a playground protected from the rain by a large over-hang. Ten minutes later, Ruth was shivering outside at a picnic table, watching the four-year-old blow off steam climbing through one tunnel to slide down another.

"Watch this!" the little girl shouted, suddenly appearing head first and landing on the carpet with a thud. Predictably, her face contorted as she began to cry.

"Sweetheart, you came out of there like a rocket. People aren't supposed to be rockets," Ruth teased gently. "Maybe you should come and eat for a few minutes until you feel better."

Jessie did as she was asked, tearfully climbing up onto the bench to take a big bite of her cheeseburger.

As a mom, Ruth felt guilty about how she had handled the care and feeding of this child over the last eighteen hours—a cheeseburger for dinner, sleeping in the car, a sweet roll for breakfast, and then another cheeseburger for lunch. But it wasn't the food that was important here. It was the playground and the chance for Jessie to be a kid for just a few minutes. Ruth knew she was asking a lot of her daughter right now, and she wasn't going to lose sight of the fact that this was all about what was good for Jessie.

"I'm going to go get some more coffee, honey. I'll be right back." The playground's only access was from inside the store, and Ruth could keep an eye on Jessie easily as she drew another cup of coffee from the large dispenser. On her way back out, she picked up a complimentary copy of the *Journal Messenger*, the local paper in Manassas. Once back at their table, she was pleased to see that her daughter had recovered from her spill and was back on the slide.

A couple of stories on the front page about local businesses and an arts and crafts fair confirmed for Ruth that this was a thriving community, yet still a small town. Flipping to the back, she found the classifieds, which included several job ads, mostly entry level or service jobs. But it was a "For Rent" ad that got her attention.

For Rent: 2BR/1B trailer furn $150 utl incl. Owner needs help w/errands & lt chores.

Ruth had figured on paying at least seven hundred a month for something already furnished, and then to have to pay utilities on top of that. *What kind of place rents furnished with utilities for a hundred and fifty dollars a month? A dump. What else could it be?*

Lowering the paper, she took a closer look at the community of Manassas. Traffic was moderate, the buildings modern. Signs to Old Town and to the Manassas Battlefield suggested that it was a tourist destination and that the city's history was a source of great local pride.

"Megan?" The little girl's new name didn't register. "Megan, sweetheart?"

The sweetheart part got the child's attention, reminding her once again that she would be called Megan from now on.

"Honey, I need to make a phone call. Can you put your shoes back on?"

"One more time?" the girl asked hopefully as she started

toward the ladder.

Ruth smiled and nodded. *You're such a trouper, Jessie.*

When she turned off the main highway, Ruth counted the rows of mailboxes on the left side of the road. At the third one, she took a left as instructed. The pavement ended almost immediately and she hugged the right side of the rutted road until she reached the second driveway on the right. She had feared from the woman's directions that the place would be way out in the boondocks, but now that they were here, it didn't seem that far out of the town at all.

"Is that it?" Jessie was sitting up straight, straining to see over the dashboard as they pulled into the drive.

Ruth saw the white frame house as soon as she turned, but the trailer in the back didn't come into view until she pulled even with the front porch. It was small and pretty close to the house, she realized with disappointment. She had hoped it would have been set back more for privacy.

Coming to a stop, she spotted a thin, gray-haired woman of about sixty dressed in jeans and an oversized denim shirt stepping from the front porch into the driveway. As she got out of the car, Ruth was momentarily intimidated by the lady's obvious appraisal, but relaxed at once when she saw her flash a smile at Jessie.

"Hi, I'm Karen Oliver. And this is my daughter, Megan."

The woman grinned broadly and stuck out her hand in greeting. "I'm Viv Walters. Did you have any trouble finding the place?"

"No, your directions were perfect."

"Good," she said, turning back to the little girl. "Hi, Megan. How old are you?"

"Four."

"Four? My goodness! I bet you're smart."

And shy. Jessie moved closer to her mother, who agreed hurriedly. "I think she's pretty smart. And she's a good girl, aren't you, honey?" Ruth knew that her daughter was slow to come around to new people.

Viv nodded her head toward the trailer. "It isn't much, but if you want to see it, it's out back."

"I'm sure it's really nice," Ruth offered politely.

The landlady chuckled. "I don't know about nice, but it's clean. I had to get inside there and scrape up all the dirt and cat sh—," she stopped herself. "Sorry. The woman that lived here before asked me if she could keep a cat. I told her yes, but then she got another one, and another one, and before I knew it, she had eight cats living in that little trailer. I had to pull up the carpet and put down vinyl, so the floor's new."

Viv didn't seem to know much about salesmanship, Ruth thought. Was she trying to find a renter or trying to warn people away?

"You don't have any pets, do you?" the gray-haired woman asked pointedly.

"No, no pets. Just my daughter and me."

"That's good. 'Course, if you wanted to have a pet, I guess that would be all right. No cats, though."

"I don't think we'll be getting—"

"Thor and Maggie don't like cats much."

Ruth looked around to see if she could spot Thor and Maggie, half expecting to see vicious Dobermans patrolling the yard.

"They're my Labradors. I had to lock 'em up on the back porch so they wouldn't jump all over you when you got here. Labradors are like that. Never met a soul that wasn't their best friend. Now if you'd been a man calling about the trailer, I might have had Thor out here with me . . . you know, just for show."

"You've had some trouble?"

"Oh, no! And I'm not liable to have any as long as they're

here. They're sweet dogs, but I don't think they'd ever let anybody hurt me. Maggie's gonna drop a litter of puppies any day now." Viv smiled when she saw the excitement in the little girl's eyes. "You want to meet 'em?"

"Maybe later," Ruth said tentatively. "Could we see the trailer?"

"Of course. Right this way."

As they rounded the house, the two big dogs let loose with a cacophony of rich, throaty barks. Through the screen at the back door, they could see two Labs—one black, the other yellow—eager to get out and meet these new friends.

Viv led them across the muddy back driveway to the trailer's wooden porch.

"You'd have this spot to park in, right here at your doorstep. I keep my Jeep in that shed over there."

As Viv opened the door, Ruth got a nasal clearing blast of disinfectant—welcome, she considered, in light of the previous renter. The older woman stepped in and flipped on the overhead light switch to reveal a small living room and kitchen area finished in the standard dark wooden paneling. An old couch, a recliner, and a straight back armchair practically filled up the entry, and the dining table was a built-in bar with two stools and room for a third. In a quick perusal of the cabinets, Ruth found an array of mismatched plates, bowls, glasses and mugs. A few aluminum pots and pans were stored beneath the stove. A tray of assorted silverware and utensils lay inside one of the drawers, and the other held dishcloths and hand towels.

"It's fully furnished, except for sheets and towels. You'll have to get them yourself."

"Just sheets and towels?"

"Yep. Everything else is here already. I mean, it's not the best stuff, but it beats nothing at all, I guess. My daughter used to live here with her husband, but then she ran off with another man, and her husband didn't want to stay, so I inherited everything.

That was almost fifteen years ago."

Ruth would have guessed the age of the furnishings, given the wear on the counters and appliances.

"Now like it said in the ad, it's got two bedrooms and one bath." Leading the way down a darkened hall, Viv once again flipped a wall switch, this time getting no response. "Damn light bulb! Oops! I did it again. Sorry."

Ruth took it in stride, sure that her daughter had picked up these words and worse from Skip. But even at four years old, Jessie had the discretion not to use them in conversation with her mother.

The first bedroom held a twin bed, a built-in vanity and stack of drawers, and a closet. Next was the bathroom, a simple tub and shower combination, with a toilet and sink, all in harvest gold. The back bedroom had windows on both sides, a double bed against the end wall, two nightstands, and a dresser with six drawers. Given the motif, Ruth found herself immensely glad that the carpet was gone. It had probably been shag, brown and orange shag.

"So it's a hundred and fifty a month including utilities?" Even for a place like this, that seemed like a good deal.

"That's right. You got water, electricity, and Jerry from the church ran the cable over here and spliced it in, so you have that too."

"And your ad also mentioned some errands and light chores. Could I get an idea of what that involves?" Ruth was starting to think she would muck horse stalls every day for a deal like this. Viv seemed like a nice lady and the trailer was plenty big enough for just her and Jessie. It was out of town, so she wouldn't really have any neighbors except Viv.

"Well, it isn't a whole lot, really," the woman began casually. Now her salesmanship was creeping in. "I can't drive at night because I don't see so good. I get most of my errands run during the day, so it usually isn't a problem. But on Wednesday nights I

61

like to go to bingo down at the church, so I need a ride. Now you can drop me off and come back for me, or if you want to try your luck, you can stick around." A crooked grin popped out as she scuffed her foot on the vinyl floor.

"That's all you need? Just a ride to bingo?"

"Well"—she hesitated—"once in a while I need a little help around the house. You know, the kind of things that are easier with two people, like holding a ladder . . . or picking up something heavy . . . or giving the dogs a bath."

Ruth gulped noticeably.

"They're usually pretty good, but they get excited and sometimes I need help holding 'em still," she explained.

Ruth quietly looked around. At one-fifty a month, she wouldn't have to worry about making the rent for a while. As soon as she got Jessie into a pre-school or daycare, she could start looking for work. Even a low-wage job would be enough for the time being if she lived here.

"Would you mind if I talked it over with my daughter?"

"No, not at all," Viv answered. "I'll just wait outside."

Ruth had made up her mind, but she wanted Jessie to like it and to feel at home. Kneeling down, she pulled her daughter close.

"So what do you think, punkin? How would you like to have that little room with pretty flowered sheets?"

"It's dark in here."

"I know, but it won't be when we open the windows." She walked over and tugged gently on the bottom of the shade. Abruptly, it flew to the top with a snap. "Oops, good thing I didn't have my nose over there," she teased, covering her nose.

That made Jessie laugh and she covered her own nose as well.

"What do you say, honey? We can make it pretty, and there's a closet for all your toys in the little bedroom. I think we'll like it here."

"Do you think Daddy will find us here?" the girl asked seriously.

"No, sweetie, I don't. Not if we keep our secret . . . Megan. Okay?" Ruth was glad to realize that her daughter understood what this big change was all about.

Finally, Jessie nodded her agreement. This wasn't as big and bright as the house she had shared with her father, but it already felt a lot happier than that one.

Together, the pair walked out onto the porch just as the rain began falling more steadily.

"Viv?"

The gray-haired woman opened her back porch door. "Did you decide?"

"Yeah, we're going to take it. I think Megan and I are going to like living here," she shouted across the back yard.

Viv smiled and waved them in. "Well come on in here and say hello to these hounds so they'll know you're the good guys."

Chapter 8

"Goddamn it!" With his blood pressure soaring and the veins in his forehead throbbing, Calvin Akers was dangerously close to having a stroke. Spencer Rollins had been right there in his clutches. Thirty more seconds and all of this shit would have been over with.

It had looked like she was going to surrender. Had he known her game, he would have had his gun ready. He would have shot her dead right there on the spot. It wasn't hard to justify killing a fleeing suspect when you had evidence that she had committed a murder already and was likely to kill again. Next time he would shoot her first and not bother to ask questions at all.

He drew his cell phone from inside his coat and angrily jabbed his partner's number.

"Mike!" Agent Pollard's job was to watch the townhouse in Alexandria that belonged to Elena Diaz. Seven of the last ten calls on Rollins's cell phone had gone to this woman, most of those to her office at the IRS. "What's going on there?"

"I'm tailing Diaz. She took off about ten minutes after the call. Looks like she's headed to Rollins's place in Arlington. Maybe they're gonna meet or something."

"Rollins is in Fairfax, headed west. She knows better than to go home." The senior agent wasn't about to admit that their quarry had made a fool of him on the side of the road. "Stick with Diaz. I'm heading your way. We'll talk to her . . . try to get something inside the house so we can keep tabs on Rollins."

"Where do you think Rollins is headed?"

"I don't know. But you saw what I saw. She's got no address book, no personal mail, no pictures. All she's got on the cell phone is Diaz and that dead guy." Akers was finally starting to calm down. "She'll be calling Diaz again. All we gotta do is wait her out."

Spencer throttled back when she exited onto Lee Highway heading west. Her sudden move had caught both the deputy and federal agent unaware, so she was long gone before either of them got back into the flow of traffic. This time, though, she wasn't going to take any chances on running up on another law enforcement officer from behind. She was a sitting duck on these interstates and highways, exposed and at the mercy of the exit ramps and crossroads. She would have a better chance of staying out of sight on a two-lane road, especially if she could get offroad quickly and into a place where she couldn't be pursued.

At the first chance, Spencer turned off the highway, heading south onto a road with moderate traffic. She needed to find a place to regroup. Her hair was wet and stringy from the rain, and the blood from her shoulder wound had soaked her shirt all the way to the collar. She wasn't going to be able to walk into any old public building and hang out unnoticed. It was bad enough that she was out here on a motorcycle where people stared at her at stoplights, obviously bewildered at why she was riding in weather like this.

When the road she was on abruptly ended, she turned west on 620, heading away from downtown Fairfax. That road became New Braddock Road, where traffic picked up a bit. Not good, she realized, looking again for something more out of the way. Most of the surface streets off to the side looked like they looped back into residential areas, which meant there was likely no thruway. It wouldn't do at all to get trapped in a place like that.

Her left arm was starting to feel tingly and numb, no doubt from the swelling in her shoulder. Every time she squeezed the clutch with her left hand, it shot pains all the way to her neck. She needed to get that stick out of her shoulder soon, or it was going to get infected. And at some point, she wanted to have a look at her ribs and hip, both of which were tender to the touch.

From highway to back road to dead end and back, Spencer rode in the rain, searching in vain for a place she could stop. Her eyes were peeled for a closed business, a parking garage or even a dugout on a little league ball field. She needed a place where she could sort out this mess. What was this all about? Had Henry really stumbled across something so sinister that he had been killed for knowing about it? What did James have to do with it all? And how were the feds involved? The questions wouldn't stop.

After several hours and endless loops, she ended up in the one place she hadn't wanted to be—on a road leading back to the interstate. With this morning's fiasco, she figured that the highway patrol and probably every other badge on earth had her description by now. Cynically, she imagined also that their orders now were "shoot to kill." Spencer couldn't risk being out here anymore. She needed to get off the road for now. After dark, she would venture out and try to call Elena again.

As she considered her limited options, she picked up the dreaded sound of a siren, the all-too-familiar threat growing louder as it got closer to where she rode. What if she had been spotted and someone called it in?

With a rising sense of panic, Spencer studied her immediate surroundings. On her left was a large wooded area; on her right, an open field. Straight ahead was I-66 and behind her was a town, filled with stoplights, traffic, and inevitably, the police. The lesser of evils was the woods on the left, so she turned down a side road to find the best place to sneak in without being seen.

The wooded area was probably only two or three acres, but it would have to do. Though most of the leaves on the taller trees were gone, the scrub pines and rhododendrons offered a little cover down low. Still, she would have to go deep into the woods to be completely hidden to anyone driving by, and then she ran the risk of coming out the other side. But all she had to do was find a place to hunker down until dark. There was a poncho in her other saddlebag that she could drape over the bike to make a tent.

Picking her way up the bank and over a fallen log, Spencer caught herself chuckling at the image of her coworkers trying to get their fancy Harleys in here. Could their big touring bikes have jumped the fence at Margadon? *Hell, no!* Could they have climbed curbs, skipped medians and changed directions on a dime? *Doubtful!* Could they clear the underbrush like the Kawasaki? *Not fucking likely!* Her last twenty hours on the dual purpose KL650 could have been a sales video. *Take that, Harley Davidson!*

Spencer was winding slowly back into the woods when she heard the siren closing in fast. Eager to get deeper into the cover, she accelerated a bit, turning back to see if she could catch a glimpse of the cruiser through the trees.

That was unwise for someone not wearing a helmet.

The instant she turned back around, she was smacked across

the forehead by a stiff branch of a barren white oak. Landing with a thud flat on her back, she watched as her bike crashed ahead into a tree. Spencer lay there for all of about eight seconds, marveling at the fact that at least she knew what had hit her. Then she took an unplanned nap.

"Elena Diaz?"

The Latina agent eyed the two men on her front porch. They were FBI—she would stake her badge on it.

"I'm Special Agent Calvin Akers, FBI. This is my partner, Special Agent Mike Pollard."

Yeah, yeah. We're all special. "Good morning. What can I do for you?" Elena didn't give an inch in her doorway. She knew this was about Spencer—her friend's Arlington apartment had been tossed by professionals—but her distrust of the FBI in this town was deep-seated. No agency was more proprietary when involved with other jurisdictions, or more protective when it came to its own.

"May we come in?" It was the senior agent who asked. Akers was a man of about fifty, slightly overweight, and with a crew cut that was mostly gray. Elena read the rugged lines of his face as a sign that he didn't take care of himself very well. She imagined him a hard drinker, a man who lived alone and ate his meals from a package or a brown paper bag.

"What's this about?" She stepped aside to allow the men to enter her townhome.

"Do you recognize these?" Akers held out the pair of leather gloves he had found during their sweep of the scene at Margadon.

Elena nodded nervously. "Those belong to a friend of mine, Spencer Rollins."

"When was the last time you saw Ms. Rollins?"

"If you're conducting an investigation, Agent Akers, I'd

appreciate a little professional courtesy here. I'm a criminal investigator at the IRS." She knew he already knew that.

"Yes, I'm aware of that. We came into custody of Ms. Rollins's cell phone and saw that most of her recent calls were to you, either here or at your office in the District. I take it you two are friends?"

"We are. Now would you tell me what this investigation is about?"

"We're looking into a murder at Margadon Industries in Rockville. A man by the name of Henry Estes was killed last night."

"Henry?" Elena couldn't conceal her shock. She had known Henry for six years and considered him to be her friend as well as Spencer's. She knew that her former lover thought of him as a brother. "What's that got to do with Spencer? She was here at a party until almost midnight." *But she said she was in trouble!*

"Well, that's just it. Estes was killed about one and Rollins showed up on surveillance cameras at twelve forty-five."

"No. That can't be." Elena knew she was somehow playing into their hands, but she couldn't stop herself. No way did Spencer do something like this.

Akers cleared his throat and then began to cough. "Excuse me . . . could I trouble you for a glass of water or something?"

Elena nodded and led him into the kitchen. The other agent stayed behind in the living room. He hadn't said a word but busied himself taking notes while the senior agent talked. He was a younger version of Akers, but not as hard, even for his years. If Elena had to guess, she would say he was married.

"Spencer had nothing to do with this. How can I prove that to you?" She handed the agent a glass of water from the tap.

Akers took it and drank only a sip, his cough magically gone. "Would you happen to know where we could find her? Have you spoken to her today? Maybe she can tell us what she knows and help us find out who did this."

"I don't know where she is." Elena hedged, but she knew that her badge didn't give her the right to conceal information from the FBI. "She called about an hour ago, but we got cut off."

"Did she say where she was calling from?"

"No. All she said was . . . something about being in trouble." Elena hated the way that sounded. Things were looking very bad for Spencer right now. "But there's no way she would have hurt Henry."

"Then would you care to speculate about why she hasn't come forward?"

Elena locked eyes with the tenacious man. She didn't like him. "No."

"Elena?"

Shit! That was Kelly, finally awake. Elena went back into the living room to greet her lover, who had come downstairs dressed only in a long shirt.

"What's going on?"

"Nothing. I'll tell you later." Elena waved dismissively and the younger woman turned and went back upstairs.

Akers handed her a business card. "You understand that your friend is involved in something very serious here, don't you Agent Diaz?"

"It would appear that way . . . but I'm telling you, she didn't do this."

"I know you want to believe that. And for her sake, I hope you're right. But you surely know that it would be best for all concerned if she were to come forward and help clear all this up. If you should hear from Ms. Rollins, please give her my direct number and I'll see to it that she's treated fairly."

Elena took the card and opened her wallet, reaching inside to pull out her own card, one that also boasted a gold shield with the title of Special Agent. "And I'd appreciate it if you kept me apprised of what you find—as a professional courtesy, of course."

"Of course."

She didn't believe him for a minute.

For the second time that same day, the injured cyclist awoke to rain pelting her face. Immediately, her right hand—now the only one she could lift—went to her forehead, where it found a sticky mass she knew was congealed blood. That had been a nasty spill and she had obviously been out for hours, since the last traces of daylight were nearly gone.

Spencer struggled to sit up, reeling at the dull ache from her newest injury. Even the slightest movement brought shooting pains that seemed to wrap around her head, and she was almost overcome by a wave of dizziness and nausea.

It was just twenty-four hours ago that she had said goodnight to Henry and walked out of Margadon, her mind already on the fun-filled party ahead. Since then, her friend had been murdered, the police had chased her all over Maryland and Virginia, she had been shot at, for God's sake, and had spent the night outside in the cold rain. Bruises and a punctured shoulder were bad enough. Now she worried that she might have a concussion or even a fractured skull.

Spencer needed help.

She struggled to her feet and reached out for a branch to steady herself. *That branch! Fuck, no wonder it hurt so bad*, she thought. It was as big as a baseball bat. Her bike lay in a heap a few feet away, but that didn't matter now. She was in no condition to ride.

As the woods darkened around her, Spencer saw that straight ahead—where she had first thought was deeper into the woods—there was a glow of lights. As she suspected, had she pushed on through the trees, she would have emerged on the other side at the edge of the town she had passed.

Steadying herself now on a tree, she stooped to the side pocket on her bike, pulling out the black poncho and dropping it over her head. It didn't matter that she was soaking wet already.

The poncho would cover the blood on her rain suit, and the hood would hide her wet hair and battered face. It was hard not to look like an idiot when you were out wandering around in the pouring rain, bleeding like something out of a horror flick. At least with the poncho, she could hide the worst of it and maybe not call undue attention to herself.

Slowly, Spencer stumbled through the woods in the direction of the light, not knowing what she would find when she emerged. With luck, there would be a phone and a place where she could be warm and dry while she waited for Elena to come pick her up. Twice, she fell. The second time she landed hard on the bruises on her left side. She had no idea how bad her injuries were. All she knew was that they hurt like hell.

Nearing the edge of the woods, the source of light came into view. It was a Wal-Mart, the giant discount department store. Even amidst a downpour on a Saturday night, the store was doing a good business, evidenced by all the cars in the parking lot. By now, Spencer's instincts demanded that she watch for law enforcement vehicles, especially dark sedans with government plates. Seeing neither in the dark lot, she scooted down the muddy embankment, finally reaching the edge of the paved road on the side of the store. This was the path delivery trucks took to reach the loading dock in the back. There weren't any cars over here and she stuck out like a store thumb coming from this direction. Thanks to the rain, there didn't seem to be any shoppers in the parking lot, so no one would see her approach.

Tentatively rounding the building, she spotted a pair of pay phones mounted on the outside wall next to the vending machines. The slim overhang high above offered little shelter from the rain, which was coming down much heavier than before. She could see the shoppers gathering inside the entrance, all waiting for the deluge to let up so they could run to their cars with their packages.

Spencer knew she must look like a fool out in the rain, but she had no choice. Turning her back to the entrance, she leaned against the wall and dropped two quarters into the phone farthest from the door. Concentrating hard on the keypad, she placed her call to Elena's home number. Anxiously, she counted the rings, almost hanging up before she finally heard the response.

"Hello?"

"Elena?" She shouted to be heard above the downpour.

"Spence, is that you?"

"Yeah," she sighed with relief. "I'm in so much trouble."

"Where are you? I'll come get you."

"I'm in Virginia, at a Wal-Mart near I-66. I'm not sure exactly where I am. I just know it's a Wal-Mart." Spencer looked around for a clue as to what this area or city was called. "Elena, Henry's dead. I saw the guys that did it. I think . . . I think it was the feds. And now they're after me."

Like she had this morning, Spencer related the truth as she knew it and waited for her friend's response. But like this morning, it never came.

"Elena?" *Not again!* "Elena?"

At that instant, the programmer realized what she had just done. The fuckers had found her cell phone and they were probably the goddamned FBI or something—maybe the CIA or the Secret Service. Whoever the hell they were, they had to know about Elena and all the calls they made to one another. Of course, if they were looking for her, all they had to do was wait for her to call her friend. They had listened in to every word and both times had cut her off just as she started to explain what had happened. By tapping Elena's phone, they had found her this morning at the gas station, and goddamn it, that was how they would find her again!

Suddenly panicked, Spencer hung up the phone and stepped back, looking at once toward the parking lot entrance for the telltale police car. *Now what?* Her bike was still in the woods. No telling what kind of condition it was in after ramming the tree. She couldn't take a chance on going back for it. They would probably be here before she ever found it again.

Her only other option was one of the cars. Hurrying as fast as she could with her injuries to the nearest row of parked vehicles, she ducked low as she looked for a hiding place. The rain was coming down in torrents.

Her first choice was a pickup truck with a small camper top, but it was locked. Likewise with the SUV two spaces over and the van parked next to it. Finally she reached a red station wagon and gave the door handle a yank. To her surprise and relief, it opened, and she quickly crawled into the back and covered herself with a black tarpaulin that was already spread out.

Waiting anxiously to see if she had been spotted, Spencer listened to the sounds around her. Occasionally a door would slam or an engine would start. The rain was obviously still keeping shoppers inside.

Five minutes passed, then five more. Warm and out of the rain for the first time all day, she gave in to her exhaustion.

As soon as the door opened, Elena charged through it. "I need to use your phone." Not even saying hello, she went straight for the kitchen and grabbed the cordless phone off the wall.

"What did you find out?" Kelly had waited all afternoon for Elena to call her about Spencer.

"They're definitely after Spencer, the FBI. Somebody killed the guy she works with last night, and they're saying it was her. Did you talk to Kaitlyn?"

"Yeah, she said Spencer blew her off right after they walked out. She got a phone call from somebody and said she needed to go."

Elena paced nervously. Spencer had said again that she was in

74

trouble and that she was in Virginia. Then the line went dead, just as it had this morning.

"Do you think she killed him, Elena?"

"No, there's no way. But I don't know how to find out what happened. The FBI agents who talked to me today asked a lot of questions, but they didn't really answer any of mine." She practically snarled as she remembered Akers's cocky attitude. "Hold on just a minute. I need to call my cousin."

"Sure."

Elena dialed the number and spoke in Spanish to a woman, then a man. After a few clipped sentences, she hung up and turned to her lover. "Spencer didn't do this, Kelly. I don't want you wondering about it, no matter what you hear. She didn't do it."

"Okay." Kelly liked Elena's programmer friend and she figured they had probably been lovers once. Elena had been lovers with nearly everyone, she was learning.

"Thanks for the phone. I gotta go back to my house."

"You came all the way over here just to use the phone?"

"Yeah, I think mine's bugged."

Chapter 9

With the rain easing up, most of the Wal-Mart shoppers were now scurrying to their cars, tired of being crammed together in the entryway. A few of the smarter ones had sent someone else to fetch the car while they waited inside.

"Okay, are you ready to make a run for it, Megan?" As much as she could, Ruth practiced saying her daughter's new name.

The little girl nodded and pulled her shopping bag close. It held her brand new Lisa doll, which her mother had rejoiced to find on sale for only thirty-five bucks.

Ruth double-checked that her daughter's coat was zipped all the way up and her hood was secure. She took the child's free hand in her own, her other carrying a heavy bag of sheets, towels and a few dry goods from the food aisle, including a jar of spaghetti sauce and a box of noodles.

"Let's hurry," she cried, jogging across the parking lot during a letup in the deluge. Quickly, she opened the passenger door and guided Jessie onto her booster seat. Next, she opened the door behind Jessie and heaved the shopping bag onto the crumpled tarp. Before the heavy rains could start again, she was in the driver's seat checking the seat belt on her daughter's side.

Just as Ruth reached the exit, two police cars with flashing lights pulled into the parking lot, sending her stomach into knots. Right this minute she hadn't broken any laws, but all that was going to change tomorrow at six o'clock when she was due back at the restaurant with Jessie. They weren't coming for her, she knew. But she wondered how long it would be before she stopped having a physical reaction each time she saw the police.

"What are they doing?" Jessie asked.

"I don't know, honey. Maybe somebody tried to take something without paying."

"That's bad. You have to pay."

"That's right."

"Can I watch TV tonight?"

Ruth chuckled and shook her head in resignation. She hadn't even owned a television when she lived in their little house. Instead, she and her daughter played games and told stories, always finishing the night with the book of Jessie's choice. But life was different when the little girl had gone back to live with her father. Barbara Drummond used the television to keep her granddaughter occupied all day, and Skip spent virtually every evening at home in front of the tube. So despite Ruth's aversion, television was undeniably a part of her daughter's life.

"It's 'may I' and maybe for just a little while," she conceded. "Tell you what. We'll have some spaghetti. Then you may watch TV while I'll put the new sheets on your bed. Maybe after that we'll find a book and have a story. Okay?"

Jessie readily agreed. Her mom was the only one who ever read her stories.

Ruth was exhausted, even though they had taken a two-hour

nap together that afternoon on the scratchy couch. It would take her a few days to get back on the right sleeping and eating schedule, but it was important to try to get into a routine again. The sooner they both got settled, the sooner they would both start putting their past behind them.

Finding the right turnoff in the dark proved a bit of an adventure. The first time, they turned into the wrong driveway, but Ruth realized it immediately and backed out. She laughed to herself at the irony. Here she was worried that Skip would find her new home, and she couldn't even find it herself. Soon they were turning onto the gravel driveway, pulling around to park between the trailer and the house. Ruth turned off the lights and reached behind her to grab the heavy bag.

"Can you take Lisa?"

"Uh-huh," the little girl agreed, turning around as the dome light came on inside the car. "Mommy!"

"What?"

"Who's that?"

"Who's who?" Ruth turned in alarm to see what her daughter was talking about, nearly jumping out of her skin at the sight of a woman's bloody face peeking out from underneath the tarp.

"She has a hurt," the child observed.

"Jessie, run up on the porch and wait for me, okay? Take Lisa and go now." Ruth was trembling with fright, her protective instincts on high alert. She couldn't comprehend why this woman was in their car, but whoever she was, she was trouble.

The four-year-old reluctantly got out of the car. "Who is it?" she turned and asked.

"Shhh . . . I don't know. Go on up there. I'll come and unlock the door and you go straight to your room," she said. Ruth had no idea what she was going to do. Clearly, she couldn't just knock on Viv's door and ask her to call the police. How would that look to be making trouble on their very first day here? Besides, the last thing she wanted was to call attention to herself and Jessie, especially since the only identification she had was a driver's license for Ruth Ferguson.

Once her daughter was safely in her room with the door locked from the inside, Ruth returned to the car and opened the back door. She shook the woman gently, hoping like hell she was only asleep. *What if she's dead!*

To her relief, the woman shifted as though pulling away.

"Hey, wake up. Come on, wake up," she coaxed.

The eyes fluttered open and squinted against the dome light. Her entire face was a bloody mess.

"Come on. You got in the wrong car or something." That was the only explanation that made any sense at all. "I can take you back, but you need to wake up."

"No," the woman moaned. "I can't go back."

"Look, you're hurt. You need to find your family so they can take you to the doctor or something," she urged. She would tell Viv that she forgot something very important and ask to let Jessie stay while she ran back to the store.

"I can't," the stranger murmured.

"Come on, you can't stay here." Perhaps a threat would work. "I'm going to call the police."

"No!" she pleaded, suddenly fully awake and obviously panicked. "No police. Please!"

Ruth knew it was an empty threat. With the stowaway unwilling to leave, she had few options open to her that wouldn't put her at the center of the very thing she needed to avoid. She couldn't very well drive back to the Wal-Mart and dump the woman in the parking lot. Thoughts of the store brought back the image of police cars pulling onto the lot. *God, is this who they were looking for?*

"Are the police after you?"

"Yes." She was barely whispering. "Trying to kill me. Please help me."

Kill you? Surely she didn't mean the police were trying to kill her. But by the battered face, it looked like somebody was. Ruth's sensibilities told her that she shouldn't get involved, but it was too late for that. Of all the cars in the lot, this woman had picked hers, so whatever problems this woman had, they were now Ruth's problems too.

But Ruth's maternal instincts were elevated in the presence of something that might be dangerous to her child. She had no idea what kind of person this woman was or how she had gotten like this. If she was the sort of person to be getting into trouble, Ruth didn't want her around Jessie. That was her pledge to her daughter—that no one would ever hurt her again. She couldn't take a chance with a total stranger.

"I need you to leave. You have to. I have a little girl."

"I won't hurt you. I just need . . . to rest."

Now Ruth's instincts were warring with her conscience. She knew she couldn't just turn the injured woman out. Something told her that a dreadful fate awaited her if Ruth didn't keep her safe tonight.

Besides, it wasn't as though she really had a choice.

"Come on. Let's get you inside."

Saying and doing that were two different things, Ruth realized. The woman was barely conscious and seemed to have little strength. She groaned and fell back in obvious pain when Ruth tried to help by tugging gently on her left arm.

After several attempts, the woman finally managed to stand. She draped her right arm over Ruth's shoulder for support as they climbed the steps and entered the trailer.

Ruth spoke to her daughter through the locked bedroom door. "Jessie, go outside and get the green blanket from the car. Bring it to my bedroom, okay?" Ruth guided the injured woman down the dark hallway to the bedroom in the back.

The child came out of her room and ran back out to the car, returning with a plastic package almost too large for her to carry.

"That's it, honey. Good girl. Can you pull the plastic off?"

80

Ruth eased the woman down to sit on the edge of the bed, holding her upright with one hand while her other released the blanket from its packaging and flung it haphazardly across the center of the bed. Lifting the sides of the nylon poncho, she pulled it over the woman's head and dropped it onto the floor. With the poncho removed, Ruth could see the trail of blood running from the deep gash above the left brow all the way down the front of her shirt.

What have I gotten us into, Jessie? What if . . . ? Ruth couldn't let herself finish the thought.

Wrapping an arm around the woman's sagging shoulders, Ruth edged her backward onto the bed and propped a foam pillow beneath her damp head. Then she lifted the booted feet and swung them to the end of the bed.

"Sweetie, I'm going to let you watch television by yourself for a while, okay? I need to help this lady."

Jessie nodded, clearly afraid of this stranger. "Will she hurt us?"

"No, honey, she isn't going to hurt us. We're going to help her feel better. Then she'll be able to go back to her house by herself." Ruth hoped it was that simple. It was bad enough to have a bleeding stranger in her home. It was worse having someone like that so close to Jessie.

She walked her daughter back to the living room, settled her into the recliner with a carton of juice, and tuned to a children's channel on the television. "You need to stay in here, okay? I'm going to help her for a little while, then I'll make some dinner. Are you getting hungry?" Ruth realized that her fear of the injured woman was contagious and hoped her more casual tone would set her daughter at ease.

"What are we going to have for dinner?"

"Spaghetti."

"Yum."

Ruth ruffled her daughter's hair, relieved to see that she was reassured, at least for the moment. "I'll be in the bedroom. If you need anything, you can call me and I'll come right back out."

Jessie nodded, already engrossed in the program.

Ruth unpacked her first aid materials from a box of toiletries and cosmetics in the bathroom. There wasn't much—some plastic bandages with pictures of cartoon characters, a few cotton balls, tape, antibiotic cream and rubbing alcohol—the standard kit for taking care of Jessie's skinned knees and elbows. She carried the items to the nightstand and returned to the kitchen for a bowl of warm water and a dishcloth. She hoped these meager supplies would be enough to treat the mysterious woman's injuries

Against the dark paneled walls of the bedroom, the overhead light didn't brighten the room very much. To get a better look at the injuries, Ruth took the small lamp from the dresser, plugged it in by the nightstand and removed the shade.

The only injury she could see was the cut above the eye, so Ruth's first priority was to stop the bleeding there. She wet the ragged cloth and began to wipe away the dried blood. The cut was only about an inch wide, just above the brow, but it went all the way to the bone. From the bruising on the forehead, it looked as though she had been hit with something blunt that split the skin. Pressing the woman's shoulder to the bed to hold her still, Ruth used a cotton ball to dab the alcohol directly into the wound.

The injured woman moaned without opening her eyes.

"Yeah, I know it hurts. I'm sorry," she soothed. Next, she gently applied the antibiotic cream and closed the wound with two narrow strips of tape. The woman shivered and Ruth folded the blanket over her. She needed now to feed her child.

"These fuckers are the Keystone Cops," Akers groused into his cell phone. "Urgent means after they've had their goddamned donuts and taken a dump. Rollins was long gone before they ever got there." The agent was driving back to the city for the night.

The situation was getting out of hand. The more time that lapsed, the more dangerous this got for everybody. As much as he hated to, he would have to put out an APB tomorrow. The risk with having somebody else pick her up was that Rollins might run her mouth and point fingers before he or Pollard could take her into custody. Still, they had to bring her in and soon.

"Diaz went out right after the call—over to her girlfriend's house—but she wasn't gone more than twenty minutes," Pollard reported. Both men had been quick to conclude that the woman who came downstairs had something personal going with Diaz. "And she came back alone."

"I don't trust that dyke. We're going to need some rookie backup to keep her under surveillance twenty-four seven. Rollins is gonna call her again. Hell, she might be stupid enough to show up at her office. We just need to make sure we're there when she does."

"Okay, I'll line up a couple of guys first thing in the morning," the junior agent said. He didn't agree at all with Akers about Rollins being stupid. She had slipped away from them three times already. Not many people could say that.

"Line 'em up tonight!" *Twenty-four seven, you moron.*

"Right. I'm on it."

"Are you going to sleep with that hurt lady?" Jessie asked innocently as she crawled into her twin bed.

"No, honey. Tonight I'm going to sleep on the couch like we did this afternoon."

"You can sleep with me in my bed," the child offered.

That was a tempting offer, but it wasn't fair to disrupt Jessie's sleep for a second night in a row. They were both still tired from being on the road all night. "You're sweet, little Megan," she smiled, nuzzling her daughter's hair. "And I love you. But I'll be okay on the couch."

"I love you too, Mommy."

Ruth pulled the door almost closed and headed back to the bigger bedroom to check on her patient. During dinner, she had become suddenly anxious that the woman might actually die in their trailer and had jumped up to find her resting peacefully, but feverish. That, no doubt, was from being out in the rain.

Maybe it would help if she got this woman out of her wet clothes. She probably should have done that in the first place, but she hadn't wanted to do more than what was necessary to keep her from bleeding to death. Pulling the blanket back, Ruth noticed for the first time that the woman was wearing some sort of rainproof jumpsuit. Why was she dressed like that? Had she been riding a motorcycle? That was the most logical explanation, and maybe the downpour would explain why she sought refuge in the car.

As she unsnapped the top, she saw a leather jacket underneath and a pale yellow shirt under that. Starting with the boots, she carefully undressed her patient, stopping when she reached the jeans and shirt. The jeans were dry so there wasn't any need to remove them. Ruth was surprised to see how much blood had dripped onto the woman's shirt from the cut above the brow.

She unbuttoned the shirt and pulled back the collar, gasping in horror as the real source of the blood was revealed, a swollen and discolored puncture wound, festering with infection. *Is this a bullet wound?* This, she realized, was the reason for the fever.

Drawing the shadeless lamp closer, Ruth could barely make out something brown and solid in the center of the wound, a stick or something. Gently brushing her fingertip across the opening, she could feel a jagged point. Whatever it was, it needed to come out and the hole needed to be cleaned.

84

She soaked a cotton ball with alcohol and dripped a little of the fluid onto the wound, causing the woman to wake up and jerk away.

"Shhh, I'm trying to help you here. You need to relax."

"It's . . . a stick . . . broken."

"Yeah, I can see that. I'm going to have to try to pull it out, and it's probably going to hurt like crazy."

"It already does," she gasped.

With the tweezers from her cosmetic bag, Ruth pinched the end of the stick and gently started to work it out. Unable to stand the pain, the injured woman flinched and tried to sit up.

"You have to be still. I'll be as careful as I can." With her left hand, she gently pressed the woman's breastbone and urged her back against the blanket. As the anguished face contorted in pain, Ruth tugged the stick, this time pulling it out amidst a new flow of blood. That would help cleanse the wound, but the alcohol would be better. As she trickled it again directly into the wound, the woman flailed, her flesh on fire.

"I got it. It's out." Ruth blew on the wound as she would her child's scraped knee. The woman calmed down and her breathing slowed. "Shhh . . . that's it. You can go back to sleep now."

Chapter 10

As tired as she had been when she had finally gone to bed, Ruth had expected a better night's sleep, even on the cramped couch. But the anxiety about being on the run, coupled with the presence of an injured stranger in their home, robbed her of the peace of mind she needed to rest. Now the sun was up, and it already looked as though today it might actually shine.

Today was Sunday. She would give her right arm to know what was going on back in Madison right now. Chances were that no one even missed her yet. Skip never contacted her over the weekend, and she had made it a point to tell her friends at work that she and her daughter planned to stay indoors and play. Friends rarely called when they knew she had Jessie, not wanting to interrupt what little time the two had together.

Coffee would be good, Ruth thought, tossing back the thin blanket as she set her bare feet on the cold vinyl floor. All she had was one packet of instant powder that she had nicked from work. She and Jessie would have to hit the grocery today.

As she shuffled over to the kitchen area, she was startled by a pounding on the door, accompanied by animated shouts from her landlady.

"Anybody up?"

Jesus! Flinging open the door, Ruth squinted in the light of day as she greeted a beaming Viv on the porch. *How could people be so jolly at this hour of the morning?*

"Still in bed, huh?"

"What time is it?" A brisk autumn breeze blew into the room, and Ruth hugged herself as she shivered.

"It's almost nine o'clock."

"You're kidding!" Maybe she had slept better than she thought.

"You're just in time to witness the miracle of birth."

A still sleepy Jessie joined her mother at the door, wearing her favorite blue pajamas. "Puppies?" she asked excitedly.

"Yes, ma'am! They're coming now." Viv had told them both yesterday that Maggie was overdue.

"Can we go see?" the little girl begged.

"Sure, honey. Let me get my"—the child stepped off the porch into Viv's waiting arms and was gone before she could blink—"shoes."

Before leaving, Ruth tiptoed down the hall to check on her patient. The cut over the woman's eye had seeped a little more blood, but all in all, it was a heck of a lot better than it had been last night. The shoulder, too, looked better, swathed in ointment and covered in a Fred Flintstone bandage. The woman had hardly moved at all and seemed to be resting without distress.

Ruth looked for the first time at the mysterious stranger in her bed—not at the patient, but at the woman. Her face was pretty, despite the swollen eye that was already turning black and blue. The hair was disheveled and stringy from being wet, but it was a nice shade of brown with auburn highlights. The woman was calm today, compared to the night before when she had been agitated and anxious about the police. The irony of that wasn't lost on Ruth, as neither she nor this stranger wanted to call attention to herself. Now if they could just get her well and get her out before anyone . . . *shit! Please don't say anything to Viv, Jessie.*

Ruth donned her shoes and robe, grabbing the same for her daughter before she bolted across the yard to the back door. In the utility room off the kitchen, Maggie was doing her thing as Viv, Jessie and proud papa Thor looked on in fascination.

"Look, Mommy, four puppies!"

"Here, put these on, sweetie." She handed the child her slippers and robe and peeked over her shoulder to have a look.

"And more on the way," Viv added, pressing a welcome mug of hot coffee into her tenant's hand. "You want cream or sugar?"

"No, thanks. This is perfect. Thank you."

The black Lab had produced two chocolate, one black, and one yellow offspring thus far.

"How many do you think she'll have?"

"A usual litter is anywhere between six and ten. I'm hoping for more because they'll fetch about four hundred dollars apiece."

"You're kidding! People really pay that much for a dog?" Ruth asked.

"Full-blooded Labradors aren't just any dog, I'll have you know. Thor's a champion, and Maggie's won Best of Opposite Sex three times." Viv went on to tell about their successes in the area dog shows. She had given that up last year when Thor won his champion status. It was a lot of work to show dogs, she explained.

Jessie watched Maggie with continued excitement as Viv led Ruth to her den, where ribbons, trophies, and photos documented her dogs' illustrious careers in the ring.

"You don't show anymore?"

"Naw, it was fun though." Viv turned out the light in the den and led them back to the action off the kitchen. "It's just that after a while, the dogs didn't seem to like it all that much, and I didn't think it was right to put 'em through all that training and grooming and traveling when they weren't having fun anymore."

That seemed like a fair response to Ruth. She had always felt you could tell a lot about people from the way they treated animals, and that, along with the easy way the woman had taken to Jessie and her, made Viv a pretty good soul.

A half hour later, Maggie's work was done—a grand total of eight puppies, all seemingly healthy and squirming contentedly. The new mother poked each one with her nose as if counting off and licked them clean while guiding them to her teats.

"I like that one," Jessie proclaimed, pointing to a fat chocolate pup on the top of the pile.

"Then I'll save that one for you," Viv promised.

"Oh, we'd better wait and see," Ruth interjected. "I don't think I can afford a dog as nice as that one, Viv."

"This one's a gift for Megan . . . and for you, of course. Thor and Maggie will like having one of their pups close by."

Pleading looks from both her landlady and daughter erased Ruth's hesitation. Jessie needed something fun in her life, and it looked like they would be sticking around for a while.

"Okay, but you're going to have to help take care of it," she told her daughter.

"Oh, I will!" the happy child promised. She had never had a puppy before.

I can't believe I let myself get talked into that so fast. To Ruth, this had all the feeling of a bad sitcom. She could already see herself walking the dog alone in the snow and cleaning up its mess. And it would probably end up sleeping at the foot of her bed. "Megan, why don't we go fix some breakfast while Maggie takes a nap?"

"I've got plenty to eat here. I bet you're not even set up in your kitchen yet. Why don't ya'll come on in and I'll whip up some pancakes and bacon?" Viv was obviously getting a kick out of having her tenants around, especially Megan.

"We don't want to be any trouble," Ruth answered, all the while thinking that pancakes and bacon sounded a lot better than cold cereal with powdered milk.

"I'm gonna fix breakfast anyway. It's no trouble at all to just add a little more. Come on and stay. Here, let me give you a refill on that coffee." Without waiting for a response, she took Ruth's mug and filled it up.

"All right, then. Thank you. We accept." But she had to talk privately to Jessie before the girl said anything about the woman back at the trailer. "Could we wash up? And then I'll come back and help."

"Sure, right down that hall on the left."

Ruth guided her daughter into the bathroom and closed the door. She turned on the water first and began to speak. "You like Viv, don't you?"

Jessie nodded happily.

Despite the self-imposed distance, Ruth had to admit that she liked Viv too.

"Sweetie, don't forget that we have a secret. Even if we like Viv, we can't tell her our secret, okay?"

"Okay."

"It's very important." She couldn't emphasize that enough. "And you know what? We have another secret, too. Do you remember last night when we found that lady in the car and she was hurt?"

Jessie's eyes grew big with fright. She had forgotten about that.

"Honey, that has to be a secret too. We're going to help her until she's all better, and then she'll leave. But we can't tell anybody she's staying with us, not even Viv. Okay?"

"Why not?"

Good question, Jessie. Damn good question. "It's really complicated, sweetheart. I guess the best answer is that if we tell somebody she's here, they might find out about our other secret."

It was complicated all right. She could tell by the confused look on her daughter's face that she had more questions. It was just that Jessie hadn't figured out what to ask next.

Spencer stirred and opened her eyes, anxious to get her bearings. She was in an unfamiliar room with brown paneled walls and windows on each side. The windows rolled out, and there weren't any windowsills. She was in a trailer. The room was narrow and sparse, with no pictures or personal items visible from the bed.

It was coming back to her. The woods . . . the call to Elena . . . the car. She hadn't expected to be driven away. She had just needed to hide for a few minutes in case the police came by, but she must have fallen asleep. It was a miracle that she was here today and not in jail.

Vaguely, she remembered the woman who had tended to her last night . . . the long blond hair, the pretty green eyes . . . the soft, comforting voice . . . *Where the hell was this place? And why hadn't that woman called the police?*

Her left shoulder hurt like a son of a bitch, but it no longer felt swollen or hot to the touch like it had when she woke up in the woods. She pulled back the collar of a T-shirt that wasn't hers, barely making out a picture of a cartoon character on the bandage that covered her wound. When she twisted her head to look at it, she was reminded of another injury, the one above her eye . . . from that branch that had come out of nowhere and smacked her.

With a colossal effort, Spencer leaned forward and swung her legs over the side of the bed. She could see her rain suit lying on the floor in the corner, along with her clothes and boots. She was very thirsty and her head pounded like a jackhammer. Pushing herself gingerly off the bed, she started for the door, growing dizzier by the step. Flailing wildly, she lunged for the doorknob, hoping to get her balance.

Then it all went black.

Elena watched impassively as her cousin helped himself to the last remnants of Friday night's party: stale chips, hardened cheese cubes, and dried-out olives. There wasn't anything Rico wouldn't eat.

"And you haven't heard from her since, huh?" he asked. As was their habit with family, he and his cousin spoke in Spanish.

"No. That was last night, right after dark. She said she was in trouble, Rico. I'm really afraid for her." The worry in Elena's voice was genuine, even if the conversation wasn't.

"Do you think she could have done something like this?"

"I don't know what to think."

Elena and her cousin kept the mindless banter going while his buddy Luis combed the townhouse for surveillance devices. In a handwritten note, the spy-wear hobbyist had already confirmed that her phone was tapped, so Elena assumed that these FBI bastards were also listening in on her cell phone and most likely, monitoring her ISP. She hoped that Spencer knew it too, and that she wouldn't put herself at risk by trying to make contact again.

"What do you think, Luis?" The IRS agent had earlier noticed the van down the street and knew that whoever was watching had seen the two men enter her home. If indeed they were listening, she didn't want them to suspect the real purpose of Luis's visit.

"I don't know. I only met her a couple of times. She didn't really strike me as the type, though." Excitedly, he motioned

Elena and Rico to the end table by the sofa, pointing toward a listening device that was affixed to the back of the leg.

"Yeah, I'm with you," she agreed. "I just wish the FBI would tell me what's going on. I tell you, those agents can be such pricks."

The word "pricks" didn't translate into Spanish, so that would save a little time for the boys in the van who were taping the exchange.

Chapter 11

All through breakfast, Ruth fought the urge to excuse herself to run back to the house to check on her patient. The injured woman had been fine when they left her, still sleeping off whatever war she had been fighting. But she and Jessie shouldn't stay too long at Viv's, she knew. It wouldn't do at all for the woman to get up and suddenly come looking for her.

Viv prepared a veritable feast for their Sunday breakfast: blueberry pancakes with warm maple syrup, bacon, cantaloupe, coffee and milk. At first, she had wanted to set everything up in the formal dining room, but Ruth insisted that the kitchen table was perfect for her and Jessie. They didn't need anything fancy at all, she said.

From the outside of the house, no one would have guessed that the simple frame structure was like two separate homes inside, divided by a long hallway that led from the kitchen to the front door. One side of the house resembled an antique museum; the other, a comfortable old shoe. The formal living room, the dining room and the guest bedroom were packed with polished antiques of dark, rich woods and brass. The overstuffed chairs and davenport weren't particularly inviting, but they were lovely to look at. Given what she already knew about Viv's down-to-earth nature, Ruth had trouble envisioning the woman living in a setting so elegant.

By contrast, the kitchen, den and Viv's bedroom held a modern but worn décor that seemed to encourage staying a while and making yourself at home. That was truer to the image the landlady presented and it was, in fact, the kind of home Ruth wanted someday for her daughter and herself.

When they were finished with the meal, Jessie returned to the utility room to watch Thor and Maggie with the puppies. Ruth offered to wash dishes while Viv dried them and put them away. Despite her growing anxiety about the woman back at the trailer, Ruth found herself relaxing in Viv's company. The landlady told her a little about the history of Manassas and offered to take them both on a tour of the community when they got settled. Already, the young mother was feeling like she and Viv could be friends.

"I guess we better get going. I need to make a list and go pick up some groceries."

"Can we take the puppy?" Jessie asked.

"No, we can't bring him home yet," she answered her daughter with a smile. "He has to stay with his mother until he's bigger so he'll be healthy."

"Can I visit him?"

"It's 'may I' and if it's okay with Viv, I don't see why not."

"You can come whenever you want, Megan," their hostess politely replied.

Ruth laughed to herself and bit her tongue not to automatically correct her landlady with "may." She liked the fact that

Jessie was exposed to an older woman who was patient and attentive. The little girl had been destined to miss out on that kind of relationship in Madison. Skip's mother was distant and stern. Ruth's own mother Mildred had never quite gotten past the fact that Jessie had been conceived outside of marriage.

"What are you going to name him? Have you decided?" Viv asked.

Jessie cocked her head sideways while she thought about it. "Brownie?"

"That's . . . okay. He's brown." Ruth nodded her head thoughtfully.

"Or Hershey?" Viv suggested. "Since he's chocolate."

"Hershey! We'll call him Hershey." Jessie squealed with delight. She had heard of the famous candy maker.

"I wonder how many chocolate Labs are named Hershey," Ruth mused.

"Probably thousands. But Cadbury doesn't really suit him," Viv laughed.

"Hey, sweetie, there's another chocolate maker you like. Do you remember his name?"

"Willy Wonka!"

"What if we called him Willy?"

"Or Wonka," Jessie argued.

"I like Willy better than Wonka," her mom answered seriously, shooting Viv a pleading look.

"I think I like Willy too," she agreed.

"Willy!" The little girl got down from the table and ran into the utility room. "Yeah, his name's Willy."

"Say goodbye to him for now, Megan. Then we need to thank Viv for her wonderful breakfast and go back to our house." Ruth stood and waited next to the back door, glancing over at the trailer to see if there were any signs of life.

Jessie did as she was told and the two headed out. Stuffed to the gills, mother and daughter climbed the wooden steps to their new home, the youngster heading immediately for her room where she picked up her Lisa doll and returned to take a seat on the couch.

"Can I watch TV?"

"It's 'may I'," Ruth corrected gently. "And yes, you may." That would give her a chance to look in on their uninvited guest. She didn't want Jessie around the woman any more than was absolutely necessary. She still couldn't image what kind of person got herself in this condition.

Ruth helped her daughter find a children's program, and then headed back down the darkened hallway. She met resistance as she pushed the door, seeing with alarm that the woman was crumpled in the entry. Ruth shoved harder, and when the door opened far enough, she rushed in to check that the collapsed figure was breathing okay and not losing any more blood.

"Hey, wake up," she coaxed softly. *Please don't die on me!* Lifting the dark head off the hard floor, she prodded, "Are you okay?"

"I think I got dizzy," the woman murmured, slowly opening her eyes to find herself once again face to face with this soothing presence.

"You need to stay in bed until you're better. Let me help you get back there." Ruth was frightened now at what could have happened—at what still might happen—and she was desperate to get this woman well so she could leave.

Spencer tried to stand, leaning heavily on her caretaker. "I'm so thirsty."

"I'll bring you something to drink. Come on, get back in bed."

Spencer collapsed again on the bed, mystified at where her energy had gone. Besides the pain in her shoulder, side and head, her legs felt like cement and the dizziness was disorienting. Lying on her back, she tried again to get a grip on where she was and what had happened to her. Last night, there had been a little girl, too.

"Here you go." The woman returned, presenting a glass of cold water and three ibuprofen tablets. "You should take these too. I think you have a fever."

Spencer tried to sit up, and the woman reached behind her to steady her back. She swallowed the tablets and started to sip from the glass, but her overpowering thirst got the better of her and soon she was gulping it down in huge swallows. Too much water too fast caused her to choke and cough, which in turn, made her clutch her battered ribs in agony. Her eyes watered as she slumped forward, the kind woman patting her softly on the back.

"You want to try again?" Ruth offered, this time holding the glass herself to control the amount.

Spencer took another couple of drinks and lay back against the pillow, tugging up her T-shirt to check out a dark purple bruise the size of two hands just beneath her left breast. She pushed down the top of her panties to reveal a similar bruise on her hipbone.

"I saw those last night. What happened to you?"

"A motorcycle wreck," Spencer answered breathlessly, "on Friday night."

"Friday night!" That was almost two days ago. "Why didn't you go to the hospital?"

The dark-haired woman shook her head. "I can't," was all she said.

"But you have to. I think your shoulder's infected and it looks like your ribs might be broken. And you need to let me call somebody and let them know you've been hurt." The last part was added with the hope that the injured woman would be more agreeable to move on today than she was last night.

She shook her head again. "No, I can't." Spencer tried again to pull herself upright, worried that this woman would call someone now that she had seen the extent of her injuries.

"Wait . . . no! It's okay." Ruth guided her back against the pillows, where she closed her eyes. "You can stay here until you're better. I won't call anyone," she promised.

"What's your name?" the injured woman asked softly.

Ruth hesitated. "Karen."

Spencer reached out and clasped her savior's hand, squeezing it hard. "Thank you, Karen." It was barely a whisper. "I'm Spencer. Thank you."

After a few minutes, the dark-haired woman relaxed and her breathing slowed, a sure sign that she had drifted off again. No doubt, her body was fighting the wound infection as best it could, but it wouldn't hurt to reapply the ointment and change the small bandage.

"Just don't die on me, Spencer. That would be pretty hard to explain," Ruth said softly, fairly sure that her words had fallen on undiscerning ears.

Ruth had no idea what to do if the ribs were broken, but she remembered one of the guys that Skip had played ball with wearing an elastic bandage around his torso. She made a mental note to pick one up when they went out for groceries. Whatever she could do to get this stranger fixed up and on her way was worth it.

Against the backdrop of cartoons, Ruth and Jessie fell asleep together on the couch, the former still trying to recover from the overnight drive from Maine. When they awoke, she began her grocery list with her new budget in mind. Ruth had plenty of money to get set up, but she needed to be mindful that the cash she had garnered might have to go a long way, especially if she had trouble finding work that would accommodate Jessie's hours in day care. The good news was that the little girl turned five next summer and would start kindergarten in the fall.

Ruth checked on the injured woman again, relieved to see her resting comfortably. Satisfied that this time she would stay put, the mother grabbed her jacket and pulled it on.

"Sweetie, we have to go to the grocery. Can you put your coat on?"

"You mean 'may I,'" the child corrected haughtily.

Ruth had to stop and think before responding. "No, not in this case, honey. You use 'may' when you're asking permission and 'can' when you're asking if you're able."

"That's too hard to remember."

"I know. But you'll get the hang of it one of these days," she said with encouragement. "You're a really smart girl."

Jessie loved hearing that from her mother. Her daddy had never said anything that nice to her. "Do you think Daddy's looking for us now?"

Out of the mouths of babes! Ruth had awakened from their nap, uneasy and anxious about the impending hour of six, the moment that she officially became a fugitive. The feeling would probably intensify over the next few weeks. There were times that she wondered if she ever really would be able to put Madison, Maine, behind them.

"I don't know, sweetie. But he isn't going to find Karen and Megan Oliver, is he?"

Jessie grinned and shook her head. "We're hiding."

"Let's go."

On Viv's recommendation, Ruth set out for the Food Lion, a chain grocery with everyday brands and many items on sale. Before going inside, Ruth checked out the pharmacy next door. The elastic bandages big enough for someone's torso were expensive, but the woman back at the trailer needed something in case those ribs were actually broken.

Returning from their errands just before dark, Jessie asked to visit the puppies. When Viv said it was okay, they took a quick peek and headed for the trailer. Once the groceries were put away, the two shared a cheese pizza as they settled in the living room for their first real night together at home.

As she finished washing the dishes, Ruth noticed the clock

over the stove. Six fifteen. Skip Drummond was a raving madman by now, probably stomping around the parking lot at the fast food restaurant and kicking trashcans. Before too long, he would drive to her house to see what was taking so long, yelling in the car all the things he planned to say when he got there. It would probably be another hour or so before he got in touch with the police, and only then so they would find her for him and lock her up for violating their court order. It wasn't like he was worried about his daughter.

"Will you play Candy Land with me?" Jessie asked, reminding her that Skip didn't need to exist anymore.

"Sure. Do you remember where we put the games?"

"Under my bed." To Jessie, this was one of the best things about living with her mom. Her daddy never wanted to play games, read stories or play with toys like her mom did. "I want to be blue!" she called.

"Then I'll be . . . What color should I be?"

"Red!"

"Okay, I'll be red."

For forty minutes, they took turns drawing the cards and marching their gingerbread men to the castle. Ruth got there first in the first game and they played again. By skipping the shortcuts, she made sure that Jessie won the second time. That was always a good stopping point.

Next was a bath and a book, and soon, the four-year-old was down for the count.

As she had done practically every hour, Ruth returned to the back bedroom to check on the injured woman once again. Spencer had slept for most of the last twenty-four hours, still fighting the infection and probably the effects of being out in the rain so long. The wounds on her shoulder and eyebrow were definitely better, though, and maybe tomorrow she would be well enough to be taken somewhere and dropped off.

After a shower, Ruth grabbed one of the pillows from the bed and headed back out to the couch. Last night, she was so tired that she hadn't bothered with more than just a thin blanket, but tonight she decided to spread out a sheet on the scratchy upholstery. With any luck, this would be her last night on the couch.

Settling in, she used the remote to turn on the television, lowering the volume so she wouldn't disturb Jessie in the next room. Flipping through the channels, she stopped for a local newscast at ten o'clock. Barely able to hold her eyes open, she listened to the report, her worst fear being that the authorities would be on her trail already, broadcasting her picture and a description of the red station wagon with Maine tags.

"Authorities in the metro D.C. area are seeking your help tonight with a murder investigation. Spencer Rollins is wanted in connection with the murder of Henry Estes, a computer programmer at Margadon Industries in Rockville. Estes was found strangled in his office on Saturday morning. Police say he died late Friday evening. Rollins, a coworker, was captured on surveillance tapes leaving the scene around the time of the murder. The suspect is considered armed and dangerous. If you have information . . ."

Ruth suddenly sat up, now wide awake and staring at the picture on the screen, her whole body trembling. The mysterious woman down the hall . . . the woman sleeping in her bed . . . whose wounds she had so carefully treated . . . was wanted for murder. She turned, her heart nearly stopping as she saw the tall figure standing over her shoulder in the hallway.

Chapter 12

"It isn't true," Spencer said, falling to a knee as she grabbed the end table for support. "I didn't do it."

"I need you to leave," Ruth pleaded, her voice shaking with fear. How could she have let a murderer into her home, so close to where her daughter slept? "My daughter . . ."

"It's not true," the woman repeated. "I didn't kill that man. He was my best friend," she said sadly, her eyes filling with tears. "I'm not going to hurt you."

"Then go to the police." Ruth had stood and taken a step backward toward the kitchen, hoping to draw the woman away from Jessie's room. "But you have to leave—right now."

"I can't go to the police."

Ruth shook again with panic. What if the authorities came looking for her here? "You can't stay here. I'm going to call the police."

"Please don't. I promise I'll go. And I won't hurt you," the injured woman pleaded, pulling herself to her feet. She was barefoot, wearing her jeans and the T-shirt Ruth had dressed her in. "But I didn't kill him. You've got to believe me. He was my best friend." Spencer didn't know what else to say to convince the woman.

"Then why can't you turn yourself in? If you're innocent, they'll let you go."

"They'll kill me." Spencer knew the words sounded absurd, but she believed them to be true. She slid over the arm of the old leather recliner, completely spent from just the short trip down the hall. "I don't really understand either. I just know that something's wrong with all of this. And it isn't just that they're saying I did it."

"But you were there. They said they caught you on tape."

"I was there. But so were the people that killed Henry. I saw them. At least I saw them in our office and he was already dead. They were talking about something . . . about whatever it was Henry found in the code. They were whispering and the lights were off. Then they saw me and started chasing me. That's how I wrecked my bike."

Something in the code? Ruth didn't have a clue what Spencer was talking about. "So why can't you tell the police that?"

Spencer sighed. She was still trying to make sense of it herself. "Because one of the guys who I think killed Henry was our boss. And the other one was some kind of federal agent. That's who chased me. A black car with government plates."

Ruth didn't say anything. She just stared with a look of disbelief.

"I got away from these guys on Friday night. I hid in a park all night, and when I went to call my friend and tell her what happened, the police showed up at the pay phone I was using. They chased me again, and this same guy—this federal agent who was in Henry's office—he shows up out of nowhere. I'm telling you, he wants me dead too. Don't ask me how, but I know he does. He even shot at me yesterday when I was trying to get away."

Ruth relaxed a little. She still didn't understand why this woman didn't come forward with her side of the story, but the sadness in her voice every time she mentioned the man who was killed—and the fact that she was still as weak as a kitten—made her less threatening than when she was looming in the hallway. "Your story doesn't make any sense."

"I know." Spencer leaned forward and held her throbbing head in her heads. "This is going to sound ridiculous . . . but can I have something to eat?"

Ruth ignored her question. "Do you have any weapons in this house?"

"No!"

"Do you have a cell phone or something? Can you call somebody to come get you?"

Again, Spencer shook her head. "I lost it when I crashed my bike. That's how they knew I was going to call my friend, because her number was in there."

Ruth stood in the kitchen sizing up the situation. This woman didn't strike her as a killer. Her story was outrageous and disjointed, but Spencer didn't seem to have a coldness that would allow her do something like that.

"I can make you a cheese sandwich. Or I have some leftover spaghetti I could heat up."

"Anything. I'm sorry I'm so much trouble. I promise, I'll be out of here tomorrow." Spencer's head was still swimming, but she needed a plan for saving her ass, and that wasn't going to happen with her lying in bed all day. "You've been . . . I really appreciate everything you've done."

Ruth took the bowl of spaghetti from the refrigerator and spooned some of the sticky pasta into a saucepan, adding a small bit of water so it would stir. The stranger wasn't so intimidating when she was sitting down with her head in her hands.

"So what do you think really happened?"

"Henry and I found a problem in one of our computer routines on Friday afternoon. We're programmers at Margadon," she explained. "He stayed late to work on it. I left to go to a friend's party."

Telling the story aloud brought unexpected pangs of guilt. If she had stayed to help Henry, maybe this wouldn't have happened.

"He called me around midnight to say that he'd found something big. He asked me to come back to the office and look at it. I had other plans and I didn't really want to go, but then he said he'd already called James, so I knew that whatever it was must have been a pretty big deal. Henry didn't get excited about much, and he was wild on the phone."

"Who's James?" Ruth scooped the now steaming spaghetti onto a plate and grabbed a fork.

"He's our boss. He's the controller, the one in charge of the inventory flow. So when I got to Margadon, it was dark upstairs. Everything was dark. And it shouldn't have been, because Henry was supposed to be working. He wouldn't do that with the lights out, so that was the first sign that something was weird. I went toward our office and I could see James and some other guy standing over Henry's terminal. I started to walk in, but they were . . . I don't know, acting funny. I don't know how to describe it, but it's like they were whispering and nervous. So when I got to the office, I could see in, and Henry was lying on the floor . . ." Spencer shuddered at the horrible image in her mind. "And he had a power cord tied in a knot around his neck."

Ruth had been waiting to hand Spencer the plate, but she set it on the counter and took a seat on the barstool when she saw that the woman had lost her composure.

"I tried to get out without anyone seeing me—I would have gone straight to the cops right then—but they saw me and the next thing I knew, they were chasing me all over the parking lot.

That's when I saw that it was a government car, like the FBI or something. I had to jump the fence on my bike. That's how all this happened," she indicated her injuries.

"Maybe they just wanted to talk to you," Ruth reasoned. "Maybe they were investigating it already."

"You heard what they said on the news. They said they didn't even find Henry until the next day. No way were these guys investigating anything."

Ruth wanted to believe every word, because if the story wasn't true, she was sharing her home with a murderer. "So tell me why you can't just go to the police now. I mean, if you told them this story, they'd be able to find these guys and figure out who's really guilty."

Spencer shook her head in frustration. "It's gotten so much more complicated than that. These guys are after me, these guys who were chasing me on Friday night. They were right there when the police showed up yesterday morning. They're calling the shots. If they didn't even find Henry until yesterday, why would the police be trying to pick me up?"

Ruth shook her head. It didn't make sense to her either.

"I think these FBI guys were waiting for me to call Elena, and when I did, they cut me off before I could tell her anything and sent the cops to hold me until they got there. 'Cause this guy who was after me showed up in no time. If they'd picked me up, I probably would have ended up dead just like Henry. They'll say I was shot trying to escape or something. I saw what they did and they have to shut me up."

"You called your friend and the line just happened to go dead when you started to tell her about it?" This was so preposterous that Ruth was starting to think that the woman was making this up as she went.

"Yeah. Look, I know how that sounds. I don't think I'd believe me either, so I know exactly why you're looking at me like that." The look was one of complete incredulity. "But I swear to God, it's the truth. Or at least it's the truth as I know it. The woman I called is an agent with the IRS, an investigative agent. She's law enforcement, just like these guys. Like I said, I lost my cell phone when I crashed the bike, so I'm guessing they found it and they know I call her all the time. Outside of Henry and Elena, I really don't have any other friends. Probably the last twenty calls on my log were to one or the other. And these guys had to be listening in when I called. Otherwise, they wouldn't have gotten to me so fast."

Ruth remembered the two police cars that were entering the parking lot at the Wal-Mart just as she left. "Did you call your friend again last night?"

Spencer nodded. "Yeah, and when they cut me off again, that's when I realized how they found me. That's why I hid in your car. I thought the police would come."

Ruth almost snorted. "Well, they did. Two cars, right when I was pulling out of Wal-Mart on the way home."

Spencer closed her eyes and sighed.

"So why do you think these men killed the guy you worked with?"

"Henry was more than just a guy I worked with. He was my best friend," Spencer said softly. "We've worked three feet away from each other for the last six years. God, he was smart. He was a lot smarter than I was, but I wouldn't have told him that. We were always bragging to each other about who was the best." Spencer chuckled. "Henry was the best and we both knew it." She swiped at a tear that rolled down her cheek. "You have no idea how unreal it is that somebody would kill a person like Henry. He never hurt a soul, even when people gave him a hard time."

"Why would they give him a hard time?"

"Henry was an albino. Assholes made fun of him a lot, but it just rolled off his back. He was one of the nicest people I ever knew."

Ruth listened to the woman talk about her friend, and as she heard her story and saw the sadness in her face, she became wholly convinced that the woman in her house was not Henry's murderer. She stood up again to get the plate from the kitchen. "Here, you need to eat."

"Thank you." Spencer had eaten a single bite of a sweet roll in the last two days. "I guess I should also say thanks for taking care of me these last couple of days and for not just calling the cops."

"You're welcome, but . . . Look, I don't mean to be unsympathetic, but you can't stay here. I can take you somewhere, to a friend's house or something, but I really don't want to be in the middle of this. I've got my own problems."

Spencer nodded solemnly. She didn't want to cause any trouble for this woman or her little girl.

"Can you take me back to where I hid my bike in the morning? It's near that Wal-Mart, back in the woods."

"Sure."

"I'll, uh . . . stay out here on the couch tonight. You can have your bed back."

"That's okay. You could probably use another good night's sleep. How's the shoulder?"

"It's better."

"And your side?"

Spencer glanced up as a little girl appeared in the hallway.

"Mommy?" Keeping her distance as much as possible, Jessie crossed the room to where her mother sat.

"Yes, sweetie. Come here." For some reason, Ruth's stomach knotted at the thought of her daughter being in the room with this suspicious woman, though she had concluded to her own satisfaction that Spencer Rollins hadn't killed anyone. However, she couldn't help but be skeptical about the rest of the story. It seemed pretty outrageous to think that the feds were really trying to kill her. It was probably paranoia—or an overactive imagination.

"Hi, I'm Spencer. You don't have to be afraid of me." Spencer set her empty plate on the floor beside the recliner.

"This is my daughter, Megan."

"Hello, Megan. Your mom and I were just talking. I'm going to leave tomorrow so you don't have to worry about anything."

Jessie wouldn't answer.

"Did we wake you up?" Ruth asked tenderly, brushing the blond curls back. "Why don't I come in and read another story? We're all ready to go to sleep now."

Spencer took that as her cue to head back down the hall. She felt a lot better now that she had eaten, but another night's sleep would be a good thing. She was still exhausted.

And tomorrow she would be a target again.

Chapter 13

Ruth was fairly sure that there had to be a shortcut or a bypass that everyone in town knew about and used to get from one end to the other, but today was not a good day for experimenting with alternate routes or getting to know the neighborhood. Until she learned her way around, she thought it best to stay on the main road. That meant one stoplight after another and many long minutes alone in the car with her enigmatic passenger.

"Where exactly are we?"

Ruth shot her passenger a sidelong glance. "What do you mean? This is Manassas."

"Yeah, I got that from the sign on that building back there. But I mean what highway is this and where does it go? How do I get back to D.C. from here?"

Beats the hell out me, Ruth admitted to herself. "I'm not sure."

"You don't ever go to the District for anything?"

"We haven't lived here very long."

Spencer considered this new bit of information. Come to think of it, Karen had shared very little about herself. Then again, it wasn't like they were friends or anything.

The three of them had eaten a quiet breakfast, and then mother and daughter had gone to the house next door to visit the puppies. The little girl stayed with the landlady when Karen said she had a quick errand to run.

"So where are you from?"

"Maine," Ruth answered nervously, knowing that her license tags had already given that away. Changing those to Virginia plates was a top priority. She would try to do that this afternoon.

"What brings you down here?"

"The usual. A bad marriage . . . a new start." None of that was a lie.

"What kind of work do you do?"

"Enough with all the questions!" Ruth groaned in exasperation. *Okay, that wasn't the right response*, she admonished herself, pushing her hand through her hair. She was going to have to deal with people's natural curiosity, and this was not a good start.

"Sorry." If there was one thing Spencer understood, it was a private nature. On top of that, it made perfect sense that this woman wouldn't exactly feel comfortable opening up to her, given their circumstances. It was a wonder she talked to her at all.

"No, it's okay. I'm just not used to talking about myself."

"It's all right. I have to learn not to be so nosy."

The pair rode along through town silently, finally spotting the turnoff up ahead for Wal-Mart.

"Here we are."

"This is where you found me in the car?" She vaguely remembered something about I-66, which she could see in the distance.

"You're kidding, right?"

"No, I really don't . . . it's just that . . . things aren't real clear to me about the other night. Getting smacked in the head can do that, I guess," she joked, touching the tape on her brow. "I really don't remember us meeting here."

"Well, that's because we didn't. You got in my car while I was in the store, but I didn't find you until I got home."

"Oh." That explained why she hadn't been pushed out and left in the parking lot. But it didn't answer why the woman hadn't called the police once she had reached home and found her there.

"Yeah, you were kind of out of it," Ruth added.

Spencer looked around in confusion. It had been dark and raining the other night, and none of this looked familiar. The store was surrounded by woods in the back and on one side, so she wasn't exactly sure where she had left her bike. But that wasn't Ruth's problem, Spencer knew. She had obviously worn out her welcome.

"Listen, I appreciate this—everything—more than I can say. When this all gets cleared up, I'll stop by and settle up for the food and stuff."

"It isn't necessary."

"I know. I just want to find a way to say thanks."

"You don't have to." Again, Ruth heard the edge in her own voice and told herself to calm down. "Really, it's okay. Sometimes we all need a little help."

Spencer nodded. "Well, if there's anything I can ever do for you . . ." She had no idea what that might be. "I'm in the book. DS Rollins in Arlington. Call me."

"Okay." Ruth pulled in and drove through the lot, which was already bustling with midday shoppers. "Where do you want me to drop you?"

"I guess at the front door. With all these people out here, it's going to look pretty funny for me to just walk into the woods and disappear." She might have to wait several hours until dark, she realized grimly. But then if she did that, she would have trouble finding her bike.

Ruth looked at the woman beside her and knew that wandering into the woods wouldn't get her half the attention her appearance would. Her eye and forehead were black and blue, her clothes were filthy, and her hair looked as though it hadn't been washed in a week.

"Why don't I just drop you over at the edge? Then you can just go straight to your bike."

"That would look kind of suspicious, don't you think?"

"Maybe," Ruth said diplomatically. "But I doubt people would notice that as much as they'd notice you walking around the store. You don't exactly blend in with your colorful face."

Spencer conceded that the woman had a point. "Yeah, I guess you're right," she sighed. Frustration seemed to be her constant companion today, and it was made worse when large raindrops began to pelt the windshield. "Oh boy."

Great! Now Ruth felt guilty about putting the woman out in the rain. But Spencer Rollins wasn't her problem, she kept telling herself. Jessie was her problem, and so was everyone back in Madison who was probably looking for them by now. She couldn't be in the middle of this, and she couldn't do a thing about the weather.

"I'm really sorry," Ruth offered.

"That's okay. I appreciate everything you did."

The Taurus stopped at the pavement's edge. Spencer grabbed her rain suit from the back and opened the door.

Ruth watched her climb out. "Take care of yourself. I hope everything works out." *God, that was lame. I hope you're not killed or anything.*

"Thanks. Thanks for everything."

Spencer closed the door and climbed the muddy bank to the

edge of the woods. Any moment now, the sky was going to open up and douse her good, but she needed to get out of sight before stopping to put on her rain gear.

Ruth couldn't shake the feelings of guilt, no matter how much she rationalized her decision. But it had to be this way. Too much was at stake now with her and Jessie, things Spencer Rollins knew nothing about. She wished she had been able to explain it all, so she wouldn't seem so callous.

Absorbed in her thoughts of the injured woman's problems, Ruth fell in behind a line of traffic, catching herself in the left-turn lane before she realized her error. The road she was on led out to the interstate. That was in the opposite direction from the trailer, so she immediately started looking for a place to turn around or circle back. A cutoff up ahead looked promising, and she followed a couple of cars as they turned.

The rain was heavier now and she turned her wipers up a notch. On her left was a wooded area. In fact, she realized, it appeared to be the other side of the same woods where she had dropped her passenger. Peering through the trees, she tried to catch a glimpse of—

Fuck! Ruth slammed on her brakes, narrowly avoiding the stopped car in front of her. *Did the idiot just stop in the road or what?*

The flashing blue lights up ahead sent a shockwave to her bones. From here, it looked like a checkpoint of some sort. Her only driver's license was for Ruth Ferguson, who was now a fugitive. It was too late to turn around without being seen, and already, three more cars had lined up behind her.

Ruth's knee bounced uncontrollably as she inched forward and saw with relief that the commotion wasn't a checkpoint after all. Apparently, it was just a minor accident of some sort, because there were yellow lights from a wrecker on the other side of the road. As she drew closer, she followed the patrolman's direction to keep right, finally seeing what all the activity was about. Two uniformed officers were guiding a red motorcycle down the embankment. Parked behind the wrecker was a black sedan with government plates.

So they found Spencer's bike.

With a sick feeling in the pit of her stomach, Ruth realized that the woman she had dropped off was at this very moment walking right into the hands of her pursuers, as a man wearing a suit and a dark-colored raincoat was starting up the bank toward the woods. He had been standing in front of the government car when she approached, and it suddenly occurred to her that this might even be one of the men who Spencer said wanted her dead. But surely the Manassas police were all over the scene and they would keep her safe, and Spencer could explain what happened.

But what if everything that Spencer had said was true? She might never have a chance to tell her story. She might be whisked away in the black sedan and killed in their custody. They would just say she tried to escape or something. It's not like it hadn't ever happened before. Suddenly Ruth felt as though she held the woman's fate in her hands.

This is not your problem, the voice inside her head said. *Your priority is Jessie. Spencer Rollins will be okay.*

Even as her conscious mind repeated that mantra, Ruth slowed and pulled onto a gravel road. When traffic cleared, she turned back toward the wrecker, looking away as she passed the patrolman again. Two quick turns later she was back at the spot where she had dropped her passenger.

Leaving the car at the edge of the pavement, Ruth got out and scampered hurriedly up the muddy bank and into the woods. She trudged through the wet underbrush, fighting the urge to call out for fear of giving their presence away. Through the heavy rain, she could make out the figure of the woman in the rain suit moving slowly in the woods up ahead. If she could just catch her before she went too far. Running faster, Ruth hurdled a fallen log and charged over the slippery forest floor in pursuit.

Spencer looked about anxiously as she scoured the woods for her bike. Her memory from the other night wasn't the best, but she didn't think she had walked this far when she came out of the woods by the Wal-Mart. Thinking she was following the wrong angle, she turned to her right, freezing in place as she caught movement behind her from the corner of her eye. Crouching behind a rhododendron, she waited and watched, shocked to see that Ruth had followed her into the woods. Standing up, she started to call out.

Frantic, Ruth ran straight toward her, waving her hands and gesturing wildly for Spencer to stay quiet and get back down.

"They've got your motorcycle," she whispered, joining Spencer behind the bush. "They're just over the rise at the edge of the road. It's the black car, just like you said."

The blue eyes grew wide at the sudden danger.

"We need to get back to my car. Let's go!"

Spencer didn't need to be told twice. Stealthily, the two women moved back through the woods, finally sliding down the slippery bank to where the station wagon was parked.

"Get in!"

Still shaking, Ruth started the engine and turned around. In seconds, they were back on the highway toward town, both gasping for breath in the wake of their near miss.

"How did you know?"

Ruth shook her head, still in disbelief at what had almost happened to both of them. "I took a wrong turn and ended up on the road on the other side. They were bringing a red motorcycle out of the woods."

"And you're sure the black car was there?"

The blond woman nodded. "With the government tags."

Spencer sighed hopelessly. "I don't know what to say, Karen. I can't believe you came back for me."

"I couldn't let you just walk into that. I still don't believe that the feds want you dead, but on the off chance that it's like you said, I just . . ."

"Thanks, for whatever reason. You may have just saved my life."

"It's her bike, no mistake about it," Pollard reported from the scene. The store's surveillance photos from Saturday night showed a blurry image of someone wearing a black poncho coming from the side of the building to the area where the phones were mounted, and then walking away in the direction of the parking lot. The pouring rain that night kept them from making a positive ID, but if it had actually been Rollins, it was doubtful she was running to her bike. Unfortunately for the investigators, the parking lot was out of the camera's range.

"Goddamn it! That means she left in somebody's car. Are you sure you cut her off before she told Diaz?"

"Yeah, I'm sure. I even got Diaz telling somebody about it on the phone, that she didn't know where Rollins was."

Akers sighed with annoyance. "We need to tighten the screws on that woman."

"Did you get the wiretap at the IRS?"

"Yeah, they set it up last night. Jeff had to clear it through channels, so Diaz probably knows about it already." Jeffrey Wilkinson was their boss, the Field Director of the D.C. office.

"So where are you now?"

"Watching the IRS building. One of us is going to have to be here the whole time Diaz is working in case Rollins shows up. And then we'll have to follow her home and keep an eye on her there."

"Why don't I head on home and get some sleep, then?"

"That's good. You can relieve me at the house at eight." A senior agent rarely pulled the overnight leg.

❧

"I think you should get in the back and cover up. It's best if Viv doesn't see you when we get back to the house."

With Spencer's only real option now gone, and with Ruth starting to get a sense of the danger the woman was in, they were heading back to the trailer. At the very least, Spencer needed some time to come up with a new plan, a plan for coming forward that wouldn't mean risking her life.

Spencer squeezed her tall frame between the seats and curled up in the back, pulling the plastic tarp over her. Ruth pulled around the house and parked in the muddy drive.

"I'll go in the house and make sure they're busy, and you sneak back into the trailer."

Ruth couldn't believe she had given in to her conscience and let this woman come back. She had so much at stake with hiding Jessie, but she couldn't bring herself to turn her back on someone who had absolutely nowhere to go. She figured that if Spencer had meant to hurt them, she would never have gotten out of the car at the Wal-Mart in the first place.

Arlene came out of the office and stole a glance at Sharon, her supervisor. The mood was grim this morning at the Bank of Madison. It was unheard of for Ruth not to come in to work or to call. When the deputies showed up and said she was missing, they all became worried that something bad had happened.

Both the teller and the supervisor talked with the officers, giving their separate accounts of their contact with the missing teller. Neither had heard from Ruth and neither had gotten any hint that she was going to run away with her daughter. As far as they were concerned, if that was what she had done, more power to her. They had both seen their friend devastated by the court's outrageous decision, and Arlene knew through the grapevine that Skip didn't care one whit about his daughter.

The deputies walked out of the office, their interviews now

complete. No one had seen or heard from Ruth Ferguson or her child since Friday night when they had left the restaurant. Either she had run off with the kid or someone had taken them both.

Sharon came back over to see them out. "You'll be sure to let us know if you find out anything, won't you? We all think the world of Ruth."

"We don't usually comment on investigations while they're still in progress, but if she turns up you'll probably hear about it." Both deputies tipped their hats to the ladies and left.

The supervisor nodded her head in the direction of the vault and Arlene followed her in.

"The mail came while you were in there talking with those two." She handed the teller the envelope, already opened.

Dear friends,

By the time you get this, Jessie and I will be gone from Madison. I don't have to tell you how hard it's been this last year to be separated from my daughter and to see her little heart get broken every time she had to go back to her father's house. Recently, things have gotten worse for Jessie. I'm pretty sure that Skip hits her, and even if it's just a spanking, I know he's not doing it for discipline. He's doing it because he can't control his temper, and one day he's bound to go too far. I'm not going to let that happen to my little girl. Don't worry about us. We're going to be fine. I just wanted you to know that nothing terrible happened. In fact, I'd like to think that something wonderful happened. Starting over is going to be good for both of us. Thanks again for everything. I'll always be grateful for your friendship.

Love, Ruth

Sharon watched as Arlene wiped a tear from her eye. That had been her reaction as well. "So do you think we ought to call the deputies back and show them this letter?"

"What letter?"

Chapter 14

"I really appreciate this," Spencer said as she exited the small, steamy bathroom, her hair still dripping from the shower. "I know I keep saying that, but I really mean it."

Ruth and Jessie returned to Wal-Mart in the afternoon to pick up a few more things for their new house, and with Spencer's last forty-five bucks, bought a few changes of clothes, including jeans, two T-shirts, a sweatshirt, and underwear. From her own reserves, Ruth picked up some socks and a size ten pair of sneakers.

"Yeah, it was self-defense. You were starting to smell," Ruth answered flatly.

Spencer's jaw dropped. For a fleeting moment, she thought the stiff woman had just made a joke. But Ruth didn't laugh or even look up from her cooking when she said it, so maybe it was just unkind.

"Viv said I could use her washer, so if you'll give me your other stuff, I'll throw it in with that blanket you bled all over."

"Thanks." Spencer disappeared down the hall and returned with her laundry, confirming with a sniff that it really was rather pungent. "Is there anything I can do to help out?"

"Sure. Why don't you stir dinner while I go put all this in the washer? We're almost ready to eat."

Spencer took over at the stove stirring a skillet filled with sliced beef, peppers and onions. The rice was ready, and a small bottle of soy sauce sat on the counter. The little girl sat on the couch with a picture book. She had barely spoken a word since returning from the store with her mother, seemingly afraid of this mysterious stranger.

"So what's your doll's name?" Spencer asked, trying to set the child at ease.

"Lisa," Jessie answered shyly without looking up.

"That's a very pretty name. One of my best friends when I was a little girl was named Lisa." That was a lie. She had gone to school with Lisa McCall, but they had hated each other's guts.

"My best friend is Brittany."

"Does Brittany have a pretty doll too?"

The little girl shrugged her shoulders, still not making eye contact. She didn't like being left alone with this other woman.

As soon as Ruth walked back through the door, Jessie jumped up and ran to her mother's side.

"Megan was just telling me about her friend Brittany."

"Was she now? She and Brittany went to the same Little School back in Maine. We're going to find a new Little School here. Won't that be fun, Megan?"

The child shook her head. She didn't want to be away from her mom, unless it was with Viv and the puppies.

"Sure it would. School's fun. You learn things and play games. You've always liked school," Ruth encouraged. "I bet you'll like it when you make new friends."

"Do I have to go?"

"Not yet. I think we can wait a little while."

Her daughter visibly relaxed at the reprieve.

"But we should find a new school soon, because I think you'll have fun."

"I want to be with you."

"I know, but I'm going to need to find a job when we find you a school."

"I don't want you to. I want you to stay home."

Ruth chuckled and sat down in the hardback chair, pulling her daughter into her lap. "We have fun when we play together, don't we?"

Jessie nodded.

"But I'm going to have to get a job soon, sweetie. We'll still have a lot of time together."

"Why can't you stay home?"

"Because people are supposed to go somewhere every day. Big people go to work and little people go to school."

"Viv doesn't go to work."

"That's because Viv's retired. She worked a long time and now she doesn't have to anymore," Ruth explained patiently.

"Spencer doesn't go."

"Well, you see, honey, Spencer's . . . lazy." She needed an explanation on the spot and hoped the other woman could take some good-natured teasing.

"Lazy?" Spencer's eyebrow shot up. *What's she talking about?*

"That's right. Lazy people just stay in bed all day and that's what Spencer has been doing." Her tone was serious, but Spencer picked up on the smirk.

So Karen actually has a sense of humor after all. Still, she couldn't believe she had suddenly become the butt of the woman's jokes.

"I think dinner's ready. Grab a seat, and I'll bring it over . . . if I can stop being so lazy," she teased back.

"See?" Ruth laughed in answer, dragging the armchair from

the living room to the bar so they could all sit together. The threesome ate quietly until Jessie asked the question that had been bothering her all day.

"Why do you have a boy's name?"

"Excuse me?"

"There's a boy named Spencer at my Little School, and he's a boy."

"Well . . . Spencer can be a girl's name too," the newcomer argued gently.

"I don't know any girls named Spencer, just boys."

"Well, now you know a girl named Spencer. It's what my mother and father named me."

"It is kind of an unusual name for a girl," Ruth agreed, as both a friendly jibe and a way of letting her daughter know that she understood her confusion.

"It's a family name," Spencer explained defensively. "I was named for my grandmother."

"So your grandmother's name was Spencer, too?"

"Yes," she answered in mock indignation.

"Spencer what?"

The programmer shifted uncomfortably. "Her last name was Spencer."

"Oh, so your first name is somebody else's last name." Ruth recognized that she was finally letting her guard down about this stranger in their home.

"No, actually Spencer is my middle name."

"Mommy, what's my middle name?" Megan asked.

"Alise. Megan Alise Oliver."

"What's your middle name?"

"Michelle. My whole name is Karen Michelle Oliver."

"So what's your whole name?" Jessie asked Spencer pointedly.

"Spencer Rollins."

"Oh no!" Ruth interjected. "You said Spencer was your middle name. So what's your first name?"

124

"Now if I told you that, I'd have to kill you."

Suddenly Jessie's eyes went wide and she jumped down to stand behind her mother.

"She's only teasing, honey." She reached around to take her daughter's hand and pull her into her lap. "You can't say those kinds of things around a four-year-old," she admonished.

"Sorry. I was just kidding, Megan. I would never hurt anybody, but especially not you or your mom."

"So what's your first name?" the child demanded.

Defeated, Spencer dropped her fork and leaned back, looking away from the twin pairs of pretty green eyes that waited expectantly. "Dolly."

"Dolly?" Ruth asked in disbelief.

"Yes, Dolly. Dolly Spencer Rollins. I'll have you know that my grandmother was named Dolly Spencer, and I'm very honored to be named for her."

"Yeah, I can tell by the way you announced it so proudly," Ruth teased. "Dolly Rollins."

Jessie squealed with laughter. "Like my dolly."

"You think that's pretty funny, huh?" Spencer couldn't believe how these two were ganging up on her.

"Yeah! I think it's funny . . . Dolly." Unable to hide her smirk, Ruth turned the question to her daughter. "Do you think it's funny?"

The little girl nodded happily.

"See there? We think it's funny."

Spencer rolled her eyes. She would try a new tack. "You're not setting a very good example for your child, teaching her to laugh at people's names."

That was true, Ruth admitted. "You're right. It isn't nice to make fun of people's names . . . even funny names."

That got Jessie giggling and her mother joined in. To Ruth, it was as though they hadn't laughed in ages.

"Okay, that's it!" Tossing her napkin on the table, Spencer

stood abruptly. "You two want to laugh? I'll give you something to laugh about." Reaching over, she dug her hands into Jessie's ribs and started to tickle. As soon as the child dropped to the floor squealing with laughter, she started on Ruth, who also dissolved onto the floor. Only the pain in her own ribs stopped the assault, as Spencer sat back down in the chair and wrapped her arms around her torso. "Now I'm warning you—there's more where that came from," she said menacingly.

Ruth caught her breath and climbed back onto her stool, pulling the child up with her.

"Okay, we give . . ." and with a very tiny voice, she added, "Dolly."

Spencer smiled and got two smiles back. It felt good to let go of the tension for the first time in three days.

"Okay, since I have to prove that I'm not lazy, I'll clean up the dishes."

"Can I . . . I mean may I watch TV?"

"Just for a little while," Ruth acquiesced. It was getting late and already time for Jessie's bath, but this was the very first time ever that her daughter had correctly used "may" instead of "can" and it called for a reward.

Spencer made quick work of the dinner dishes, waiting for one last glass. "Are you finished with your drink, Megan?"

"Uh-huh." The little girl jumped up and stretched to grab the glass so she could take it to the sink, accidentally tipping it over so that it rolled off the counter and shattered on the floor. "Uh-oh!" The barefoot child started to pick up one of the pieces.

"No, Jessie! Don't move." Ruth picked her daughter up and ushered her to the couch.

"I'm sorry," the child whimpered. Being sorry got her nowhere when she did things like this around her father. He yelled and spanked her when she broke things. Her mother wasn't like that, but it was hard not to be afraid that she might get mad.

126

"It's okay. I'll clean it up. I just didn't want you to get cut by the broken glass."

Spencer had already started sweeping the glass into a dustpan.

"I'll do it," Ruth offered, stooping to hold the dustpan.

"I don't mind. It's just one less dish I have to wash, and that's good because I'm lazy," Spencer joked.

Together, they mopped up the mess and gave the floor an extra going-over. Soon after, the mother and daughter disappeared into the bathroom to get ready for bed.

An hour later, Ruth emerged from her daughter's bedroom to find Spencer spreading out the sheets on the couch. "You don't have to sleep out here. I don't mind the couch."

"No, you should have your own bed. I'm better now. I don't hurt all over like I did, thanks to you."

Ruth looked the tall woman from head to toe and measured the couch with her eye. "So do your legs unscrew, or does your head come off?"

"You really are quite the comedienne tonight, aren't you?"

Ruth smiled and dropped into the recliner.

"It's been nice to laugh for a change," Spencer said quietly. In fact, their fun earlier seemed to have changed the whole atmosphere here in the trailer. All three of them were more relaxed. It was almost like their living together was just ordinary.

"Yeah, Megan and I haven't laughed much lately either."

Spencer leaned over to pick up one of the pillows and immediately clutched her side. Those ribs were still tender.

"That reminds me. I got a bandage for you at the drugstore. I meant to give it to you this morning before I turned you out in the rain." Ruth got up and went into the other room, returning with the package. "I thought it might keep you from straining your side."

"Thanks." Spencer looked at the sticker on the package. Karen had paid almost ten dollars for the elastic wrap, and Spencer was deeply moved by the kindness of the gesture. This woman didn't really know her at all and she didn't seem to have a lot to spare. Spending that kind of money to help a stranger was very generous. "When I get everything sorted out, I'll pay you for this and everything else."

"You don't have to, really."

"But I want to."

Ruth thought about what that would mean. Spencer's friend was a federal agent. That might be trouble for her and Jessie.

"So . . . who's Jessie?" Spencer asked without a hint of reproach. "Or should I ask who's Megan? And who's Karen?"

Ruth sighed heavily. She realized when she and Jessie were in the bathroom that she had called her daughter by the wrong name in that brief moment of danger. Her first instinct was to deflect the question with simple lie, but it wasn't forthcoming. Her next thought was to just put the subject off-limits. She owed Spencer Rollins no explanations at all. But instead, she found herself wanting to open up, wanting to explain things so that Spencer could understand why she had been so insistent about not wanting her here.

"Megan and Karen Oliver were two little girls that died a couple of years ago in a boating accident. Their grandfather had savings accounts for them at the bank where I worked, and Jessie and I needed new identities when we left. I was able to get their social security numbers from the accounts." She shook her head at the irony. After all that business with Jessie making sure she didn't tell anybody, here was Ruth telling the first person who asked.

"Your husband must be some kind of beast if you have to run away and change your names."

Ruth nodded without looking up. "He never could deal with Jessie not being Little Miss Perfect all the time. He didn't have much patience for kids."

"So you left to get away from him."

"We're divorced. But he got primary custody."

128

"Wha—? You're kidding!"

"I wish. He told a bunch of lies at our hearing. He said that I left Jessie home by herself, that I would sometimes go days without changing her or feeding her. He put on this big act and the judge swallowed it hook, line and sinker. Skip didn't want Jessie. He never wanted her. He just wanted to make sure I didn't get her."

"So you kidnapped her?"

Again, Ruth nodded, tears filling her eyes. "She hated living there. She would scream her head off every time she had to go back. And then a couple of months ago I started finding bruises on her arms and legs. She always said she fell. I just wasn't going to let that happen to her anymore."

Now it made sense why Ruth had taken her in without calling the police. Spencer reached out and laid a comforting hand on her shoulder. "I'd have done the same thing. I think anybody would."

"Well, I guess now you can see why I was sort of . . ."

"Yeah, I can see that my being here complicates things for you," Spencer said seriously. "I'll get out as soon as I can and I won't tell a soul, Karen. Or should I call you something else?"

"My name's Ruth. But I need to move on from that. Jessie and I both do, so it'd be best if you just called us Karen and Megan."

"Sure, whatever you want." Spencer was suddenly struck by the irony of their respective circumstances. "So both of us are hiding out and we end up together. Pretty amazing coincidence, huh?"

Ruth shook her head and chuckled. "Yeah, like either of us didn't already have enough excitement in our lives."

"I know I really do complicate things for you, Ruth, but if I'd ended up in anyone else's car that night, I might be dead by now. I really do owe you, and if there's anything I can do when this is over to help you and your daughter, I will."

"I don't think there's anything anybody can do," Ruth said,

obviously discouraged. "And I'd like to help you out too, but . . ."

"I know. You can't be in the middle of this. I understand. Like I said, I'll get out of your hair soon, I promise."

"I don't . . . you can stay here until you're better, until you decide what to do. We just have to be careful about people finding out is all."

"I know, and we will. I really can't thank you enough for all you're doing. You've been more than generous." From the sheepish look she was getting from Ruth, Spencer figured she had probably said thank you enough to make the woman uncomfortable. It was time to lighten the mood. "Go on and take the bed. I'll be okay out here." She gestured toward the couch. "Besides, I'll be sleeping in late tomorrow on account of I'm so lazy."

Chapter 15

Spencer woke before dawn, her mind racing with the bits and pieces of information she had about what had gone down on Friday night. Everything was still confusing but one part was becoming increasingly clear. Those federal agents had no business being at Margadon on Friday night unless they were called there by James to help him deal with what Henry had found in the code. His discovery was a secret so important to James and the agents that they killed him in order to protect it.

Even if she had doubts before, the news that they had reported finding her friend's body on Saturday was proof that there was some kind of cover-up in place. Why hadn't James shown up on the surveillance tapes too? Spencer wasn't about to overlook as coincidence the fact that she had been named as the murder suspect and that the agents who were there on Friday night were the very ones looking for her.

Was Ruth right about her going forward? The scary part of that was thinking she would be taken into custody and handed over to those guys right away. It wasn't likely that anyone would believe her story. She didn't have any proof that the agents had been there, or James either, for that matter.

Getting out of this mess called for a careful plan, and she approached that like she did her programming tasks. First, she needed to step back and get the big picture. No matter what the circumstances now, where did she want to end up?

That was easy. She wanted to see Henry's killers brought to justice. She wanted to stop whatever it was that was going on at Margadon that had made Henry's life expendable. And she wanted her own life back.

Rummaging through the kitchen drawers, Spencer found a drawing tablet and a few crayons, selecting the blue one because its point was the sharpest. At the top of the page, she wrote Henry's name. Beneath that, she scribbled fragments of the things he'd said:

somebody fucked with it
it's calling a different global
it's backing out the cytokines
skimming the books
hidden field

The programmer stared at the words for a long time, trying to imagine each of the steps her partner had taken to find the problem. His call hadn't come until almost midnight, so it must have been an arduous process. But following the trail had gotten him killed.

With that thought, Spencer added one more note:

already called James

That was why Henry was dead, because he had called James. So that meant that James knew about the changes in the program, and therefore, what the program was doing. But he couldn't have done this on his own. He would have needed another programmer, since his own skills were rudimentary at best. Come to think of it, James had never struck her as being the brightest bulb in the pack anyway, so it was likely that he was just along for the ride by virtue of his position as controller. If this was a scheme to skim the books like Henry had said, they needed someone like James to cover the gaps in inventory. But there had to be others involved, someone in production and probably even their supplier.

What didn't make sense at all was why the feds—

"Will you get me some juice, please?"

Preoccupied with her analysis, Spencer was astonished to see the pajama-clad child standing before her clutching her doll. She had no idea how long the little girl had been standing there.

"Well, good morning!" Dropping her papers, she got up and went to the kitchen. "You want some cereal too?"

Jessie shook her head. "Toast and jelly."

"Toast and jelly," she repeated. "That sounds good. Maybe I'll have some too."

Minutes later, they were sharing breakfast when Ruth stumbled down the hall. Spencer didn't know the other woman very well, but by the look on her face, Ruth was really pleased to find them sitting together in the kitchen.

"Is there coffee?"

"Yes, there is. It was made by the Lazy Lady."

That got a giggle out of Jessie and a smile from her mom.

"What kinds of things do you have to do today?" Spencer asked casually, vacating her stool at the kitchen counter so Ruth could have a seat. She crossed the room to the couch, which was wrecked by her night of fitful sleep.

"I have to get my car registered and get a new driver's license.

Do you want me to pick up anything while I'm out?"

Anyone listening to their casual banter might have thought they had been married fifteen years.

"Yeah, can you bring me a notebook of some sort? I borrowed a few pages from Megan's tablet. I hope that was okay."

"Of course."

"And maybe you could find me something a little more adult to write with?" She held up the crayon she had been using.

"You mean like markers or maybe colored chalk?" Ruth teased. "I have a pen in my purse you're welcome to use. Anything else?"

"Gee, I was thinking more like a computer." Even that wouldn't help, though. What Spencer needed to figure this out was access to her own terminal at Margadon, and that lay within an impenetrable firewall.

"Are we getting a computer, Mommy?" Jessie asked with excitement.

"No! She's being silly. We can't afford a computer."

Spencer leapt off the couch and began pacing. "Henry sent it to the server!"

"What?"

"All I need is access to a computer. Henry sent it to the server. I'm sure of it."

"What are you talking about?"

Now excited, she explained. "Henry and I used to do a few jobs on the side, you know, contracting with small companies to write code. But we couldn't park that kind of stuff at Margadon, so we bought a server and set it up in Vienna. When we wanted to work on Margadon stuff at night or over the weekend, we'd send it there so we could both have access. I bet Henry sent what he found to the server."

"Whatever it was you just said . . . how can you find out?"

"I need a computer with a modem."

"Well, we don't have either one. Even if we had a computer, I

134

don't have a phone."

"We need some kind of Internet café."

"What about a library? Don't they have computers?"

Spencer nodded. "Yeah, but they're public buildings. They might have some kind of surveillance. If they've got my picture . . ." She didn't want to spell it out in front of the little girl. "The thing is, if they already know about the server, they've gone after it by now. And they might be watching it, waiting to jump on the IP if I log in."

"I understood about every third word of that."

Spencer took a deep breath and thought about how to explain this. She usually took for granted that everybody knew this stuff. "Basically, what I meant was that if they know about the server, they could be using it for bait. See, when you log on to the Internet, the computer you're using broadcasts what's called an IP. It stands for Internet Protocol. Whoever provides your Internet service assigns you a number that other people on the Internet can see if they have the right program. Since people at home usually pay for their service with a credit card, the service provider can match the address of the credit card with the IP."

Ruth nodded slowly, but still had a blank look.

"Which means they can figure out where your computer is. So if I were to log on to the server, they could track the IP to wherever I was."

"So they could find you."

"Theoretically, yes. But there are some ways you can hide your IP." Spencer's brow furrowed as her plan for checking the server started to take shape. "The trick's going to be getting access to a computer."

"Okay, I need to get going on this car stuff. I have no idea how long we're going to be gone, but if you figure out how we can get to a computer, we'll go when I get back."

"Can I stay here with Spencer?"

"No, honey. You have to come with me."

"Why?"

"Yeah, why?" echoed the programmer. She was perfectly capable of taking care of Jessie for a few hours.

"Doh! Both of you. Viv doesn't know Spencer is here, and she knows I wouldn't go off and leave you by yourself."

"Oh," the others said together.

" . . . so I told him like, I'm not gonna do that, and he goes, well why not, and I go, I'm just not, so then he goes . . . Oh, shit! Not again! Melanie, I gotta go. There's a cop behind me and he's pulling me over. Bye!"

Sixteen-year-old Carrie Porr had been driving less than two months, and this was the third occasion on which she had been stopped by the police. The first time, she had gotten a stern warning about rolling through a stop sign. The second was for a series of vehicle safety violations: one headlight and both brake lights on the old Plymouth were out, the tires were nearly bald, and one of the windshield wipers flopped aimlessly in the rain. For all that, she had gotten ticketed, but it convinced her father to buy her something a little more road-worthy.

That was how she came to be driving the brand new Saturn. At least it was new to Carrie. They had picked it up from her dad's friend Dick Huggins in Farmington on Sunday.

"License and registration, please," the uniformed officer demanded.

"I just got this car." She dug out her license and the bill of sale. The registration hadn't arrived in the mail yet. "What'd I do this time?"

"Step out of the car, please."

"What'd I do?" Carrie practically shouted. Some of her friends had warned her about cops who stopped women for no reason, just to bribe them into having sex so they wouldn't get a ticket.

Ignoring her question, the officer studied the bill of sale, matching the vehicle identification number from the brass strip affixed to the dash beneath the windshield. It was definitely the car they were looking for, the one that had belonged to Ruth Ferguson.

"Miss Porr, I'm going to have to ask you to come with me."

Oh my God! Shaking with fear, she pulled out her cell phone. "I'm not going anywhere till I call my daddy."

"Is your father Harold Porr, the owner of this car?"

"Yes."

"Then he's going to have to come to the station, too, I'm afraid."

Oh shit! She must have really done something awful this time. While the officer double-checked her license and bill of sale, Carrie peeked at the grill to see if she had a bicycle or something stuck there.

The cranky four-year-old stormed into the trailer, went straight to her bedroom, and slammed her door.

"There is no need to slam this door, young lady," Ruth said sternly as she followed her daughter into the room. "I know you're tired and that you didn't have a good time. I didn't have a good time either, but you heard me promise Spencer that I'd take her somewhere when we got finished."

Spencer held her spot on the couch, feeling guilty to learn that she was the cause of the child's consternation.

"Can I go see the puppies?"

"It's 'may I' and I don't think so, because I'm not very happy with the way you're acting right now."

The pouting child responded with a mumbled apology.

"I think you need to sit in here awhile and think about how you've behaved. Maybe if you took a little nap, you would feel like being nicer."

Jessie kicked off her shoes and curled up on her bed. Ruth watched her settle down, the teary green eyes a sure sign of remorse. She walked over and gave the little girl a soft kiss on the forehead. "I love you, sweetheart. I know it wasn't fun, but you'll feel better after you rest."

Spencer sat perfectly still, looking sheepish at having witnessed such a personal moment between mother and child. Ruth plopped tiredly in the recliner.

"You're wicked," Spencer teased softly, bringing an easy smile to her new friend's flustered face.

"That was my toughest Mommy act."

"It had me peeing in my pants."

"Stop."

"I'm not kidding. Remind me never to cross you."

Ruth shook her head, still chuckling. "So Karen Michelle Oliver is now licensed to drive in the state of Virginia, and her car has brand new plates."

"Congratulations. How'd you pull that off?"

Ruth couldn't conceal her smugness as she related her scheme. "I bought the car two weeks ago for cash from a private seller in Augusta. That's about fifty miles from where we lived. I asked him to write me a receipt and I filled in my own name—Karen Oliver, of course. And I told them at the DMV that I'd never had a license before, that I was always afraid to drive. I showed them a copy of a birth certificate I made for Karen Oliver and they tested me. That was all it took."

"Pretty slick."

"Yeah, it helps when you get in a long line of people who are abusing the poor clerk behind the counter and you're the first person who treats him like a human being."

"Catching flies with honey?"

"You got it. So Jessie's—I mean Megan—is going to be a lot more pleasant after a nap. She'll want to go look in on the puppies for a few minutes, and then we can go. Did you figure out where you could get on a computer?"

"No. Without a phone book or anything, I couldn't even guess what's around here. How would you feel about just riding around a little and seeing what we find?"

"That's okay. But I need to take her somewhere to play for a while. Waiting in that line for three hours was torture."

"Sure. Maybe we'll see a park or something."

Ruth looked at Spencer with gratitude. *How could anyone think this woman was a murderer?*

Viv was pleased to see the pair standing inside the porch at the back door. It was nice to have these two as tenants, and she loved seeing the pure joy on Megan's face each time the little girl peeked in on the puppies.

"Come on in. They've missed you today."

The excited child made a beeline for the room off the kitchen where Maggie and her pups had settled.

"This is the highlight of her whole day," Ruth said. "I took her with me to the driver's license office and I thought we were both going to go nuts."

"You're welcome to come over whenever you want. Or she could stay here with me the next time you have to run out for something."

"That's very kind. We don't want to be any trouble."

"I wouldn't have offered if it was any trouble. Say, I've got your laundry back here."

"Oh my goodness! I forgot all about it. I'm so sorry."

"That's okay." Viv handed over a small basket of folded clothes and the blanket. "Those were some awfully long jeans in there," she remarked casually.

"Uh, yeah . . . I sometimes wear them long because I like to roll 'em up. You know, cuffs."

"Uh-huh," she said skeptically. "Look, Karen. I know you got somebody else staying over there. I heard the toilet flush after you and Megan left."

Ruth could feel her face redden.

"Now I don't really understand why you haven't said anything about her, but I guess you had your reasons. It's your business. But you don't have to be sneaky about it. Makes me think you've got something to hide."

Ruth stared at the floor, ashamed to meet her landlady's accusing look. *If she only knew.*

"She's just going to stay a few nights. I'm sorry I didn't say anything."

"You don't have to be sorry. That's your home over there and you can have company stay whenever you want. You don't need my permission. But this sneaking in and out isn't necessary. You should go get her and bring her over. "

"Okay." Ruth started out the back door, but stopped. "Viv, how did you know it was a she?"

The gray-haired woman chuckled. "I would have noticed any boxers or briefs."

Ruth hauled the laundry basket up the steps, balancing it on her hip to open the door. "My landlady knows you're here and she wants to meet you."

"How?"

"I forgot the laundry and she found a pair of jeans that were about two feet too long for me. And she heard the toilet flush when Megan and I weren't here."

"Great. Are you in trouble?"

"No, but she wants to meet you, so come on."

"Fuck!"

"What?"

"What if she's seen me on TV?"

"Pull your hair back or something."

"Oh yeah, that'll do it," she said sarcastically. "I'll look like a whole different person. Who did you tell her I was?"

"I didn't tell her anything. I just said you were staying here a few days. She's kind of irritated that I didn't mention anything."

"So, what? Am I a friend of yours from Maine? A relative? Help me out here."

"You can be a friend from Maine, but you're living here now and you lost your job. I didn't tell her much, so you get to make up whatever you want. Just remember that Megan may get curious and start asking questions, so you better keep it simple."

With Ruth in the lead, Spencer nervously walked in through the back door of the house. To her infinite embarrassment, her new friend introduced her as Dolly Rollins, which brought a snicker from the little girl and a renewed threat of tickling from Spencer.

"Where in the world did you get that black eye?" Viv asked.

Spencer shrugged. "I ran into a tree a few days ago. It's not serious, though." She wished later that she had been more forthcoming about her bruises and injured shoulder, as that might have staved off the landlady's next request.

"To tell you the truth, I'm glad there are two of you over there. I could use some extra hands with the storm windows now that it's turning chilly."

Their plans for looking for Internet access were scuttled when Viv directed them to the shed where the windows were kept, showing them where to find the glass cleaner and the ladder. For the back porch, she had gotten a roll of heavy plastic, which had to be measured, cut, and stapled all around.

"Don't worry about Megan," Viv said. "I'll keep an eye on her. We'll watch the puppies and maybe play around a little on the computer."

Computer?

Elena clenched her jaw tightly when she stepped up onto her small front porch. These fuckers weren't even putting up a pretense about their invasive surveillance. Catalogs and flyers were scattered at her feet. In her mailbox were two utility bills and a letter from her aunt in New Jersey, all of which had been opened.

It was the same at her office. Elena nearly hit the ceiling when Kristy from the mail room delivered a bundle of envelopes that had already been pilfered. The agent's protests to her boss had been spirited, to say the least.

Chad Merke directed the Criminal Investigations Division of the IRS. He was none too happy with the FBI's request to monitor his agent's communications and he was downright pissed about the van outside that shadowed her every move. But his hands were tied thanks to a favor he owed the Bureau when he had convinced them last year to trade a collar for testimony in a drug case.

The tenacity of these investigating agents would be commendable were it not for their overbearing arrogance, which seemed to Elena to be more over-the-top than usual—even for the FBI. Something about this investigation didn't sit right, and the longer she thought about it, the more she came to think how odd it was that the FBI was the agency taking the lead. It wasn't unusual for them to investigate murders in the D.C. area, because they didn't have to worry about crossing into someone else's jurisdiction. But it typically involved a direct request from local law enforcement, and that could take a couple of days. These guys were on the case—and at Elena's door—within four hours of when Henry's body was discovered, that according to her source at the Montgomery County Police Department.

What was it about this case that had the FBI so interested? Elena had no doubts at all about her former lover's innocence, but something had her spooked about why Spencer was hiding. If she was involved in this somehow, she would have come forward to explain herself. Elena was sure of that.

All these questions, all these doubts. They had prompted Special Agent Diaz to launch a little investigation of her own.

142

Chapter 16

"Would ice help?"

Spencer shook her head. Her ribcage was screaming at her from all the activity with the storm windows yesterday afternoon; and when they had finished, Viv presented them with a new list of chores for today.

"Too late for that."

"You shouldn't have done all that work without wrapping it up. That's why I got the bandage."

"I know," she groaned. Ruth had advised her twice to stop, offering to wrap the elastic around her ribs. "I'll do it today. But I might need some help."

"I don't know about you, but I'm not all that eager to get started," Ruth said, peeking past the curtain to the house. "I'm afraid if we get finished with this stuff, she'll find even more for us to do."

Spencer chuckled. "I think we're being punished for me hiding over here. The chores are going to keep coming until she's gotten her pound of flesh."

"You're probably right." Ruth picked up the elastic bandage and gestured for Spencer to lift her shirt. "You need to be careful with this. If they're broken, they'll never heal if you keep stretching."

"I think they're just bruised. They don't hurt like they did a couple of days ago." Spencer grimaced as the bandage was pulled tight across the dark contusion. Still, she got a nice jolly from the warm hands.

"How's your shoulder today?"

"It's much better, Dr. Ruth." As soon as she said it, the image of the diminutive sex therapist popped into her head and Spencer snorted.

Her caregiver said nothing, her only response a hard yank on the elastic.

"Ow! Not so tight!"

"Sorry." She wasn't really.

"Do you think Viv will let me use her computer?"

"I don't see why not. Tonight's bingo night, you know. I think you should have to come along for that before you're granted computer privileges."

"Well, I would volunteer, you know, but since my picture's on the news as a wanted murderer, it might be best if I pass," Spencer answered sweetly, batting her eyelashes with exaggerated innocence.

"Excuses, excuses." Ruth moved around behind the injured woman to attach the metal fasteners. "You know, you were asking me the other day about how to thank me for letting you stay here. What if you took Viv to bingo every Wednesday night?"

"What, you don't like bingo?"

"Puh-leaze!"

"It'll be fun. You just need a positive attitude."

"Yeah, right. That reminds me, would you watch Jessie tonight so I don't have to keep her out so late?"

"Sure. But I think she's still afraid of me."

"Well you did threaten to kill us both, as I recall," Ruth joked. "But she likes you all right. She doesn't ask just anybody to play Candy Land." In fact, Jessie had insisted the night before that Spencer play too, because somebody had to be green. When the mother-daughter pair trounced the newcomer in consecutive games, Spencer had been a very good sport. It was the first time in ages that Ruth could remember having fun with her daughter and another adult.

On the surface, Spencer was proving to be a really interesting person, easy to be around. Ruth could sense those times when the programmer's thoughts would turn to her dilemma, and she wished there was more that she could do to help. It really touched her that Spencer seemed to have also taken on her problems with Skip, thinking ahead about what she might be able to do to help Ruth and Jessie when she got her own business taken care of.

"I appreciate all your help with Viv's chores, but you really do need to take care of this. Let me do the heavy lifting today, okay?"

"Sure. Thanks, Ruth."

"And stop calling me Ruth."

"You're all wet!" Jessie declared, as if either her mom or Spencer might have been unaware. Viv had grossly misrepresented the enormity of the dog bath task.

A happy Maggie joined her hungry puppies while Thor preened nearby. The dogs really did smell a lot better, but the same could not be said for Ruth and Spencer.

"Dibs on the shower," Ruth called as the threesome walked

across the drive to the trailer.

Spencer muttered a few choice words under her breath, ever cognizant of the presence of a four-year-old.

"What was that?"

"You don't want to know." She was exhausted, but at least Viv had agreed to let her use the computer tonight while they were at the church. She wanted to look for a job, she had said.

Viv had them back over for dinner, and soon after, the landlady and Ruth left to seek their fortunes at the Goodwill Christian Church.

Spencer finished the last of the dishes and helped Jessie find the children's channel on television. She felt guilty knowing that Ruth didn't like the idea of using the television as a babysitter, but she needed to take advantage of this chance to get online. At least she could be together with the child in Viv's den.

In the last three days, Spencer had discovered a surprising fondness for the little four-year-old. She had never been around children much. Elena had lots of nieces and nephews, but she had never really gotten much one-on-one time with any of them. Jessie was fun—a genuine dose of playfulness with the frankness only a child could possess. One of the things that made her so endearing was knowing that she had survived a rough start in life. It made Spencer's blood boil to think that her father had raised his savage hand to such a precious little girl.

And then there was Ruth. In no time at all, Ruth felt like a lifelong friend. What else could you call someone who would put at risk everything she held dear to help a total stranger? After what Ruth had told her the other night, Spencer was still amazed that the woman had come back for her in the woods. With all she and her daughter had at stake, Ruth should have put her head down and kept driving. That's what most people would have done. The fact that she didn't spoke volumes about the kind of person she was.

Spencer thought again about Jessie's father. What kind of man couldn't appreciate a woman like Ruth? Not only was she a great mother, she was fun to talk to, a hard worker . . . and awfully easy on the eyes. Spencer had always been attracted to blondes, but it had been a long time since she had met one who was more than a casual fling. In fact, it had been a while since she had met somebody that she wanted to get to know beyond just a physical attraction.

Spencer mentally scolded herself for where her thoughts had gone and turned her attentions back to Jessie and to the task at hand. "Let me know if you need anything, okay?"

Jessie didn't answer, already absorbed in the cartoon.

With a small smile, Spencer spun around in the office chair to start to work. She was glad to see that Viv accessed the Internet through America Online. That made it a lot less likely that her location could be traced. Viv had stored her password for automatic access, and in only a couple of minutes, Spencer was on the Internet. She went first to the website for the *Washington Post* to read about Henry's murder. Skimming through the story, she sought clues for who else might be involved and what the possible motive might have been. Predictably, executives at Margadon were expressing all the appropriate shock and sadness at the killing, but one comment stood out:

"I don't think anyone really could have predicted this, but in hindsight, I'm not completely surprised by what has happened. In my own interactions with Miss Rollins, I could see that she had a volatile temper, and even Mr. Estes had told others that she believed the people at Margadon were out to get her."

The reporter had spoken with Stacy Eagleton, a senior product manager at Margadon who had primary responsibility for the Kryfex contract. In her six years at Margadon, Spencer had spoken with Eagleton no more than five times, mostly to provide technical updates on the program she and Henry had written. *Even if I did have a volatile temper—which I don't—you would never have seen it.* Added to the absolute bullshit about her purported paranoia, that preposterous assessment about her temper put Eagleton at the top of her list of those involved in this conspiracy. And Eagleton had a background in programming.

Before she left the article, Spencer turned on the printer and waited for it to warm up.

"Is your show good, Jessie?"

The girl nodded absently and then her eyes grew wide. "You called me Jessie!"

"Oops! I made a mistake. Your name is Megan." Spencer doubted she would ever think of the pair as Karen and Megan again, but she needed to help them keep their cover.

"How did you know my name was Jessie?" the child demanded.

"It slipped out the other night when you broke the glass," Spencer answered calmly. "Remember when your mom shouted at you because she was afraid you would hurt yourself?"

Jessie nodded.

"She called you Jessie, so that's how I knew it was your name."

"But you can't tell anyone, 'cuz it's a secret."

"I won't tell anyone, I promise."

Feeling thoroughly reprimanded, Spencer turned back to her work. Once she printed the news story, she took a deep breath before taking the next step. Accessing the server was an enormous risk, but she was pretty sure that she could get to it without giving herself away. AOL assigned a random IP for every session, so it would take a crackerjack agent days—maybe even weeks—to trace her location if she also went through a public proxy. By the time they found her, she would have what she needed to figure out what was going on and why Henry was

148

killed.

No one except Spencer and Henry knew of the server's existence. Sure, if these guys were really good, they would have been able to peel back the layers on the computers at Margadon and find it. But if they were *that* good, they would have caught her by now. To find the hidden server, they would almost have to know to look for it. When she and Henry routed things from work out to Vienna for remote access, they routinely cleaned up the log file at Margadon so no one would know.

The company's security team would have a fit if they knew that internal documents and programs had left the local network, but both programmers knew their server was secure, and that proprietary information was not at risk. Besides, they never stored company data, just bits of their code. The way they saw it, Margadon's security measures were overkill.

Of course, she was only assuming that Henry had sent what he found to the server. If he hadn't, then she was back to square one. According to the *Post* article, the authorities were virtually certain that she was the murderer. Even if she came forward with her story of James and the federal agents, Stacy Eagleton had already painted her as a delusional paranoid. She needed the code as proof.

"I hope you sent it, pal." She whispered the words to her friend.

So now the big question was, if Henry did send the files, did he have time to erase the entry in the log file before he was killed? *Of course he did.* He did that automatically after every upload or download, just as she did. It was part of their procedure, just like logging off. *Routine.*

With another deep breath, Spencer typed in the URL for a public proxy, a site that allowed her to surf the web anonymously. From there, she opened the browser and keyed in the FTP for the server. Her index finger hovered over the "enter" key as she gathered her nerve. Henry was a slave to detail, the most meticulous person she had ever met, she kept telling herself. No way would he have left the record in the log file. She tapped it and waited for the directory of files to appear.

There it was—a folder of documents sent Friday night at 11:33, about ten minutes before Henry had called her at Elena's. He had probably called James by that time, but that gave him plenty of time to clear the log file. Had he not, the feds would have taken this folder down, she realized with relief.

With a few clicks of the mouse, Spencer downloaded the files he had posted. They were programs, page after page of the documentation and application commands that managed the inventory at Margadon. Henry had uploaded more than eighty pages that he thought were relevant to the problem, eighty pages that he would have wanted her to see.

Spencer logged off when the download was complete, hurriedly reloading the paper tray. Anxiously, she sent each of the documents to the bubble jet printer and waited for the output. At four pages per minute, this was going to take a while.

The first seventeen pages were the first part of the global program they had written almost four years ago to execute all of the appropriate modules. As she glanced at the intricate routines, she recalled the fun they had together when they were working on it. It was right after they were hired in Rockville, and Henry had—

"What are you doing?"

Spencer was surprised to find that she had a small visitor standing over her shoulder.

"I'm just printing some things to read later. Is your show finished?"

Jessie nodded and yawned. "What's it about?"

"It's about . . . it's a mystery story, like a puzzle with words. I have to figure out all the pieces."

The little girl had come to stand closer and was now leaning against the programmer. Spencer reached out and swept her into her lap.

"Are you getting sleepy?"

Again she nodded. "When's Mommy coming home?"

Spencer looked at her watch. It had been more than a half hour since she had accessed the server. The fact that their door hadn't been broken down by the feds was a good sign.

"Not for a little while, but I'm finished here." Still holding the four-year-old in her lap, Spencer scooped up the last of her papers. A few more clicks and she shut down the computer. "Why don't we go back to the trailer and I'll read you a story that's more interesting than this one? You wanna do that?"

The sleepy child nodded one more time, seemingly very much at home in these long arms of the woman who had frightened her only a few days ago. Spencer carried her into the kitchen, where they said soft goodnights to the dogs and then exited to the trailer.

"I can't believe this! I go to bingo every Wednesday night and I'm lucky if I win once a month. You win on two cards your first night." The two women were almost home from their big night out.

"Beginner's luck," Ruth explained, feeling a little guilty . . . but not a lot. It was about time she got a break. "Tell you what. I'll spend my winnings on dinner, if we can cook and eat at your house."

"You've got yourself a deal. And I'll go you one better. You spend your winnings on a fat turkey, and I'll do all the rest. Thanksgiving's the week after next, you know."

For the first time, it hit Ruth that Manassas was her new life, that she wouldn't be sharing holidays anymore with her parents, or with Skip's family. With a few simple words on a whim, Viv Walters had just made her part of a new "family," and it felt better than any family Ruth had ever had.

Ruth smiled as she pulled behind the house and saw the light on in the trailer. It was almost ten o'clock, but she was sure that Jessie would be up waiting for her return. No matter how sleepy she was, she always liked the security of knowing that her mother was near before going to sleep.

"I appreciate you taking me. Maybe some of that luck of yours will rub off on me next week."

"Maybe so."

"Well, I'm gonna get on in the house and catch the news. I'll see you in the morning." Viv caught the worried look on her tenant's face. "I won't have any more chores for a while." She chuckled and disappeared into her house.

Inside the trailer, Spencer had begun the task of retracing her partner's steps. He had uploaded three copies of their global program, the first of which was their Master, the original program that they kept in the Documentation folder. By the heading at the top of the page, she could see that the second copy was the one they kept in the Run folder, the one they had invoked on Friday to process the executive summary. The Run version had a few patches, things they had recoded as prices or packaging changed. All of the patches were logged in the Doc folder as well, but not within the Master document. As near as Spencer could tell, the third copy was exactly like the Run version. According to its time stamp, it had also been invoked on Friday. Since Henry had placed all three copies on the server, he had likely found changes between the Master and the Run that weren't supposed to be there. *But what was the third copy for?*

Among the other documents he had sent were the patches and several pages of macros, the shortcuts they had written so that the program would run more efficiently and error-free. The last few pages were unfamiliar, but just as she was starting to review them, she heard the Taurus pull up in the muddy drive.

"Did you have a good time?" she asked as Ruth came through the door.

"I cleaned up," the smiling woman bragged. "I won the

Coverall and the Eight States."

"I take it that's a good thing?"

"It's a very good thing," she proclaimed, digging out her winnings as she swaggered across the room. "It means I paid forty-five dollars for three cards and I won $132, so that's $87 in the clear."

"And you obviously had a good time. Can't beat that."

"Where's Jessie?"

"Bathed, storied and down for the count," Spencer answered smugly.

"You're kidding." Ruth went down to the hall to see for herself. Sure enough, the child lay sound asleep, her Lisa doll cuddled at her side. "I bet she pitched a fit about me not being here at bedtime."

"Nope. She got tired, so I put her to bed. Hope that was okay."

"Yeah." Ruth was pleasantly surprised that Jessie had gotten her bath and gone to bed for Spencer. "So were you able to get online?" It was a stupid question, she knew, since the programmer had stacks of papers all over the kitchen counter.

"Yeah, but it's going to take me awhile to find what Henry was talking about." Spencer turned back to her work as Ruth settled into the recliner.

"You mind if I watch the news?"

"No, go ahead."

Ten minutes into the broadcast, the Margadon story was updated to include video of police recovering Spencer's motorcycle. An intensive search for the suspected murderer was underway in the Manassas-Centreville area of Virginia, where Rollins was seen placing a phone call from Wal-Mart. Her picture—the one from her employee badge—was shown on the screen along with that of Henry Estes.

Spencer grew nauseous as she watched the clip, just as she did every time she was reminded of her friend's horrid death. It was unimaginable that someone would kill a person like Henry, or that anyone would think *her* capable of such a vicious act. But more than to prove her innocence, she wanted the animals who had done this brought to justice.

"Oh my God!" Ruth shouted suddenly, leaping from the chair and out the door.

"What?"

"Viv! She was going in to watch the news too."

Ruth raced across the yard and pounded on the back door, shouting for her landlady to hurry.

Inside, Viv Walters had just gotten the fright of her life when she saw the picture of the woman wanted for murder. At once, she had grabbed the phone, intent on calling 9-1-1 to say that Spencer Rollins was in the trailer behind her house. Only the pounding on the door stopped her, as she realized the danger for Karen and her little girl. She rushed to the screened-in porch and threw the bolt to let the frantic woman in.

"I just . . ." Viv pointed absently at the television, the shock apparent on her lined face.

"It isn't true, Viv. Spencer didn't do it," Ruth said, gasping for breath.

"But they said—"

"No, it isn't true."

Behind her tenant, the tall stranger was approaching slowly from the trailer. Fear gripped the older woman as she imagined the worst, and she instinctively pulled Karen inside and started to close the door.

"She's right, Viv. I didn't kill that man," Spencer said softly. "He was one of my best friends."

The calm in her voice was contagious, and the landlady loosened her grip on Ruth. "Why are you hiding then? Why don't you just go to the police and tell them you're innocent?"

"Because the guys who killed her friend *are* the police and they're trying to kill her," Ruth explained. "It's true. I know it's hard to believe, but they're after her, Viv. She's staying here because nowhere else is safe."

Spencer could see that the older woman wasn't convinced. "I'll leave if you need me to. I won't give you any trouble at all. Karen can take me tomorrow and put me out on a street corner if that's what you want. You both have already done more for me than I have a right to ask. But just please don't call the police tonight." Her request was as much for Ruth as it was for herself.

"What are you going to do?"

The programmer waved the papers that she had printed earlier. "I have to prove that somebody else did it. That's why I needed your computer tonight. I have the evidence in these printouts, but I haven't figured it out yet," she pleaded. "I'm sorry that I lied to you, but I'm not lying now." Spencer stepped onto the screened-in back porch as Viv stood shaking in the kitchen doorway. "I'll tell you everything if you'll let me come in, and you can decide if I stay or go. I promise, I'll do whatever you say."

Viv nodded hesitantly and stepped aside to let Spencer and Ruth into the kitchen. At the kitchen table, the programmer explained in the simplest way possible how she came to be hiding out with Ruth and what she needed to do to clear her name. She showed her bruised ribs and the wound on her shoulder as proof of the chase.

"These people are dangerous—and I think a couple of them are FBI agents. They murdered my friend. I don't know why they're involved in this, but I intend to find out." She gestured to the stack of printouts on the table. "The proof is in there somewhere. The night he was killed, my partner called me and said somebody was skimming the books. They messed with our program to cover it up, and I have to find what they did. I need a little more time, Viv, but I'm going to bring those people to justice. Please trust me. I promise you that I'm not the person they say I am."

Over the years, Viv had gotten pretty good at sizing people up. You had to do that when you rented to strangers. There was nothing about Dolly Rollins—Spencer was her real name—that remotely suggested she was capable of something like this. "I believe you," she said simply. "I was miffed about you hiding over there, and I admit I didn't trust you at first. But I can see now why you did."

Ruth watched the exchange, feeling guilty now about her own lies to the obviously compassionate woman. She wanted to come clean about the secrets she kept, but her situation wasn't like Spencer's. Regardless of how she justified it, there was no misunderstanding or conspiracy about what she had done—she had kidnapped her child.

Akers jiggled his key in the lock, irritated as always that the tumblers inside the deadbolt didn't turn when he expected them to. The lock was cheap and worn, like much of the Landover townhouse. Replacing the deadbolt was an easy fix, but home maintenance was low on Akers's list of personal priorities.

When the bolt finally slid, he entered the darkened foyer and struggled out of his raincoat. Methodically, he emptied his pockets of his wallet and change, removed the gun from its holster beneath his armpit, and unclipped the badge from his belt. All were placed in their usual positions on the table near the door and he continued to the kitchen where his hand sought the light switch between the refrigerator and the wall.

"Hello, Calvin."

The agent's heart nearly stopped when he recognized the two men in dark suits sitting at his small dinette. He knew why they were here, and it never occurred to him to wonder how they had gotten in. These men worked for Yuri Petrov, who owned the largest casino in Atlantic City.

"You're working late. Big case?"

"You could say that." Though Akers worked hard to compose himself, his shaky voice gave away his nervousness.

The shorter of the two men stood and approached the agent, stepping close enough to seal his exit from the small kitchen. "You know why we're here, don't you, Calvin?"

"Of course," he answered, still trying to exude confidence when he had none. The payment on his gambling debt was overdue. "It's Wednesday."

"That's right . . . two days after Monday. And you do remember what's so special about Monday, don't you?"

The agent nodded. "Yeah, I was gonna call, but I've been tied up with work." In an effort to appear casual, he opened the refrigerator and reached inside. "You guys want a beer or something?"

"Sure." The intruder amiably took the offered beverage.

Before Akers knew what was happening, the short man smashed the long-necked bottle against the doorjamb and pushed its jagged edge into the stubble beneath the agent's chin. Akers knew better than to resist and steeled himself as he felt the blood begin to trickle down his neck.

"We got beer in Jersey, Calvin. We came to talk about the money you owe. Mr. Petrov doesn't like to be kept waiting."

The taller stranger now stood beside the dinette, tossing one of Akers's cheap carving knives from hand to hand with nonchalance.

"He'll get his money," the agent rasped, relieved to feel the pressure lessen as the broken bottle was pulled away. At once, Akers raised his hand to the wound, stemming the flow of blood with his index finger.

"Of course he will. But the question is when."

"I'll have it for him by Saturday." First thing tomorrow, Akers would lean on Pollard for a quick loan of ten thousand dollars. That would cover not only this week's payment to the casino head but next week's as well. They should have this Rollins business resolved by then, and the money from Margadon would flow again.

"Saturday is five days late. You do realize that the interest on Mr. Petrov's generous loan is substantial." For markers such as Akers's, the standard penalty was one thousand per day, with a ten thousand dollar limit. Reaching one's limit was unhealthy, to say the least.

"I'll have it—ten thousand on Saturday."

"Very well." The man tossed the bottle neck into the sink, where it clanged against the stainless steel. "But understand this, Calvin. You're worth more than ten thousand dollars as an example to those who think they can skip out on their debts."

"I'm not skipping out on my debt. I'll have the money."

"See that you do."

The two men left through the kitchen door and Akers sank onto the floor in a heap, his hand still pressed against his neck. With the heat on after what went down on Friday night, Thayer had called him over the weekend to say that their usual Monday surprise—seven thousand dollars apiece—wasn't going to be delivered. Stacy Eagleton thought it best if they laid low until Spencer Rollins was brought in—and silenced.

If they didn't find the programmer soon, Margadon wasn't going to matter much to Akers.

Chapter 17

Clutching her doll, Jessie shuffled sleepily down the hallway toward her mother's room. Yesterday, Spencer had gotten her breakfast while her mommy slept, but today, Spencer was still asleep on the couch.

"Mommy?" she called softly.

"Hey, sweetie. Come on in." Ruth lifted the blanket and Jessie crawled onto the bed, snuggling against her mother's warmth. "How did you sleep?"

"Fine."

It was a miracle that the little girl had slept through all the commotion last night. When her mother and Spencer returned to the trailer after talking with Viv, they stayed up mapping out what Spencer would do next. Ruth heard all about Margadon Industries, and the programmer walked her through what she thought was going on. If she could prove they had been cooking

159

the files, she could show why Henry was killed, and possibly, by whom.

"It's like this. We have these computer programs to keep track of production. Margadon makes pharmaceuticals . . . drugs. You need certain amounts of A, B and C to make D. We track everything by lot number so we not only know how much A goes in, but what box it came out of, and where it ends up. You ever hear those stories about products being taken off the shelves because there's something wrong?"

Ruth nodded.

"Well, that's how we know which lot numbers are affected when something like that happens. We might find out that there was something wrong with a shipment of B, so we have to recall all of D that was put together with that shipment. You with me?"

"I think so. You wrote some sort of accounting program to track what went into pharmaceutical products and then you found a problem with it."

"Exactly! But what we found—what Henry found—was that we weren't putting enough of one of the active ingredients into the batches of Kryfex that we're making for a government contract. But then, somebody messed with our program so they could cover it up. That way, they're billing the government the full amount, but they're shorting the key ingredient, which also just happens to be the most expensive ingredient. And somebody is pocketing the difference."

"Spencer read me the kitty cat story and made all the meow sounds."

Ruth laughed at the image of the programmer losing her usual serious demeanor. "Did you like that?"

"Uh-huh."

"I'm sorry I got home so late last night, honey. But I won."

"You did?"

"I certainly did. And I'm going to buy us a big turkey for Thanksgiving, and we're going to eat a nice dinner at Viv's house. Won't that be fun?"

Jessie smiled in agreement. "Will Spencer be there too?"

"Maybe, if she wants to. You like Spencer, don't you?"

The little girl nodded. "She's funny."

"Oh yeah? What does she do that's funny?"

"She tickles me and she plays games with me."

"I like Spencer too. You think we should go wake her up?"

"Uh-huh. And she has big feet."

"Big feet?"

"Yeah, come see."

Holding her daughter's hand, Ruth walked into the hall, immediately covering her mouth to suppress the laugh. Indeed, Spencer's size tens hung over the end of the couch, blocking the path to the living room. Tiptoeing back into the bedroom, the conspirators laid their plans.

Each armed with a cotton swab, they crept back down the hall, stooping low to take turns trailing the swabs softly across the instep of the bare feet. Mother and daughter worked hard to contain their giggles as the toes curled, the feet twitched, and the legs jumped.

"Someone is going to be very sorry," a deep voice threatened from around the corner.

Jessie squealed and ran into her room. Ruth followed and huddled with her daughter on the bed, bracing for the inevitable onslaught. Spencer made good on her word, suddenly appearing in their doorway, her face etched in mock fury. After five full minutes of frenzied tickling, the woman with the big feet returned to the living room, avenged and now wide awake.

"My granddaughter's been kidnapped, and I want to know what you're going to do about it!" Roland Drummond, Sr. bellowed. He was furious at the ineptitude of the local police, but that paled next to his opinion of the social worker who had persuaded the judge to allow unsupervised visitation. Ruth Ferguson didn't care about that child. She was obviously bitter about the divorce, and only wanted to hurt and embarrass his son.

"I assure you, we're doing everything we can, Roland," the sheriff pledged. "I've contacted the FBI, and they're sending an agent over this afternoon to go over all the details. Once they put their pictures out there, there won't be any place to hide. I promise you, we'll bring 'em back here."

"And when you do, I want that woman in jail! She ought never see the light of day again after this. And if she hurts one hair on that precious little angel's head . . ."

Skip hung back, perfectly content to watch his father take the lead in berating the investigators. Over the last few days, it occurred to him that the best possible outcome from all this would be that they never found either one of them. Sure, it would mean that his ex-wife would get undue satisfaction from thinking that she had beaten him. But the real truth was if they never found her, he wouldn't be saddled with a child to raise, but he would have the support and sympathy of all the people in Madison instead. Having Ruth run off with Jessie was exactly the freedom Skip was looking for.

Off and on all day, Spencer studied the printouts, still not understanding the paper trail her partner had created. She asked herself again the two fundamental questions. What was different between the Master and the Run? And why was there a third copy—a copy that was invoked on Friday in addition to the Run?

She also took a look at the program of macros Henry had appended. It was amateurish at best, but still, James was incapable of writing it. If Stacy Eagleton was involved in this, she was the likely author of this new code.

"You making any progress?" Ruth asked, returning with

Jessie from a tour around town with Viv.

"A little, but not much," Spencer conceded. "I know the key is in here somewhere. I'm going to have to go through all this line by line."

"Can I help?"

"Karen? Dolly?" Viv was calling them from the back porch.

Ruth went to the door as Spencer rolled her eyes. "I still can't believe you told her my name was Dolly."

"Can you two help me with something?"

With Jessie in tow, both women walked over to the house, where their landlady promptly directed them to the burned out overhead light in the kitchen.

"It just popped when I turned it on," she explained.

Ruth and Spencer retrieved the ladder from the shed, the taller of the two climbing up to disassemble the dirty fixture. That started Viv on a crusade to clean all the fixtures, and before they knew it, their afternoon was gone and they were back in the trailer, exhausted.

"She's a slave driver," Ruth moaned as she dropped onto the couch. "At least this wasn't as hard as some of that other stuff she had us doing."

"And we don't smell like dog."

"Right."

"To tell you the truth, I really don't mind helping her out, considering all she's doing for me." Spencer took the recliner and leaned forward. "And I'll do everything I can to help you and Jessie when I get out of this. I hope you know that, Ruth."

Ruth managed a small smile. Spencer had literally forced her way into their lives, and Ruth was now content to let her stay there. Though she knew nearly nothing about this woman, she felt close to her, closer in fact than she had to anyone for a long time. A shared sense of urgency bonded them, sort of "us against the world."

"You don't owe me anything, Spencer. I've liked having you

here . . . once I got over the 'bleeding murderer in my house' thing. And when I saw what you were up against, there just wasn't any way I couldn't try to help."

"Thank you. And I meant what I said about trying to help you too. Maybe my friend Elena can figure out something."

Ruth wasn't sure she wanted Spencer involving anybody else. The more people who knew about her and Jessie, the more at risk she was of being caught. "If it works out that way, that'll be great. But even if you can't help, I know you're going to get out of this mess. And when you do, I hope we'll still be friends."

"We will be," Spencer said sincerely. "So you think you'll stay in Manassas?"

"It's as good a place as any, I guess. Where do you live?"

"I have an apartment in Arlington, near the District. But I'm originally from North Carolina."

"How'd you end up here?"

"A job. Right after college, I took a job in McLean. That's where I first met Henry. That company went under, and we applied as a team to Margadon. Been there ever since."

"Is your family still in North Carolina?"

Spencer's eyes went far away with the simple question. "No," she answered quietly. "My parents died in a fire about four years ago."

"Oh, I'm so sorry. I shouldn't be asking so many questions."

"It's okay. It still hurts like hell sometimes, but I have a lot of good memories."

Ruth stood up and patted her new friend's shoulder. She felt awful for stirring up something so obviously painful. "I should check on Jessie."

As she looked in on her napping daughter, Ruth's stomach clenched with anxiety at the thought of something so horrific happening to those she loved. Now, she understood why Spencer had no place to go, no one to turn to but the friend she had tried to call. And she knew too what a loss Spencer must feel for the friend who had been murdered.

"You want some coffee or something?" she offered, returning to the kitchen, where the programmer was once again poring over her code.

"Yeah, that'd be nice." Spencer was amazed at how comfortable she felt with Ruth, so much so that she had been ready to talk about losing her mom and dad, something she had done only with Henry and Elena. Her two closest friends had kept her sane through the tragedy.

"So what about your family? Where are they?"

"Oh, you don't want to hear about my family. My own father stood up at Jessie's custody hearing and told the judge he thought she would be better off with Skip because I had always been difficult to control."

"Were you? Difficult, I mean. I know the part about Jessie is a crock."

"I wasn't difficult compared to most teenagers. But my parents had rules out of the Dark Ages, and the price of even bending those rules was more and more distance between us. It was like they didn't even want me to be their daughter anymore if I couldn't be perfect."

"So they were strict."

"They were way past strict. If they'd had their way, I'd still be in a chastity belt at twenty-five years old."

"Wow, how'd they feel when you got married? Were they okay with that?"

"Hardly," she scoffed. "See, I did the getting married-getting pregnant thing out of order."

"And that just added to what they already believed about you." Though her loss was tremendous, Spencer doubted that it was even half the void this woman had felt. At least she had been close to her folks and had always known she was loved and accepted.

"I guess. All I know is I won't miss them. It's true that you can't miss what you never had."

Spencer put her papers down and went into the kitchen where Ruth was gathering a stack of vegetables from the refrigerator. "Can I help with dinner tonight?"

"I'm just going to make some soup. Here . . ." She pulled a pound of hamburger from the meat tender. "You can brown this in that pan while I chop these. Or if you want, you can just stand there and keep me company."

Spencer smiled, ripping open the package. "I think I can handle this without doing too much damage."

"So tell me about your friend, the one you tried to call the other day."

"You mean Elena? Gosh, what can I tell you about Elena that wouldn't send you running and screaming?" she joked. "I told you she was an IRS agent, right? Mostly she investigates ill-gotten gains. She looks for people who seem to have more money than they should."

"Like drug dealers?"

"Exactly. They're the easiest to find, because most of them don't have jobs. The tougher ones are money-launderers, white-collar criminals, government officials on the take. They all go to work every day, so they have to do something really stupid to get tripped up."

"It sounds like an interesting job."

"She likes it. She gets to carry a gun. She says it helps her pick up . . . chicks." The last word she said tenuously, realizing too late where the conversation would go from there.

"She's a lesbian?" Ruth's question was surprisingly matter-of-fact.

"Yeah. And . . . so am I."

Ruth felt the words as much as she heard them, a shudder traveling through her body like a strong wind. In her mind, a transformation took place, as though the real Spencer Rollins had been fully revealed to her in that instant. The result was utter fascination. Miraculously, she managed not to cut off her thumb.

"So, you and Elena . . ."

"No. We were, but that was a long time ago. We're just friends now. Well, not *just* friends. We're good friends. She knows this is all bullshit. And even without me telling her what to do, I know she's already trying like hell to find out why these guys are after me."

"She sounds like just the sort of friend you need right now."

"That's for sure."

Ruth had calmed the butterflies, though she had no idea where they had come from. It didn't make sense that Spencer's disclosure would have unnerved her like that.

"So what happened with you two? How come you're not still . . ."

"Lovers?"

Ruth nodded. Another soft tremor rippled through her.

"Basically, she dumped me."

"Dumped you? Why would she dump you?"

"That's what I said!" Spencer said haughtily and they both laughed. More seriously, she explained, "Elena's just a really unique person and she's a great friend to have. But she's one of those people who has to be in control of everything all the time. And she knows she shouldn't try to control other people, so she keeps them at arm's length. I think I may have scared her, though . . . you know, threatened her independence. I know she loved me, but she couldn't go forward, and I was ready for a commitment. That's what love is about for me."

"I never really understood people who thought being in love was like being tied down. Of course, I doubt I'll be worrying about it again. I'd rather spend the rest of my life by myself than take a chance on losing Jessie again."

"You shouldn't have to spend the rest of your life alone, Ruth. All you need is to meet somebody who cares about you and Jessie both, and that's what you'd want even if you weren't hiding out, isn't it?"

Ruth shrugged, not looking up. "To be honest, I haven't really thought about that kind of thing in a long time."

"People sometimes find it when they aren't looking."

"What about you? Are you looking for that kind of thing? Somebody to spend your life with?"

Spencer was taken off-guard by the question, but she didn't know why. "I guess so . . . but I don't really expect to find it."

"Why not?"

Now it was Spencer's turn to shrug. "You know how it is. All the good ones are taken." *Or they're straight.*

"That can't be true, Spencer, or you wouldn't be by yourself." Ruth couldn't believe something so bold came out of her mouth.

Spencer's natural inclination was to take that as a pass and answer in kind, but she bit her tongue. This conversation had gotten too serious. "Maybe I should hire you as my agent. Let's see . . . you'll be responsible for identifying the eligible pool of potential partners, screening them beforehand for compatibility, and then you have to handle all the negotiations."

"Negotiations?"

"Yeah, like where we live, who cooks, who cleans. How much time each of us would get with our friends . . . that kind of thing. You'll be like one of those headhunters, but instead of looking for a job, you're looking for a mate."

"If I were you, I think I'd want somebody with a better track record." Ruth grinned at her new friend. "And maybe a little more experience matching women to each other."

"Nah, people are people. The dance is the same. All you have to do is keep the focus on my good qualities."

"I guess I could do that. So you got a résumé?"

Ruth and Jessie were long asleep as Spencer waded through the pages, line by line. She finally found what she was looking for on page fourteen of the Run copy. It was a simple command, adroitly embedded within another command so that it didn't alter the number of lines in the program. It redirected the entire process to a different global Run file. That's what the third copy was! So every Friday, Spencer or Henry would run their global, unaware that it contained a command for the switch. Whoever had done this was pretty fucking clever.

Henry had followed the redirect to the new global, which called an unfamiliar macro as it processed the Kryfex data. The new macro was in the stuff Henry had appended. It stood out like a sore thumb because it was written in a totally different style from their program.

Coding style was unique, much like handwriting. Programmers like Spencer and Henry relied heavily on loops and macros to minimize not only the processing time for the computer, but also the keystrokes used in the commands. It was a favorite game for both of them to see who could write a particular program using the fewest lines of code. Invariably, the final product would be a combination of their best efforts.

Other programmers, especially those with less experience, were more rigid, repetitive in their detailed logic so that each routine was clearly delineated on the page. Such programs typically took longer to run, and were, to Spencer, a royal pain in the ass to patch, because each routine had to be addressed individually. It was an example of the latter style that leapt out from the stack of papers she held. Neither she nor Henry would have written a command in such longhand.

So there it was, the evidence that had gotten Henry killed. Someone at Margadon—most likely Stacy Eagleton—had toyed with the global module they used for the run, redirecting the process to a new global, one Spencer and Henry hadn't even known existed. That global file was a carbon copy of their own, but an additional routine was included to inflate the number of cytokine units by twenty-five percent. Another macro contained a few lines of code that reduced the order for the Kryfex cytokines, but the cost was unaffected. And in a third macro, one she didn't recognize at all, the additional payment was then redirected off the books, presumably into a third-party account. The accountants and auditors would never know because the net profits were unaffected. From what Spencer knew about cost per unit for the cytokines, that meant someone was pocketing about sixty thousand a week.

In the notebook Ruth had bought her, she began to put the pieces together.

Ruth awoke in the night, surprised to see the light still streaming under the door. It was almost three a.m. Getting up to check it out, she found Spencer slumped at the kitchen counter, her papers scattered about the living room and the notebook marked in red.

Gently, she shook the broad shoulders. "Hey, you need to go to bed."

Spencer lifted her head and looked around. She couldn't have been asleep more than a minute or two. She stood and stretched, and then started to collect the papers she had sorted on the couch. "I have to keep all this straight."

"Just leave everything. Go on back to the bedroom and get in the bed."

"No, I'll sleep on the—"

"Go on. It's okay," Ruth quietly insisted, taking the papers from Spencer and giving her a nudge toward the bedroom. She set the papers down and took the coffee cup to the sink.

Within minutes of lying down, Spencer was sound asleep on the double bed in the back bedroom. She never even noticed when Ruth got back in bed beside her.

Chapter 18

The sound of cartoons—and the unmistakable smell of coffee—wafted down the hall and into the back bedroom, where Spencer Rollins had just enjoyed her best night's sleep in a week. Seeing the covers thrown back on the opposite side of the bed, she realized she hadn't spent the night alone. But she might as well have, given her near-comatose state.

But it was definitely interesting that she had been invited to share the bed, especially in light of yesterday's revelation. Immediately, she chastised herself for any leap of logic she was tempted to make, but the warm, fuzzy feeling lingered nonetheless.

Spencer stared at the ceiling as she went over in her mind the proof that Henry had found. The secret global program included a routine that inflated the number of cytokines for both the executive reports and the accountants. The full bill was paid to the supplier, who carved out the extra dollars for all of the players. Best she could tell, the players were James, Stacy Eagleton, probably the cytokines supplier in Arizona and the line producer in Little Rock. The missing link was to the feds, the guys who had killed Henry and who now wanted her dead. The only connection she could think of was that this was a federal contract—the Kryfex was going to Ethiopia in exchange for the military base. A federal contract meant government supervision and auditing. *But why was it the FBI?*

"So you're awake." Ruth appeared in the doorway, coffee mug in hand.

"Yeah." Spencer pushed herself up in the bed. She was still in yesterday's T-shirt, but her jeans lay on the floor.

"Did you figure things out last night?" Ruth sat on the edge of the bed and handed her the mug.

"Thanks. I think so. I still don't quite know why the feds are involved, though. I mean, it's a federal contract, but that doesn't explain those guys being on the take too."

"Isn't that what your friend does? Didn't you say she tried to find people with . . . what was it? . . . ill-gotten gains?"

Spencer nodded pensively. Elena would have access to all kinds of information. She could probably figure out exactly who was involved in this. "I need to find a way to get this stuff to her."

"Can't you just mail it?"

Spencer shook her head. "No, these guys are probably watching her and checking her mail. I know they were tapping her phone. They're waiting for me to contact her again, and if it's as bad as I think it is, they can't afford to have me tell her what I know."

"What if you mailed it to a newspaper or something?"

"I thought about that. A newspaper could raise some questions, but they aren't going to attach much credibility to accusations by an alleged murderer. Besides, they don't have the authority to go digging into people's finances like Elena does. If these guys have been skimming the books like Henry said, she can find it."

"Maybe . . ." Ruth couldn't believe she was really going to say this. "What if I took it to her, like to her office or something?"

"No way. I don't want you involved in this. Besides, you've already done more than enough." Spencer was adamant. It was too big a risk.

"Spencer, I'm already involved. If these guys find out you've been hiding here, they're not going to just let me go tell everybody what you told me. The way I see it, the only way out of this for both of us is for you to prove that those guys are the real murderers."

For the first time, Spencer realized with alarm the position she had put them all in. Ruth was right. If they thought she knew something, she was in danger too. And so were Viv and Jessie. "I need to get out of here before they find you." Quickly, she threw back the covers and grabbed her jeans.

"No! Listen to me."

Slowly, Spencer sat back down, surprised at the forcefulness of the smaller woman's voice.

"They don't know me. Elena doesn't know me. Why can't I just make an appointment with her to talk about my taxes or something and hand her your stuff?"

Spencer shook her head. "She doesn't do that kind of thing. The only people who talk to her about taxes are looking for a plea bargain."

"Well think of something else, then. But you're not just going to leave, not until I know you're going to walk out of here to someplace safe."

Spencer had a flash of how Jessie must feel when her mom put her foot down.

Akers winced when he saw the lighted number on his cell phone. He dreaded the tirade that would start the instant he answered the call.

"This is Akers."

"It's about goddamned time you took my call!"

"I've been in meetings."

Stacy Eagleton recognized a lie when she heard it, but she had more important nuts to squeeze. "What's the status of Rollins?"

"We've got her picture out there. I just got the okay to throw in a reward, so unless she's hiding under a rock, we're a big step closer." He figured that would placate the bitch.

"You better hope so! You and Pollard have a hell of a lot more at stake here than the rest of us."

Akers slapped his phone shut when Eagleton ended the call. *She doesn't know the half of it!* Stacy Eagleton was still sitting on the operation waiting for this to blow over, and had made it clear that no one was getting paid until Rollins was taken care of. She was sweating the notion of the programmer implicating all of them in a contract scheme. But Akers was a hell of a lot more worried about Petrov. Though he had paid up on Thursday— $5,000 for the principle and another $3,000 in penalties— Petrov's henchmen had made it clear that missing another payment next week wouldn't sit well with their boss. The late fees would probably double, which meant that one reached the $10,000 penalty limit in half the time.

He only owed $7,000 more and had $2,000 left over from what Pollard had fronted him. If they got this wrapped up before the weekend, the cash would flow again on Monday and he could pay the balance and get these guys off his back.

Akers was confident that he and Pollard had the Rollins situation under control, even if they didn't have her in custody. If she started making noise about somebody tampering with the program, she wouldn't be able to prove it as long as the program wasn't operational. And if she couldn't prove their scheme, it would cast doubt on everything she said. Akers was certain they could all stand up to scrutiny if she started making accusations. They had put together a pretty good case: Eagleton's commentary on her paranoia and temper, video of her fleeing the scene. They had effectively gotten rid of anything that even suggested someone else might be to blame.

But Akers couldn't afford for this to drag out. He needed to be able to get the operation up and running again. The only way to do that was to bring Rollins in—dead.

Ruth sat at the kitchen counter reading Spencer's typed, six-page story, stopping when she got to the attached sheets of code. "Overall, I think it's pretty clear. I understand every word . . . well, except for the part about calling globals and macros. You might want to spell that out a little bit."

Spencer had worked all afternoon at Viv's computer writing down what she knew of the events and her theories about the players. The involvement of the feds was the murky part, but she kept coming back to Kryfex being a government contract.

"I think Elena will know what most of this means. If she doesn't, she'll be able to ask someone at the IRS to go over it with her." The programmer made some additional notes in the margin and reread the difficult section.

"That's much better," Ruth agreed. "So all you have to do now is figure out how to put this in Elena's hands, right?"

"Right. She'll be able to take it from there."

"So how do we get it to her? Is there anyone you know who can pass it on? Any of her friends?"

"Nobody I can think of, but I'm still working on it. The important thing is to make sure it doesn't end up in the hands of the guys who did this. Right now, that server might be the only evidence left. If they find out about it, they'll go after it and that's it."

"So we have to get it to Elena without them knowing."

"I have to get it to Elena—not you." Spencer scooped up her papers and set them aside. "But I think there's something else we ought to do too."

"What?"

"I think we should tell Elena about you and Jessie and ask her to help."

"Oh, no. I don't think so." No way was Ruth going to confess to being a fugitive to a federal agent.

"Look, if anyone can help you—if anyone *will* help you—it's Elena."

"Why would she help me? She doesn't know me from Hedda's house cat."

"But she knows me. And she'd help you because I asked her to."

"You're forgetting one very important fact here, Spencer. I'm not being set up here like you are. I'm guilty of a felony. I kidnapped my child and fled across state lines. The feds are probably looking for me now, too. And if Elena finds out, she may have to turn me in, whether she wants to or not."

"No, she won't! Elena cuts deals with criminals all the time to get a bigger fish. She has the authority to do things like that. She wouldn't turn you in if I asked her not to." Spencer needed to make her see that Elena could set things right. Ruth shouldn't have to be on the run. She had done nothing to deserve the way the system had treated her, and that needed to be fixed.

"What could she possibly do, Spencer? The IRS isn't going to get a custody decision reversed."

"I know. But she might be able to look into some things, lean on a few people, throw a little weight around." Spencer knew she was probably being unrealistic about what was possible, but she also knew that Elena would do whatever she could. "What if she helped you and Jessie hide for good? Really hide! What if she could close all the little loopholes and lapses so that nobody could ever put it together? At least you'd have peace of mind and

176

not have to be looking over your shoulder every day for the rest of your life."

"Fine, if you think she can do that, maybe you can talk to her about it someday. But not now. Right now, getting you out of trouble is what matters."

"But you and Jessie matter too. This has to be a package deal. That's what makes it work. She'll have to help you then."

Ruth was afraid to let herself hope for that much, but she couldn't deny that this was worth the risk. It might be her only chance ever to break free of Skip Drummond once and for all. "Okay, but I'll only do it under one condition."

"What?" *Anything.*

"You let me take it to her." Spencer started to protest, but Ruth put up her hand. "That's the only way I'll agree to do it."

"Something stinks here, Chad." Elena slumped uninvited into the leather chair across from her boss's desk, her hands clutching a manila folder. All of their conversations about the Spencer Rollins case took place in his office because hers was bugged by the FBI.

"I sympathize, but what can I do? She's called you twice already."

"No, I mean really stinks. It's bad enough that they probably listen to me pee, but I think there's more to this than just a fugitive on the run."

In the eleven years they had worked together, the supervisor had learned to trust this woman's instincts. Elena was dogged when it came to investigation and had a nose for sniffing out trouble. "You got something in that folder?"

"Yeah," she admitted. "I've been doing some digging on my own and I came across something pretty interesting for Special Agent Michael Pollard." That was the agent who had approached her boss.

"What are you doing poking around in Pollard's business? Just because he's working this case? We don't do things like that, Agent Diaz. You know better," he scolded.

Yes, she did know better, but something about this case wasn't right, and it wasn't just because Spencer was their prey. "Chad, this is not a case of me abusing my authority. It's about me having my own suspicions. That's what you pay me for—to play my hunches and catch the bad guys. Right?"

"You're stretching it, Elena." He folded his arms defiantly across his chest. "So what have you got?"

"Agent Pollard is pulling down about $115 thousand a year, but he and his wife are pretty extended. They've got four kids in private school and a mortgage on· a five-bedroom house in McLean."

"So?"

"So they just bought a vacation home in Eastern Shore, about $200 thousand—for cash."

"Cash?"

Elena nodded.

"So this Pollard, he's still working this case?"

"Yes, he is. In fact, I think he's sitting out in the van. You want me to go get him so we can ask him how he got his hands on that much money?"

Merke leaned forward and rested his chin on his hands, intrigued by the information Diaz offered, but stopping short of considering it as evidence. "So I gather that you think his new house and his interest in Spencer Rollins are related?"

Elena sighed, closing the folder and tapping it rhythmically on her knee. "I know it's a stretch, Chad, but hear me out. First of all, Spencer didn't kill Henry. They were best friends, but even if she had hated his guts, Spencer wouldn't have done something like that. I know her, and you know what I just said is the absolute truth."

The agent stared down her boss until he finally nodded his

agreement.

"Second, she tried to call me twice to tell me what was going on. Both times, the calls were cut off, like whoever was pulling the strings didn't want me to hear her side of the story. That's pretty desperate if you ask me, and it happened before those assholes ever got a warrant to tap my phone. I told you already that I thought it was pretty amazing how fast they got on this case. You know how hard it is to get the Bureau to take jurisdiction."

Chad nodded again, conceding her point.

"Third, if she didn't kill Henry Estes, who did and why? You know as well as I do that the answer in a case like this usually comes back to one thing—greed. And I don't like it that one of the agents who wants her caught, who wants to keep her from talking, just paid that much cash for a vacation home."

Ruth and Spencer managed to get through the evening without talking about the code, about Elena, or about Ruth's running away with Jessie. The words were just beneath the surface, but without a resolution, there was no need to keep beating a dead horse. Spencer stridently refused to allow the young mother to make the delivery unless they came up with a foolproof plan for getting her in and out without risk of being caught.

When the dinner dishes were done, Jessie brought out her new dinosaur puzzle and spread the pieces on the floor. Since Ruth was running back and forth to Viv's doing the laundry, Spencer sat down on the floor to help. "Helping" a four-year-old with a puzzle meant grouping pieces by color and giving lots of hints. Ultimately, Jessie would be the one to place each piece.

The tension between Spencer and Ruth was nearly palpable, and when Jessie was finally ushered to bed, there was no way to avoid having it out.

"You're being stubborn," Ruth said, her anger at Spencer not concealed.

"I'm not going to let you do it." Spencer shook her head and sighed. "Will you take me to the Franconia-Springfield station tomorrow morning?"

"You're going to risk everything by just going out there and turning yourself in?"

Spencer nodded, but wouldn't meet the other woman's eyes. "If she isn't expecting me, maybe they won't be either."

"You're just going to walk into her office?"

"Yeah . . . you know, I was thinking that maybe I should do what you said and write a letter to the *Washington Post* and leave it with you. If you don't hear from me again, you should drop it in the mail or something."

"I don't believe this! Do you hear how ridiculous that is? A letter to the paper isn't going to mean a goddamned thing if something happens to you. It's too dangerous for you to go. I'll take it."

"I can't let you do that."

"But they aren't looking for me. Not these guys, anyway. I bet they couldn't care less about Karen Oliver."

Spencer shook her head in frustration. "She wouldn't even bother to see you unless you had—" Spencer stopped herself, her mind racing with a new idea. "Unless you told her you had information on Roscone. That would get her attention."

"Who's Roscone?"

Chapter 19

Elena resisted the urge to make an obscene gesture, waving instead toward the gray panel truck that had been parked illegally on Constitution Avenue for the last five days. The boys inside had watched her building and monitored her phone and Internet account all week. Despite her outrage at the intrusion, she was stuck with the surveillance, as the FBI was almost certain that Spencer would contact her again.

Flashing her ID to the guard at the desk, the towering woman bypassed the elevator in favor of the steps, just as she did every day. Three flights of stairs were nothing given her usual exercise routine. Each day, the thirty-seven-year-old agent pushed herself to her physical limit and then pushed a little more, always reaching to be stronger, faster, better. She was as tough as any field agent at the IRS, and to her infinite delight, she was often taken too lightly, adding to her advantage.

"Morning, Elena."

"Hi, Thomas." No one was more underestimated than Special Agent Thomas Fennimore, her bespectacled assistant of the last three years. It took Elena almost a year to realize that Thomas's bumbling demeanor concealed his incredible savvy, and she eagerly took him on when other senior agents balked at what they perceived as ineptitude.

"I found something I think you're going to like," he offered, following her into her windowed office. He waited in the doorway expectantly until she bought a clue and followed him back out.

"I could use some good news." Automatically, the two exited the office area and went back into the stairwell where they could talk without fear of being overheard.

"It's about Pollard and that other guy, Agent Akers. I got my buddy over at the Bureau to run a little query on work logs, and they were the agents assigned to do the background checks for the Kryfex contract at Margadon."

"The what?"

"Kryfex. Margadon developed it for the Dawa virus, and the U.S. is shipping it to Ethiopia in return for an air base. And since it's a big contract, they did background checks."

"Do you know who they talked to? Did they ever talk to Spencer?"

"I don't have that list yet. I can start pulling it today, though. I doubt Spencer would have been interviewed. They usually only do the higher-ups."

"That's good work, Thomas. Go ahead and follow up. Did you find a money trail for Akers?"

"Not yet, but I'm working on that too."

"So what was the judge's name?" Spencer was typing the story of how Ruth and Jessie had come to be on the run.

"The judge's name? You really think that's relevant?"

"I don't know what's relevant. I just want to give Elena as much information as possible. Maybe she can talk to him about the facts."

"What facts?" Ruth grumbled. "His name was Howard . . . Malcolm Howard. I can still see his snarling face when he told me he was going to hold me in contempt if I didn't keep quiet while Skip was spewing his lies."

Spencer typed the name into the account, and reread the whole document aloud from the screen.

"Is that everything?"

"As far as I know."

"Okay, here it comes." She hit the print key. "Are you ready to go call?"

They had agreed that it would be best for Ruth to go alone, and place the call from a pay phone somewhere in Reston. Calling from Manassas might raise a few eyebrows, especially since they had found Spencer's bike in the woods nearby.

"Ready as I'll ever be."

Without a word, Thomas dropped a fresh folder on his supervisor's desk. His cocky grin told her that he had gotten some dirt, and the tab read "Special Agent Calvin Akers."

The report documented plane tickets to Las Vegas, hotels in Atlantic City, even a trip to the Atlantis Resort in the Bahamas. Calvin Akers had a gambling habit. That's why there was no money to be found.

The phone interrupted Elena's joy, and her eyes went at once to the digital display: a pay phone in Reston. A lot of her information came from pay phones because tipsters liked their anonymity, but every call she got these days made her think of her friend on the run.

With no small measure of sarcasm, she announced, "There's

the phone, boys. Got your tapes in? Ready . . . set . . . go!" She picked up the receiver, and pressed the blinking button. "Hello, this is Special Agent Elena Diaz with the Internal Revenue Service. How may I help you?"

"Uh . . . Agent Diaz . . . I . . . uh . . ."

"Yes?" It wasn't Spencer, she realized with a mixture of relief and regret.

"I was wondering if you were still interested in information about George Roscone."

Roscone? Yes, she was interested. Hell, yes!

"Who am I speaking to?" George Roscone was a District prosecutor who had scuttled a very big case against two drug-dealing brothers a couple of years ago by leaking her investigation to the press. She was certain he had been bought off, and set out to prove it by trying to locate the money. After eight months of finding nothing out of the ordinary, she had reluctantly let it go when Chad not-so-subtly suggested that she redirect her budget to something that would bear fruit.

"I'd rather not say. I want to be anonymous. For now, anyway. Can I do that?"

"My office will work with you to maintain confidentiality. But before I can guarantee that, I need to know what kind of information you have, and how you acquired it."

"Okay . . ." Ruth needed to make all of this believable, so she had practiced in the car on the way to Reston. She wanted to come off as nervous and uptight, and that was easy enough if she just borrowed from her recent experiences. "I used to work in a bank in the District, and you subpoenaed all of Mr. Roscone's statements. Right after that, my boss asked me to keep an eye on his account, and see if anything happened."

"So did something happen?" God, she really wanted Roscone.

"Well, not exactly. See, I got laid off not long after that. But I moved out to Virginia, and a couple of weeks ago I started work at another bank."

Sometimes, it was like pulling teeth to get people to talk. "And what does this have to do with George Roscone?"

"He came into my new bank the other day. He has an account there. I know it was him because . . . well, I always thought he was really handsome." Spencer had told her to put that in because Elena used to go on and on about what a "pretty boy" Roscone was.

This was definitely the kind of tip Diaz was interested in, but if he had another account, she really didn't need this witness. All she had to do was launch a new query, and watch it come up. It took a lot of resources to track accounts and transactions, but it was easier when she knew in advance what to look for.

"But the thing is, he doesn't go by George Roscone. He uses another name on this account."

Holy shit! Diaz nearly fell out of her chair. This was the best break she had gotten in a year. "Can you give me the name that he uses, and the name of the bank and the branch where you work?"

"I . . . well . . ."

"What is it?"

"It's just that I've been laid off for a while, and I was wondering if maybe there was a reward or something."

Elena was used to requests like this, especially from tipsters on the bottom rungs of the economic ladder. A few thousand dollars meant a lot to somebody who lived from hand to mouth, and it was nothing compared to the costs of twenty-four seven surveillance of suspects and round-the-clock audits. Thank God her boss saw the advantage of a few dollars wisely spent. "I might be able to swing a small reward for you. It's all going to depend on what kind of information you have, and what we're able to prove in court."

"I have copies of his statements for the past two years. And he's just started making big deposits and withdrawals again."

Elena was practically salivating. She spun around to look at the clock. It was a quarter after five on Friday evening.

"I'd be very interested in having a look at those. If you'll give me your name and address, I'll come pick them up tonight."

"No, I think I'd prefer to meet you somewhere, and show you what I have. Really, I want to do the right thing, but if there isn't a reward, I don't want to be involved." She hesitated for effect. "I could get in a lot of trouble for this at work, probably even lose my job."

"I know, and I really appreciate you coming forward with this. Can you meet me somewhere tonight?"

"Tomorrow would be better. I'm on my way home, and I have things I have to do tonight."

Great! Elena thought. Wouldn't want to interfere with a Friday night date when justice was as stake.

"Okay." A situation like this called for kissing ass, and Elena could do that when she had to. "Can you come into the city, or would you like to meet somewhere else?"

"What about somewhere on the Mall, like the Metro stop at the Smithsonian?"

That would work very well for Elena. The Smithsonian was across the Mall from her building. "How's nine o'clock tomorrow morning?"

"I can be there then, I think." Ruth didn't want to appear too eager. "If I can't make it, is there a number I can call?"

Elena quickly rattled off her cell phone. "How will I find you?"

"I'll put all my copies in a blue folder."

"Okay, then. I'll see you tomorrow morning. This is a good thing you're doing. I wish more people would take their civic duty as seriously as you." That was the standard speech Elena gave when people provided her with information. She hoped the woman would take it to heart.

"Just see if you can get me some reward money. I really need it."

"So what do you think?" Agent Pollard, who had spent the last nine hours inside the surveillance van, welcomed the chance to step outside and talk with the senior agent on his cell phone. They were both back on the day shift now that they had the rookies doing overnight surveillance at Diaz's condo.

"I'm not sure, Mike. Who's this Roscone guy?"

Pollard flipped through the dossier on Agent Diaz. "He's a DA. She's been working his case to see if he's on the take."

"That sounds just like the IRS, doesn't it?"

"So, you want me to follow up on this one?"

The agent in charge knew it would be a waste of time and resources. "Nah, I wouldn't bother. It doesn't have anything to do with Rollins. But this Roscone guy . . ."

"Yeah?"

"Tip him off." Akers hated Diaz.

Chapter 20

"You don't have to do this, Ruth. It isn't too late to change your mind." The two women stood next to the Taurus, both uneasy about what the day might bring.

"It's no big deal. I'm going to drop this off, and be back here inside of three hours."

"Elena's gonna shit a brick when she finds out the Roscone stuff is bogus. I think she'd rather have him than me," Spencer joked nervously.

"I doubt that. Look, don't let Jessie watch cartoons all morning, okay? Take her over to see the puppies or something."

"You bet." Spencer locked her serious gaze onto Ruth's anxious face. "Thanks for this, Ruth."

"You're welcome."

Spencer wrapped the smaller woman in a nervous hug, which was heartily returned.

Ruth got in and started the car, but didn't close the door, her eyes still lingering on the angular face of her friend. "This is the beginning of the end, Spencer. It'll all be over soon."

"I hope so, for both of us." Spencer closed the door and stepped back, waving goodbye as she watched the Taurus pull away. Not that they would needed any reminders, but both of their lives were riding on the meeting with Elena.

Ruth realized it. She had been thinking all morning about what was at stake for both of them. Coming forward about her identity was a big step, but after their talk last night, she had finally agreed to put all her faith in Elena, trusting that the agent would never let Spencer down.

Last night had been . . . interesting. When it came time for bed, Spencer had gotten the sheet and blanket from the closet to make up the couch, and it struck Ruth as silly that she would do that. They had slept together in the double bed the night before. Why not again? Spencer joked that while she had no problems sharing a bed with the likes of someone as pretty as Ruth, she should keep in mind that sleeping with a lesbian was theoretically the same as sleeping with a man.

Ruth refused to let it be a big deal, though. She put on her gown like she always did, while Spencer pulled off her jeans to sleep in her panties and T-shirt. If anything, Ruth was more comfortable sleeping with Spencer than she had ever been with Skip. Spencer didn't hog the bed, and it was nice that they had gone to sleep facing each other. She had always hated the way Skip turned his back to her every night.

Why am I thinking about this so much?

When she reached the Metro station at Franconia-Springfield, the end of the Blue Line, Ruth parked the station wagon in the garage. A twenty-minute ride would take her to the Smithsonian, but Spencer had suggested she get off earlier at the Federal Triangle, and walk across the Mall from the opposite direction, right past the IRS building. It would make her feel

189

more in control of this meeting if she weren't so predictable.

When she boarded the train, she flipped open the blue folder to examine its contents one last time. The first few pages were bogus bank statements, meticulously formatted on Viv's computer to look like the ones Ruth used to see at the Bank of Madison. Underneath those statements were Spencer's report and the annotated pages of code. The last page was the typed note that Spencer had encouraged her to include, the story of Ruth Ferguson and Jessie Drummond. In her recounting of events in Madison, Ruth didn't reveal her new identity. They had also agreed not to divulge where they were staying until Elena gave assurances that she could help. If there was nothing she could do, Ruth and Jessie would move on, since it meant the feds would then know that they were in the area. Her anxiety compelled her to remove it from the folder. But as she considered again Spencer's infinite trust in Elena, she slipped it back inside.

When the Federal Triangle station was announced, Ruth stepped off the train and followed the signs to Constitution Avenue. She was awed by the stateliness of the buildings around her. As she walked toward the Mall, she began to make out the tops of both the Capitol and the Washington Monument. When she finally stood between those two landmarks, she could see the National Gallery, the Smithsonian and even the top of the White House. Standing in this majestic place was almost breathtaking. She hoped that one day soon, she could bring her daughter to explore this wonderful city.

Ruth was fifteen minutes early for her meeting. Already, the Mall was bustling with tourists, and having all these people around helped her relax a bit. In the distance, she located the Metro stop for the Smithsonian and the bench where Spencer said she should wait.

After only five minutes, she spotted a woman walking from the direction of the IRS building that she just knew was Elena Diaz. She was as Spencer had described: very tall, curly dark hair, with large brown eyes. She was dressed in tailored slacks and a turtleneck, the black blazer no doubt concealing the gun tucked beneath her shoulder. Ruth held the blue folder conspicuously in front of her and waited to see if she would catch the woman's eye.

Elena was vaguely aware of a woman sitting on the bench and was almost past her when she glanced sideways and caught the blue image. Stopping short, she turned and strode purposefully toward her.

"Are you waiting for Elena Diaz?" she asked.

The blond woman nodded once and dropped the folder to her lap as the agent took a seat beside her on the bench.

"Would you mind showing me some identification?" Ruth asked tensely.

Elena smiled and pulled her badge from her waistband, flipping it up to reveal her official photo ID. "Is that for me?" She gestured toward the folder.

Again, Ruth nodded without speaking. She was much more nervous about this than she had ever imagined she would be. It was sure easy to see why Spencer had been attracted to Elena. The Latina woman was gorgeous and appeared strong and confident. Spencer had used the word "independent," which seemed to fit.

Elena took the folder and opened to the first page, scanning the information with excitement.

"Where's the name? And where's the bank's name?" she asked pointedly, working hard to conceal her agitation.

"I just wanted to show you what I had so we could talk about the reward." Ruth leaned over and slid her finger beneath the bogus spreadsheets, opening to the first page of Spencer's report. "There's more here," she said.

Elena's eyes grew wide as she realized what she was seeing, the salutation *Serpiente* confirming its authenticity. Spencer had sent this woman to talk to her.

Automatically, she looked up, locating in her peripheral vision the surveillance van that had dogged her all week. Those guys never seemed to take a day off, she groused to herself. The asshole was probably watching her through binoculars, but she doubted seriously that their conversation was bugged, especially since this woman had waited for her on the bench instead of at the Metro stop where they had planned to meet. Still, they shouldn't take a chance.

"Look, you did the right thing to bring this to my attention, but I'm going to need to look at it and talk to some people before I'll know about the reward. Are you okay with having to wait a few days?"

"I can wait. I'm okay for now."

That was the best news Elena could have gotten. Spencer was safe and out of sight, and she had obviously made a friend who was willing to go out on a limb for her. "Is there a way I can get in touch with you if I have any more questions?" How could she contact Spencer?

Ruth squirmed on the bench as she contemplated her predicament. If Elena really could help Spencer, she needed a way to reach her.

"What if I call you back on Monday? Is that enough time?"

Elena pulled out a business card. "I think so. I should be able to ask around by then. Here's my direct number and extension." Elena scribbled the information on the card and pressed it into Ruth's hand. Standing, she offered her hand and one last message of thanks. "I really appreciate your help on this. I'll do everything I can to get you some kind of reward."

Pollard lowered his binoculars and chuckled to himself as the blond woman descended into the Metro station. By the time Diaz got her warrant, Roscone would have wired the money out of the country into an offshore account.

Ruth pushed her ticket through the electronic turnstile at the Smithsonian station, constantly checking the crowd to see if she was being followed. Spencer had advised her to take a circuitous route back to the Blue Line, so she hopped off at Metro Center, changing to first the Red Line, then the Yellow, finally jumping back to the Blue at Pentagon City. She had been one of only a handful getting off at Chinatown, so that gave her confidence that her mission was a success. Nonetheless, she had to calm her shaking hands before she could start the car and pull out of the garage into traffic.

Mission accomplished.

"I can't believe you did all that by yourself," Ruth remarked to a very tired and sore Spencer, who had spent the morning stacking firewood on the back porch for Viv.

"It gave me something to do besides climb the walls while you were gone."

"Well, it wasn't too smart, considering that your stomach is still black and blue and your shoulder has a hole in it," she scolded, taking up a position behind Spencer so she could massage the aching shoulders. Jessie sat at the kitchen counter coloring in a new book.

"I know, but what could I say? They dumped it in the driveway and left. Viv couldn't get her car out, and you couldn't have gotten yours in."

"You could have at least waited for me to help."

"I was going crazy," she reiterated. "So tell me everything. What did Elena say when she found out the Roscone shit was bogus?" A hard squeeze from Ruth reminded her that the four-year-old was present. "Sorry."

"We didn't talk. Well, we did, we just talked about Roscone.

She acted like she was nervous about us being overheard, so I played along."

"But you showed her the papers? You're sure she saw my note?"

"Yes, I gave her everything. And yes, she saw your note."

"Boy, she must be under pretty tight surveillance if she wouldn't even talk to you." Spencer winced when the firm hands found a knot at the back of her neck.

Ruth felt the flinch and zeroed in on the spot, pressing it gently with her thumb until she could feel the muscle start to release.

"So what's the plan for seeing her again?"

"You were right about the reward. That gave us a good excuse, because she said she'd have to check on it and I should call her back." Ruth then remembered the card she had shoved in her pocket. "Come to think of it, she gave me her card."

Ruth dug the card out of her jacket, admiring the gold-embossed shield. Turning it over, she found a note.

"Oh, I didn't see this. Look what she wrote." She handed the card to Spencer.

Elena had scribbled a few words of encouragement and a warning: *Hang in there, Spence—we're working on it. No contact is best for now.*

"I knew it! She's already on it. What'd I tell you?"

"I can see why you trust her. There's something about her that gives off confidence and authority. And she sure did seem glad to hear from you." Ruth resumed her shoulder massage.

"How could you tell?"

"I don't know exactly. It was like her shoulders relaxed and her voice got softer."

Spencer chuckled. "I can't believe you picked up on that. I've seen it before too, just like you're describing. That's when I first realized that her tough girl stuff was an act."

"I don't think it has anything to do with not being tough. I think she just cares for you, and she's probably been pretty frantic herself about all of this." In her voice was a trace of admonition. It was clear that the agent's feelings for Spencer were genuine, and if Ruth had to bet, she would say they went beyond the friendship Spencer described.

"I'm sure she has. I'm really lucky to have her out there on my side. And I bet you can see now why I wanted you to put all this other stuff in her hands. If there's a way to fix things for you and Jessie, she'll find it."

After meeting Elena for herself, Ruth found herself nursing a glimmer of hope after all. "Even if she can't, at least I trust her now not to turn me in."

Unexpectedly, Spencer reached up and covered a hand that worked her shoulder. "Ruth, no matter what happens, I really appreciate what you did today."

She liked the familiarity of Spencer's hand on hers. "You know, you've got to stop calling me that. You're going to confuse my daughter, and Viv's going to start asking questions."

"Sorry, but you're just not a Karen," Spencer said sheepishly. "And Jessie's not a Megan, either."

"I know, but if Elena can't help us on this, we have to be Karen and Megan Oliver from now on . . . Dolly."

"That was low."

Ruth grinned at Spencer's glower. With no warning at all, the most peculiar feeling came over her and she found herself fighting the urge to lean down and kiss those pouting lips. *Where the hell did that come from?*

Ruth laid awake that night thinking about what had come over her earlier. Spencer was stretched out beside her in bed, the slow, deep breaths a sure sign that she was asleep. Ruth had never been drawn to a woman before, not emotionally and certainly not sexually. All of her sexual urges up to this point had been for men. One man, actually, and that was Skip. But she hadn't exactly been attracted to Skip when it came to emotions. As far as Ruth was concerned, in the three years they were together, they never really connected at all.

What she felt for Spencer was such a contrast to all of that. It was definitely emotional, and it wasn't like any of her other friendships. When her friends were sad or happy, she could easily share that with them. But with Spencer, she did more than share, and none of it was conscious. When this woman beside her felt something, she felt it too. It didn't matter if it was anxiety, relief, frustration or hope. Ruth took it on, and in her mind, that made them closer than just friends. Whether Spencer felt that way or not was anybody's guess, but she never gave off any kind of warning for Ruth to keep her distance.

Now, the sexual thing . . . well, that was new. If she were honest with herself, she would have to admit that she had gotten her very first flicker of that the moment Spencer told her she was gay. But was it really sexual? It was just an urge to kiss her.

Whatever it was that was jolting her now, it was kind of exciting to think about. And when she considered what the enigmatic woman had said jokingly about her willingness to share a bed, she wondered if maybe Spencer felt a little spark or something.

On the other hand, maybe all of these strange feelings were just stress and concern for Spencer's safety. After all, the programmer had been practically at death's door just a week ago, and today's meeting with Elena had brought all of that danger to the forefront of her thoughts again.

Or maybe I'm analyzing everything to death and I should just go to sleep.

Spencer awoke to a dull throbbing in her left arm. In the night, Ruth had migrated across the center of the bed to rest her hand and cheek on the injured shoulder. The wound was over a week old and had been feeling better for the most part, but the pressure was definitely unpleasant.

Carefully, she pulled away, hoping not to wake her companion. Ruth would probably be mortified to find herself sleeping like this, she thought with a chuckle. But Spencer had to admit, it was kind of nice to get a cuddle, even if it was unintentional.

As soon as she extricated her arm, Ruth rolled over, pressing her backside against Spencer. That was impossible to resist, and with little thought at all, Spencer turned onto her side, wrapped her arm around the smaller body and fell right back to sleep.

Chapter 21

Just like the Sunday before, the occupants of the trailer were awakened by robust pounding on the front door.

"Pancakes and bacon in ten minutes!" Viv shouted.

Jessie rushed into the back bedroom to find her mother and Spencer untangling awkwardly. "Viv is making pancakes again!"

"So we heard," Ruth answered sleepily. "You better go pick out something to wear, don't you think?"

The child happily raced back to her room to get dressed as the grownups pulled themselves from the bed.

Ruth had awakened just before dawn to find Spencer wrapped completely around her, a long, bare leg draped between her own. She had felt no inclination at all to pull away. Lying with Spencer like that just seemed perfectly normal, like an extension of Spencer's protective nature. Now, she looked over at her bed companion, who was rubbing her face to wake up. "I never figured you for a cuddler."

"Sorry," Spencer answered sheepishly, embarrassed now about getting caught with her arm wrapped around her friend. "I guess I drifted a little in my sleep."

"I wasn't complaining. I just didn't know if you always did that . . . or only sometimes."

Spencer didn't often spend the whole night with someone, so that was kind of hard to answer. "I don't do it to just anybody. I'm sorry if it bothered you." Obviously, Ruth wasn't aware of her own migration to the center of the bed.

"It was all right. You're very easy to sleep with. You should put that on your résumé."

Spencer relaxed at the change in tone. *You have no idea how easy I can be.* "You think that's an important trait?"

"It is to some people."

Spencer stopped herself from asking if it was important to Ruth. "Gee, what shall I wear today?" She swung her bare legs out of bed and picked up her last clean T-shirt and yesterday's jeans.

Right on time, the threesome walked through the back door at Viv's, Jessie making a beeline to see the puppies. Willy was getting quite a belly and hadn't yet shown any interest in playing. Viv had said that Labs were like that for the first few weeks, but that they spent the rest of their lives making up for it.

"It's supposed to be pretty today, probably one of the last nice days before it turns cold for good." Viv had laid out a huge breakfast, and everyone was digging in. "I was thinking a picnic might be a good idea."

"A picnic!" Jessie exclaimed. She and her mommy had gone on picnics a lot when they only saw each other on the weekends.

"Yes, a picnic," Viv went on. "It's a little bit chilly, so I bet there won't be a big crowd out there."

Spencer shook her head. "I don't think I should go, but you guys ought to. It would be fun."

"Why can't you go?" Jessie demanded.

"Because I don't want people to see me," Spencer answered simply, not realizing the questions that response would raise.

"Why not?"

Ruth nervously kicked the brunette under the table. It wouldn't be good to get into a hiding discussion around Viv. Jessie would let the cat out of the bag for sure.

"Because I'm supposed to be at work. But I'm not because I'm . . ."

"Lazy!"

"That's right."

Viv left the kitchen and returned immediately, tossing a cap and sunglasses on the table beside her tall guest. "You know, I was thinking we could drive down I-66 in the Jeep to Front Royal and then take Skyline Drive south until we found a nice place to stop. There are a lot of pretty lakes out there with picnic tables and trails."

"I wanna go!" Jessie shouted. "Please!"

Even Ruth was a little anxious about being seen, but she knew she had to get past that. The whole reason for running away was so they could have a new life. What was the point of that if had to live it in hiding?

"Okay, I'll go too," Spencer announced, slipping on the glasses and hat.

That sealed it for Ruth. They were going on a picnic.

Spencer sat in the back seat of the Jeep Cherokee with Jessie, the two of them poking each other and laughing until Ruth threatened to have Viv pull over and put them both out. The drive to Front Royal was otherwise dull and uneventful, but things perked up when they reached the parkway. Even with the trees already bare, the lakes and woods were beautiful.

"I haven't been over here in ten or twelve years," Viv said.

"Tell us about the last time," Ruth prodded.

The landlady blew out a deep breath. "It was with Sheila. That's my daughter. We used to come out here when she and Robby were little. Robby's my son. He lives in Richmond now. Last I heard Sheila was in Kentucky or Ohio or someplace."

"You don't see her anymore?" For Ruth, estrangement from parents was familiar territory.

"I guess it's more like she doesn't see me. But the last time she was home, I brought her out here for a drive because we'd always had a good time here when they were little. I wanted to have a good time with her again for a change. We were always fighting about one thing or another." The landlady sniffed and blinked back tears.

"So where did you two leave things, Viv?" Spencer asked softly from the back seat.

"We got along up until the day she left, but both of us were holding back, trying not to go off on each other. Then that last day, all . . . heck broke loose, and she walked out telling me she wasn't coming back." Viv tried to gather herself. She was driving, after all. "And she hasn't."

"I'm so sorry." Ruth put her hand on the woman's shoulder.

"I'm not," she sighed. "Well, I'm not sorry she hasn't come back like that. I am sorry for a lot of the choices she made. But she's the one that's got to live with herself, not me."

The foursome rode along quietly for several miles, Jessie pointing out cows and horses as they came into view.

"What about Robby? Do you see a lot of your son?" Spencer was looking for a way to get the conversation back on something more upbeat.

"He comes up every two or three months. He works maintenance at the capitol. It's a good job for him. He didn't get blessed with a lot in the sense department, but he works hard and he's always checking in."

"Does he have a family?"

"He got married about three years ago to an older woman. She's good for him. But I don't think they're planning on having children."

"You never know," Ruth offered.

"No, I've given up on having any grandkids. You better watch out, though. I'll spoil that one back there if you let me." Viv nodded her head in the direction of the four-year-old in the back seat.

Ruth was so touched by the statement that her own eyes suddenly filled with tears. "That'll mean a lot to her, Viv. And to me, too."

"Somebody's already spoiled her," Spencer piped up. "She's so rotten she smells."

"I do not."

"Do too."

"You're lazy."

"So what have we got?" Chad had the entire team gathered in his living room on Sunday afternoon for an update. Elena had driven straight to his house after her meeting with Ruth on Saturday morning, knowing that her FBI surveillance team would assume she was going to discuss the break in the Roscone case. A call to Chad on her cell phone guaranteed that.

"So far, it's checking out. The program does just what Rollins says," their systems expert said. "And the parts that she said were inserted really stand out. It's pretty obvious they were written by someone else."

"Is there any way to know when this bogus program went into operation?"

"Not from this, but we can probably find it on the server at Margadon. It'll have a time stamp." This time, it was their network expert who spoke up.

"What if they've altered it?" Elena asked.

"We've got tools to determine that sort of thing," he explained. "Unless you really know what you're doing, it's pretty hard to get rid of something completely. But even if you can, you leave a big ugly mark that says something's been changed."

"Okay, so that part's coming together," Chad continued. "What have we got on the finances?"

This was Elena's domain. She had been handed three auditors yesterday afternoon, and they had all worked into the night and throughout the day today. "Well, as you already knew, we've got evidence of large amounts of cash moving through the hands of two FBI agents, Akers and Pollard. We have major purchases of high-end luxury items—cars, boats, houses—in the last fourteen months for Peter Crowell, the cytokines supplier, and for Adam Huffman, the production manager in Little Rock. James Thayer has been making weekly deposits of seven thousand dollars into a savings account."

One of her auditors chuckled. "I'm surprised he didn't just go with direct deposit."

Everyone laughed and turned their attention back to Elena. "But we've come up empty on Stacy Eagleton."

"Are you certain she's involved in this?" their boss asked.

"Spencer seems to think so. She clearly fabricated her statements for the newspaper to throw more suspicion on Spencer. Why would she do that if she weren't involved?"

"Maybe she just doesn't like Spencer," he countered, trying to be objective. "Or maybe she was just repeating gossip. You know how these stories sometimes take on a life of their own."

"That's possible, Chad," Elena conceded. "But she happens to be the manager for the Kryfex contract. I don't like that coincidence."

"Agreed. So we'll keep looking. What's our next move?"

"I want to bring Spencer in and put her in protective custody."

"Fine. Do it." Chad could see the wisdom of getting their star witness out of harm's way.

"And I think we ought to do the same for the informant and her child."

"Why do they need to be protected?"

"Because these guys have a habit of killing people who know things." Elena would wait until later—much later—to fill her boss in on the fact that Ruth Ferguson was wanted in Maine for kidnapping.

After driving an hour on the parkway, Viv pulled off at a stop called Elkwallow, where a short walk led them through the woods to a picnic table near a lake. No one was hungry after the huge breakfast, but the novelty of eating outside was too exciting for Jessie to put off, so they all had an early lunch.

"Can I go feed the ducks with Viv?" the child asked when she had finished her chips.

Ruth didn't answer, just cocked her head and raised her eyebrows in question.

"May I go feed the ducks with Viv?" Jessie clarified.

"Yes, you may. That was very good that you remembered."

She hadn't remembered, but Spencer had been mouthing the words behind her mother and that reminded her of what to say. The little girl crawled off the bench and grabbed her bread scraps. Viv had brought a whole extra loaf of bread.

"How about you? You want to see where that trail goes?" Spencer invited.

"Sure." Ruth walked over and told her landlady where they were going, asking if she would mind watching Megan. Viv just waved her away as if it were a given.

"I really like Viv a lot, don't you?" Spencer started.

"She's great. Just look at her with Jessie. She's so patient and sweet. It's hard to imagine her daughter turned out so badly."

"Well, somewhere along the way, Sheila made the wrong

choices."

That comment hit home for Ruth, and she began to shake her head. "I sure wish I could go back and choose over."

"Don't be so hard on yourself. Look at that." Spencer turned and looked back through the bare trees at the four-year-old gleefully feeding the ducks. "That was a good choice."

"Jessie's probably the only thing I did right."

"It's going to work out, Ruth," Spencer assured, draping her arm around the shorter woman's shoulder for a quick hug. Like Viv, she had hoped that today they could all set their problems aside and have fun. But some problems were too big to outrun, she guessed.

"So what about you? Did you ever do anything that made your parents pull their hair out?"

Spencer was delighted when Ruth answered the hug by wrapping her arm around her waist. Something was going on here. She wasn't sure what it was but it felt very nice.

"Probably the worst thing I ever did was to pick State over Duke or Carolina," Spencer answered with a chuckle.

"Why was that such a big deal?"

"My father taught statistics at Carolina, and my mother was on the faculty at Duke's med school. They went back and forth for years about where I'd go, and I blew both of them off."

"So is that really the worst thing you ever did?"

"Mmmm, probably. I was a good kid and we were pretty close. I liked my parents. We did a lot of things together."

"How'd they handle you being gay?"

"They were okay. College professors tend to be more liberal than most, I think. They both liked Elena a lot. Even after we split up, she'd still come home with me for long weekends at the lake and Mom would trash her for letting me get away. Elena was always threatening to pull her taxes."

"That sounds like so much fun. I can't even imagine playing around and joking with my family like that," Ruth said sadly.

"Then maybe it's time you got a new family."

When they reached a footbridge crossing a narrow stream, Spencer took Ruth's hand and led her onto a smaller trail that went away from the lake. Still unsure if she was imagining things, she loosened her fingers but didn't let go.

Instead of dropping her own hand, Ruth asserted herself, gripping tighter to keep the connection.

Silently, they walked deeper into the woods, both very aware that there was something brewing between them. After Spencer's disclosure that she was a lesbian, their interactions had moved to a more personal level with Ruth's teasing about building a résumé to attract a suitable partner, the easy hugs and touches they shared and especially their comfort at sleeping together so closely.

This kind of progression wasn't Spencer's usual path to intimacy. But then, it was rare that her sexual encounters led beyond just more of the same. Not since Elena had she met someone she wanted to care for, someone she wanted to really share herself with. Ruth was sparking feelings inside her that went past the physical attraction she was used to. Whether Ruth knew it or not, she was sending out some inviting signals. And Spencer had no idea how to deal with them.

They followed the stream to the trail's end, where a cluster of boulders formed a small waterfall.

"Want to sit awhile?" Without waiting for an answer, Spencer grabbed the smaller woman's waist and hoisted her onto a smooth rock where Ruth parted her knees to allow her to step between them. It was an intimate position, and when Spencer felt the other woman's arms snake through hers to hook behind her back, she knew Ruth understood where this would lead.

Now at eye-level and only inches apart, both women gave in to the attraction, and their faces began to slowly move together. Spencer brought her hands up and slipped her fingers through the soft hair at the base of Ruth's neck, drawing her forward. Their kiss was light and tender, a simple declaration that they both felt this.

❦

George Roscone gave the burgers one more turn and mashed them flat with the spatula, the dripping juice causing the fire underneath to flare. This would be his last cookout for a long time, maybe even the last one ever with this family he loved.

Last night, George had lain awake long after making love with his wife of thirteen years, despising himself for his greedy pursuits. No one in his family suspected his duplicity, but one way or another, they would probably all pay for his mistakes.

Nearby, George, Jr. and his twin sisters were playing together on the jungle gym. Would they ever get past their father's crimes? The family would probably lose the house and have to go to Indiana to live with his wife's parents. George was probably headed for a federal prison.

Elena Diaz was closing her net. Somehow, she had found out about the other accounts, though he didn't have a clue who it was that had called to tip him off about it. It would be far better if he turned himself in now and begged for a plea bargain, even if it meant risking the wrath of the drug cartel. Surely, the government would help him if he offered evidence against the bigger fish.

Tomorrow morning, he would walk into Diaz's office and give himself up. But today, he was a family man.

After their tentative kiss, Spencer reined in her impulses, afraid that her surging desire would lead her to demand too much, too soon. Ruth needed time to realize what was happening and to decide if she really meant to go there.

They didn't talk for several long minutes, but they held one another close. Ruth's head rested on Spencer's shoulder and her hands gently stroked the taller woman's back.

"So this is how you operate, huh? First you cuddle, then you kiss."

"Sometimes it's the other way around." Emboldened, Spencer added, "But it's especially nice when they go together."

"I think you ought to play that kissing thing up on your résumé."

"Even more than being easy to sleep with?"

"It's a tough call. Both are important skills to have."

Spencer chuckled, grateful for the levity that had eased the awkwardness of the moment. She leaned back to take in Ruth's playful expression and was definitely encouraged by what she was reading in the warm green eyes. When had things changed between them? *When did I start to feel this way?*

"I guess we should be getting back."

Ruth's statement brought Spencer back from her musings. They had been gone from the picnic site for almost a half hour. She helped Ruth down from the boulder and took her hand again. "It's been nice to get away today. I don't think I realized how much I needed some time to rest my head . . . and to let it go somewhere nice for a change." She squeezed the smaller hand.

"I think we all needed it." Ruth dropped her hand and wrapped her arm around Spencer's waist as they emerged onto the wider, main trail. "Do you really think there's a chance that Elena can do something for Jessie and me?"

"I honestly don't know. But if she can, she will." As they drew closer to the picnic site, the women could see the landlady on the shore of the lake, breaking off bread crumbs so the delighted child could feed a family of ducks. "I think you should say something to Viv."

"What do you mean?"

"I think you ought to tell her who you are and what you're running from."

Ruth shook her head. "I don't want to put her in the middle of this. Besides, the more people who know, the more we're at risk."

"I understand that, but just thinking about things right now. What if—God forbid—something happened to you? Would you want Viv to just step forward and say 'Here's her little girl. Her family lives in Maine.' Or would you want her to protect Jessie from going back to her father?"

"What if she doesn't want that kind of responsibility?"

"Look at her. I think you'll see the answer to that."

Spencer was right about the bond that was growing between her landlady and her daughter. "You really think I should?"

"Yeah. And it would probably take some of the pressure off Jessie about keeping things so secret."

When they got back to the picnic site, Spencer invited Jessie to walk with her to see a pool of guppies in the creek. That gave Ruth the opportunity to talk with Viv.

"I need to talk to you, Viv . . . about Megan and me."

The older woman's face grew serious.

"We're hiding. I took her from her father in Maine and ran away. He was hurting her, and she hated being with him." Ruth braced herself for the woman's judgment. "If you need for us to leave the trailer, we will."

Viv ignored her offer. "Are you both all right now?"

"Yes, but we can't ever go back."

"Why would you ever want to?"

"I-I don't. To tell you the truth, I hope she forgets all about it when she's older." Shamefully, Ruth went on to apologize for not saying something sooner.

"I can't say as I blame you. You must be scared half to death about them finding you."

"Sometimes I am. That's one of the reasons I wanted to tell you who we really were. If anything should ever happen to me, I don't want Jessie—" Ruth let her daughter's name slip. "That's her real name but I need to stop calling her that. I don't want Megan to end up back with her father."

209

"She won't if I have anything to say about it."

"I sort of hoped you'd feel that way," Ruth said gratefully. "I really hate putting you in the middle of all of this, especially on top of everything that's going on with Spencer."

"I don't care if I'm in the middle of it. You'll want Megan to go live with Spencer, though, right?"

The landlady's conclusion shocked her. The two of them looked over at the edge of the woods, where Spencer and Jessie were laughing and playing tag.

"I guess we have to work all of that out."

In all the excitement of the day, Jessie missed her nap and barely made it through her bath without falling asleep. Once she was down for the night, Ruth closed the bedroom door and returned to the living room, her breath catching at the sight of Spencer staring at her from across the room.

She was sitting in the straight back chair, her long legs stretched out in front and her arms folded across her chest. It was a commanding posture. "Can we talk about this afternoon?" Spencer asked.

The electricity between them had filled the air when they walked back into the trailer. Every look, every gesture, every casual touch only served to heighten its charge. And now, they were alone again.

Ruth sat down on the arm of the recliner, her sheepish look giving away her lack of confidence. "Okay."

"Are you all right about it?"

"Sure," she answered in a small voice. Ruth was unable to move her eyes from the tacky symmetrical pattern on the vinyl floor.

Spencer chuckled softly and leaned forward, dropping her forearms to her knees. "Look at me, please."

The green eyes slowly rose and met hers.

"If it makes you too uncomfortable to even look me in the eye, I suppose asking where you want to go next with this is kind of pointless."

Ruth grimaced, not at Spencer's words, but at her own confusion. Her head was saying one thing, but her heart seemed to be saying something else altogether. And after the kiss in the woods today, her body was chiming in as well. She found herself inexplicably drawn toward this woman, driven to care for her and compelled to have her physically close. "I don't know. But this afternoon was nice," she admitted.

"I thought so too. But I don't want to lead you somewhere you don't really want to go. We're both under a lot of stress right now and maybe we aren't using our heads like we should."

Ruth nodded in agreement, still barely able to meet Spencer's gaze. "Where do you want it to go?"

The silence was almost deafening as Spencer considered her response. "I haven't known a lot of women like you," she answered softly. "You're brave and you have a good heart. And I think you're beautiful. For somebody like me—a lesbian, in other words—it's just natural for feelings like that about another woman to grow into something more than friendship . . . but I understand if that's not for you."

Ruth laughed quietly. "I haven't even gotten around to worrying about whether that part's for me or not."

"So what part are you worrying about?"

Ruth sighed. "I feel like . . . I don't know. I feel guilty for even thinking about something for myself when I have Jessie to look out for. She's my priority."

"But she's safe now."

"I know. I just . . ."

"Look, Ruth. You don't need to give me a reason. I didn't mean to put you on the spot. I just wanted you to know how I felt. And you're right—the important thing is for you and Jessie to feel safe."

"But it's not just that," Ruth blurted. She wasn't used to having somebody ask her how she felt and actually listen to her answer. "I'm worried about feeling this way after such a short amount of time. I've only known you a week and I already feel closer to you than I ever did to my husband."

Spencer rejoiced inside at Ruth's admission. "Isn't that good?"

"Well, yeah." Seeing Spencer's smile brought one to her own face.

"We don't have to rush into anything, Ruth . . . especially something you aren't sure about. Like you said, we have a lot of other things to take care of right now. This will work itself out if we let it."

"I feel so stupid."

"You're not stupid at all. Everything you said makes perfect sense. We can take our time and see what happens. I'm not going to just disappear when this is over. You and Jessie are way too important to me for that."

Ruth smiled at that. It was nice to really feel like someone enjoyed you and wanted to be there with you. And it made her heart soar that Spencer was so kind and caring when it came to her daughter. Jessie needed that in her life.

Spencer stood and stretched, one hand holding her still-bruised ribs. "Tomorrow's a big day. Maybe we should turn in."

"Do you realize that this might all be over for you tomorrow?" Ruth reached for the light switch beside the sofa, but Spencer stopped her.

"I think I should stay out here . . . on the couch."

Ruth sighed, her face sporting an incredulous look. "That's silly. You don't have to do that. We can handle—"

"I think I should. Now that I know what it's like to kiss you, I don't think I'll be able to sleep with you beside me like I did last night." Spencer leaned forward and placed a soft kiss on Ruth's cheek. "Goodnight, Ruth."

Chapter 22

I'm falling in love with her.

Spencer knew it as sure as she knew her own name. She lay on the couch watching daylight come, asking herself over and over why she hadn't just gone back to the bedroom when Ruth had asked her to. Chances were, they would have given in to what they had been feeling all day yesterday and made love.

But that would have been a mistake. Spencer wanted more from Ruth than just a sexual experience, and until they both were sure that their feelings weren't just a reaction to the stress they were under, it was better to take it slow. Ruth wasn't ready, and the more Spencer thought about it, neither was she. If there was one lesson she had learned from falling in love with Elena, it was that offering her heart to someone who wasn't ready to accept it hurt like hell.

Before Spencer knew what was happening, the four-year-old

was beside her, a pillow in one hand, Lisa in the other.

"Hey, Jessie." She lifted the blanket and the child climbed underneath and settled in. A few minutes later, the television was on, and both had drifted back to sleep.

That's how Ruth found them an hour later. She was captivated by how easily Jessie had taken to Spencer. Her daughter was usually very slow to warm up to strangers, but there were a few exceptions, such as Viv and now Spencer. Ruth hoped there would be enough memories like this for her little girl that she would soon put the others out of her mind.

She studied the lines and curves of the sleeping woman's face, pleased to see a peaceful look. Spencer had worn a lot of strain over the last nine days—had it only been nine days? *Why do I feel like I know you so well?*

Spencer stirred and found herself under Ruth's watchful gaze. "Is she asleep?" she mouthed silently, a finger pointing to Jessie.

Ruth nodded and made a gesture as though she were taking a picture of the scene. Then she patted her heart, which Spencer took to mean that she and Jessie looked absolutely adorable. She winked at the child's mother and they both smiled. Something passed between them that said things were good.

When breakfast was ready, Ruth nudged her daughter awake and they disappeared into her bedroom to get dressed for the day. Spencer headed into the bathroom to wash up, emerging in yesterday's T-shirt.

"I guess I'll do laundry this morning," she announced, dragging the armchair to the kitchen counter. "I'm officially out of clothes."

"That shirt does look a tad familiar." Ruth leaned over and sniffed, scrunching her nose.

"Your mom thinks she's funny, Jessie."

The little girl had returned her attention to cartoons and paid the grownups no mind.

Ruth trailed her fingers against Spencer's hand, just to make a connection. "I guess I should go call Elena when we get finished. You think she's had enough time to look into all that stuff we gave her?"

"Knowing her, she's been on it since Saturday."

"So what's the plan?"

"Just call her and see what she says. Oh, and I wouldn't use the same phone you used last time. Remember, you said you were headed home, so your bank should be somewhere else."

This time, Spencer wrote the directions for a shopping center in Fairfax where Ruth would again find a pay phone and place her call directly to Elena's office.

Before Ruth left, she led the other woman down the hall to the bedroom and closed the door. Wrapping her arms around Spencer's waist, she laid her head on the taller woman's shoulder. "Today could be your last day here, you know. You might actually get your life back. I bet you can't wait."

Spencer squeezed her tightly. "You aren't getting rid of me that easy. I'm going to hold you to what we talked about last night. I want to see where this goes."

"Me too." Ruth leaned back, her eyes darting back and forth between Spencer's eyes and mouth as their faces grew closer. "Kiss me again," she whispered. When they came together, her lips parted. She could feel Spencer's tongue raking her teeth in sweet demand and she sucked it gently into her mouth.

When their kiss ended, they looked at one another with bold resolve, neither doubting where their emotions were headed.

"Be careful," Spencer said.

"I will. See you back here soon."

Thomas Fennimore reshuffled the papers on his desk, pushing his glasses up for the hundredth time today. Anyone walking by his cubicle would be appalled at the apparent chaos, but Thomas knew exactly where everything was and what it meant to his case.

His case.

Elena had given him his own case, a story and a loose set of clues beneath which he *might* uncover wrongdoing. Eager to prove himself, he had worked until midnight on Saturday and all day yesterday, pulling records and cross-checking, and laying all the pieces end to end.

Thomas understood greed, but his favorite flaw was stupidity. Unless he was mistaken, Drummond Appliances was guilty of both. As neatly as he could in his excited state, he filled out the request form for travel expenses and two local auditors in Madison, Maine.

Silently, he laid the forms before his boss, grinning broadly as she signed her approval. He was about to speak when her phone rang.

A pay phone in Fairfax, Virginia.

"Internal Revenue Service, Special Agent Elena Diaz. How may I help you?"

"Agent Diaz?"

It was the woman who had come to see her about Spencer, Ruth Ferguson.

"Yes, this is Agent Diaz," she said calmly, waving at her assistant to alert him to the call.

"This is the woman who talked with you the other day about George Roscone."

"Yes, thank you very much for calling back. I had a chance to look over the papers that you gave me, and that's exactly the sort of evidence we're looking for. I've gotten approval for a reward, but we need to move quickly. Can you come to my office?"

Chad had approved her plan to pick up this informant and drive immediately to where Spencer was hiding. From there, they would be ushered to a safe house to await the execution of the warrants.

"Can I still be anonymous?"

"You can remain anonymous," the agent assured. Obviously, that meant her informant didn't quite trust where she stood. Her apprehension was understandable, considering she was wanted for felony kidnapping.

"I'd rather not come to your office. Should I meet you in the same place?"

No, that wouldn't work. They needed to be further away from the surveillance van and close to a place where Ruth could be whisked away by a waiting car. They couldn't risk being tailed. "What if we met at the Lincoln Memorial, by the vendors on Independence Avenue?"

"Okay, I can do that. What time?"

"Can you come now?" Elena was getting anxious.

"Does it have to be right now?"

"Once the decision is made to move ahead on something like this, we try to get things done as quickly as possible. We just don't want to leave any opportunities for things to go wrong at the last minute," Elena explained, her patience running thin. She understood the apprehension, but Spencer's life was at risk, and so was this informant's. "I really need for you to trust me on this."

"Okay, by the Lincoln Memorial. I'll come now."

Returning the phone to its cradle, Elena sat back and sighed. This danger for Spencer was coming to an end. The events of the past few days had been a wake-up call, one that made her acknowledge how she truly felt about the beautiful friend who had once offered her heart.

This case was going to rock the District hard, and Spencer wouldn't enjoy the attention at all. When it was all over, they should get away for a while. Maybe they could go to one of the islands for a couple of weeks. They could sun and swim, and who knows, maybe reconnect.

"Elena?" the intercom crackled.

"Yes?"

"There's someone here to see you. He says he wants to turn himself in."

The baffled agent stood and poked her head into the hallway, craning her neck to see the reception area. There stood George Roscone.

Pollard stepped back into the van after his walk across the Mall. He didn't feel comfortable talking to Akers with the technician present, so his habit was to go outside and walk around when he had something important to discuss.

Akers was pissed this morning because of the new asshole he had received, courtesy of Stacy Eagleton. They had two more days to find Rollins or she was pulling the plug on everything.

"Did I miss anything?"

"Not much." The technician took off his headphones and got up for a soda from the cooler. "That woman called back about Roscone. She's going to meet Diaz at the Lincoln Memorial. Diaz got the reward approved for her."

"Wonder why she's meeting her there?" At least if Diaz was out of the building, they could take a break from the phones.

"The informant still wants to stay anonymous. She wouldn't come to the office."

"Hmm." That was odd . . . not that they were meeting somewhere, but why the Lincoln Memorial and not the bench where they met the other day? "Rewind that tape, let me listen."

The technician did as he was asked while Pollard settled in with the headphones. The agent played it three times and didn't like something about what he was hearing. The informant hadn't even asked how much the reward was.

"Hey, Jack. Is today a bank holiday?"

"If it was a bank holiday, you'd be here by yourself," the technician chuckled.

Then why wasn't this informant at work?

218

Pollard needed to take another walk and talk with his partner about this Roscone informant. He had a sinking feeling that this woman wasn't who she said she was and that Spencer Rollins was trying to get under their radar.

The urgency in the IRS agent's request to come immediately was unmistakable, but it was the last thing Ruth had expected—or wanted. There was something about moving ahead so fast that was unsettling, but she wrote it off as nervousness about being on the run. She needed to trust Elena, especially now that the agent held her fate in her hands.

There wasn't time to go back to the trailer and tell Spencer what was happening. She would worry, but maybe Elena could find a way to get in touch with Viv and let her know things were all right. Or maybe they were ready to bring Spencer in. That would get her out of danger and they could go after the real killers. Whatever they had planned, the agent was expecting her, and if she didn't show up she might miss a window for ending this peril.

From Fairfax, Ruth drove to the Franconia-Springfield station, the same place she had parked the other day. Before buying her ticket, she studied the layout of the Metro system, looking for the closest stop to the Lincoln Memorial. The Arlington Cemetery stop was just across the bridge and the closest from her end of the Blue Line. With a five dollar fare card in hand, she boarded the train and settled in for the ride.

It would be over soon, she repeated in her head as she jostled back and forth in the orange vinyl seat. At least it would be over for Spencer. The more she thought about her own situation, the more she doubted there was anything anyone could do. Even if Elena let her walk, she and Jessie would definitely need to find a new home, she concluded dismally. The respite of the last week would be over, along with that glimmer of hope she had for a new start here with friends like Spencer and Viv. She and her daughter would have to try again in a new place.

When the Arlington Cemetery stop was announced, Ruth stood up and exited onto the platform. A tall escalator took her to street level, where a chilly breeze prompted her to pull up the collar on her jacket. She could see the back of Lincoln Memorial at the other end of the Memorial Bridge.

As she started across the Potomac, she had second thoughts about her choice of an approach. This was a very long bridge. She hated being out in the open, and once on the bridge, she had nowhere to run if there was trouble. Ruth chided herself for her paranoia and forged ahead.

Elena is waiting at the other end and it will all be over soon.

As she neared the end of the bridge, a black sedan pulled silently alongside her. A suited man in a trench coat emerged, flashing his badge as he blocked her path on the bridge.

"Michael Pollard, FBI. Get in the car, please."

Ruth's heart began to pound as the blood left her face. They were FBI!

"In the car, now!" he ordered sharply.

Shaking and dazed, she hesitated until he grabbed her arm forcefully and shoved her to the curb. There he opened the back door and guided her inside. Sliding in beside her, the agent shut the door and the car picked up speed as it crossed the bridge and turned the corner onto Independence Avenue.

Elena continued to pace the area around the Lincoln Memorial, scanning the crowds of tourists for the blond woman who had called her almost two hours ago. For whatever reason, Ruth Ferguson had changed her mind about keeping their appointment.

Either that or the FBI agents were on to her ruse and had picked her up en route. If that was the case, both Ruth and Spencer were in grave danger.

Chapter 23

Ruth caught a glimpse of the lettering over the main glass doors as the car slowed: *Federal Bureau of Investigation*. The sedan turned and started down a ramp to the underground garage. The short ride had been quiet, so quiet in fact that she still didn't know if this was about Spencer Rollins, Ruth Ferguson or Karen Oliver.

"I don't have the evidence with me," she offered.

Neither man responded as the driver pulled into a marked space near the elevator. When they stopped, he got out and opened her door, uttering his first words.

"Step out of the car and place your hands behind your back."

Continuing to shake, she stood and slowly turned around. Too slowly, it seemed, as the driver pushed her shoulder hard to bring her hands together for the cuffs. Next he patted her down, removing her car keys and the small wad of bills she had stuffed into her back pocket. Roughly, he seized her elbow and thrust her toward the elevator.

When they reached the fifth floor, the agents escorted her more casually down a hallway of offices to a small interior room—an interrogation room from the looks of it. Six chairs sat at a rectangular table underneath an array of fluorescent lighting. The agent who identified himself as Pollard pulled out a chair and indicated that she should sit. He looked vaguely familiar—he might have been the one she had seen that day when Spencer's motorcycle was recovered, but she hadn't gotten a good look.

Ruth took the chair and leaned back uncomfortably on her arms, her hands still bound by the metal cuffs.

"Are these really necessary?" she asked.

Again, they ignored her, stepping back into the hallway and closing the door.

Fine! Her mind had been spinning all the way over about how she was going to play her part. These assholes had just helped her decide. She wasn't going to tell them jack shit about anything. Thankfully, she had thought to leave her billfold in the glove compartment of the Taurus. If this wasn't about Karen Oliver, they would never find Jessie. For that matter, they wouldn't find Spencer either.

The driver, the surly one with the crew cut, came back in and took a seat opposite her across the table. "Why don't we start with your name?"

"I have nothing to say to you."

"Look, lady! We're the fucking FBI. You're in a shitload of trouble and the only way you're going to get out of it is to answer my fucking questions. Do you hear what I'm saying?"

This time, Ruth didn't reply at all.

"So let me ask again. What is your name?"

"Hearing problem?" she mumbled.

Akers's jaw flinched in anger. He needed this woman to tip

her hand, and that wouldn't happen if she didn't talk at all. "Very well, then I'll start. I'm Special Agent Calvin Akers of the FBI. Special Agent Pollard and I are conducting an investigation in conjunction with Elena Diaz, an agent with the Internal Revenue Service. You spoke with her from a pay phone in Reston on Friday afternoon, claiming to have information on one George Roscone. On Saturday morning, you met with Agent Diaz on the Mall and passed her a folder, purportedly containing evidence regarding Mr. Roscone's accounts. You called Agent Diaz again this morning from a pay phone in Fairfax and you were on your way to a second meeting at the Lincoln Memorial when we intercepted you. That is what we already know. What we are missing is who you are and why we should believe that you have knowledge of a bank account belonging to Mr. Roscone."

"I was promised a reward," Ruth answered, sticking with her original story. As soon as they mentioned the calls—which they had obviously listened to—she realized that this was almost certainly about Spencer. If they really were working with Elena as they had implied, they would have known what was in the folder.

"And there is a reward. Your reward is that you will be allowed to leave once you have given us the information we seek."

Ruth fell silent again. The clock on the wall said eleven forty-five. Spencer would be expecting her. If she didn't show in a couple more hours, the programmer would get worried and take action. Maybe then, Elena and her team could find her and end this before the FBI learned her true identity.

"Of course, if it's money that interests you, I do happen to have a case I'm working on that involves a twenty-five thousand dollar reward." He pulled from his pocket a photo of Spencer Rollins and pushed it across the table, looking carefully for her reaction. "Do you know this woman?"

Ruth looked at the photo as if seeing Spencer for the first

time and shook her head. "No."

"Have you seen this picture before?"

"No."

"Do you ever watch the news or read the newspapers?"

"No."

"Surely, you've seen the news at least once or twice in the last week, haven't you?"

"Not that I remember." Ruth needed to stop answering his questions. He seemed to be having too much fun, as though she were playing into his hand somehow.

"Have you heard about a recent murder at Margadon, the pharmaceutical company in Rockville? The victim was an albino." That was the sort of information that people would have remembered. "His picture was in the paper too. Did you happen to see that? He looked just like somebody had powdered his face, you know what I mean?"

This man was despicable, Ruth thought. "No," she repeated furiously.

That had gotten a nice rise, he thought. One would almost think she had known Henry Estes personally to evoke that sort of angry response.

"'Course, he wasn't white like that when we found him. He was sort of purple, what with that little hitch knot around his neck." He watched with satisfaction as the woman's face reddened.

"Did you happen to know Henry Estes?" he asked. "I mean, you look a little like you're getting pretty upset at hearing about all this."

"I'm not used to hearing people talk so callously about the dead," she answered coldly.

Akers chuckled. "I guess we do get a little desensitized to these sorts of things after a while. But then, there's the other end of that spectrum, where we learn to be very sensitive to things. Over the years, I've developed quite a sense of smell, especially for rats. And that's what I'm smelling here. See, I'm not buying this story about Roscone. I think you're perpetrating a hoax on the good people of the IRS, and I'm prepared to hold you here until I learn otherwise. Am I clear on that?"

"Now that you're finally accusing me of something, I suppose this would be a good time for me to ask for an attorney." Ruth knew there was no way in hell that her wish would be granted, but she needed a little more leverage against this son of a bitch.

"I'll be happy to summon an attorney for you. Who shall I say is calling?"

She stared back at him, a look of rage on her face.

"You're getting nothing until I get a name."

"Then you can consider these my last words to you," she sneered, "Calvin."

Spencer looked at the clock again, miserable to see that only three minutes had passed. Ruth was late—very late. The shopping center at Fairfax was only thirty minutes away, forty-five in heavy traffic, but it wasn't rush hour. She had been gone over three and a half hours.

Even if Elena had called her into the city, she would have known that they were worried and would have found a way to call Viv or something. If for some reason Ruth wasn't in Elena's hands, she was probably in unspeakable danger.

"Jessie?" Spencer tiptoed into the bedroom to wake the napping child. "Sweetie, we need to go over to Viv's. I have to go out for a little while. Can you finish your nap there?" As she talked, she gathered the sleepy child in her arms, picking up the Lisa doll and the soft pink blanket the little girl used for her naps.

Stumbling onto the porch, the pair was met by Viv, who held the door and directed them to the guest room. Jessie settled down quickly and went right back to sleep.

"Viv, I need to borrow your car. Ruth should have been back by now. I have to go see about her. I may have to make a call to my friend."

"Won't they be listening? Maybe I should go."

"No, it doesn't matter. If those bastards have picked up Ruth, I don't care what happens to me. I need to have my friend get her out before they find out about Jessie."

"Be careful," the older woman advised, handing over her keys. "And don't do anything foolish."

In twenty minutes, Spencer was sitting at the shopping center. There was no trace of Ruth's car, which at least meant that she hadn't been picked up while she was on the phone. But if she wasn't here, where had she gone? Ruth didn't know D.C. well enough to find her way around. She knew the Wal-Mart, she knew the shopping center in Reston where she had called from last Friday, and she knew the Franconia-Springfield stop on the Metro. If she had gone to the city to meet Elena, her car would probably be in the garage at the end of the Metro line.

The programmer spun the vehicle back onto I-66, hopping onto the Beltway and heading south for the Franconia exit. As she approached the parking garage, she was reminded of Viv's admonition not to do anything foolish. Driving into a place where it was possible the agents were waiting certainly fell into that category. If they had figured out who Ruth was, they would use her as bait. Spencer needed to be smarter than that, for both their sakes.

Turning off Franconia Road, she stopped in a small strip mall, where a pay phone was mounted under the awning near an ATM machine. This needed to be fast—she had to get the hell out of there in a hurry. Thankfully, the assholes looking for her wouldn't recognize the Jeep.

Nervously she dialed Elena's cell phone and waited.

"Are you sure she didn't just get cold feet?"

"I thought about that, Chad. But when I got back here, I found out that Pollard wasn't in the van," Elena explained.

Her boss raised his eyebrows in question.

"I walked over there and knocked on the goddamned door!"

"And you're assuming the reason he's not there is because he went to intercept our informant?"

"Pollard is always in the van. Except when he's sitting in his car watching my house. If he's not there, it's because he's doing something more important. And he just happens to do it when our informant goes missing? You know how I hate coincidences."

"I wish I had a little more." They had agreed when they got their case together, they would involve the senior FBI field agent who supervised Akers and Pollard, Chad's equivalent for the Bureau. Chad was sure his counterpart would help if their evidence was solid, but the first instinct of any agency would be to circle the wagons.

"If we could—"

The cell phone in her pocket interrupted her thought.

"It's a pay phone in Franconia," she said. "This is Special Agent—"

"Where is she?"

Spencer! "I don't know. She was supposed to meet me and she never showed." Elena was pacing the room, waving her arms excitedly to let them know who was on the phone.

"They've got her, Elena. You have to get her out of there."

"I'm working on it. You need to come in. You'll be safe here."

"I can't!" She had to protect Jessie and Viv. They knew enough to get killed for their part in this. "Not yet. I'll call you when I'm ready."

Abruptly, she hung up the phone and raced for the Jeep. She needed to get the hell out of there before the police arrived. She had no way of knowing that the technician who had monitored her call was left without specific instructions as to what to do if she contacted Diaz. That sort of decision usually fell to Agent Pollard, who had gone out to attend to some business. The technician's duty was to log the exchange and copy the tape. But just to be on the safe side, he decided to call Pollard on his cell phone.

Ruth had been left alone in the room for almost two hours when the two agents finally reappeared.

"We have good news for you . . . Miss Ferguson." Akers delighted in the look of shock on the blond woman's face. "That's right. It seems one of the interns in the hallway recognized you from your picture on our recent update and he thought to offer his congratulations for making your arrest."

Ruth glared at the two of them defiantly. There were no conditions under which she would reveal where her daughter was. Even if they sent her back to Maine and locked her up forever, Jessie was going to be free.

"So maybe we should take a step back and re-evaluate your situation. You've got a little girl you'd like to keep. You've also got some information I'd like to have. Sound like an even trade to you?"

"I'm not telling you where my daughter is. I don't care what you do with me."

"Let's forget about your daughter for a moment. Hell, just for the sake of argument, let's assume that I don't give a rat's ass about where your daughter is. What I want to know is what you know about Spencer Rollins."

"Nothing! I don't know anything. It was just a scam for the reward. I needed money."

"How did you know about Roscone?" He still didn't believe her, but here was her chance to convince him. Now that he knew what she was running from, he was starting to think she wasn't what they were looking for after all. This wild goose chase was wasting time they could be using to find Rollins.

"I used to work at a bank in Maine. We were all talking one day about how the police sometimes got subpoenas to look at people's accounts." Ruth was flying by the seat of her pants.

228

"One of the other tellers had a friend who lived around here and she said her friend was told to watch somebody's account. She said he was a DA or something . . . so I got to thinking about it when I decided I was going to run away."

The agents looked at her skeptically, but appeared to be listening.

"I read some old newspaper stuff about it on the Internet, like the IRS was pissed that he told the papers they were doing something with those drug guys. One of the articles said it was Diaz's case." Ruth didn't want to wander far from the facts if she could help it. "I thought I might be able to get some money from it if I strung her along. That's why I wouldn't tell her anything."

For what felt like an hour, the agents traded questioning looks until Akers finally slapped his knees and stood.

"Take her upstairs and lock her up. And call the boys in Maine to come take out their trash."

Despite his satisfaction at capturing a kidnapper, Akers was once again frustrated at the dead end on Spencer Rollins. She had been out of sight for more than a week, and it was starting to look like she might just disappear altogether. Apparently, they had overestimated her ties to Diaz, and with every day that passed, their money-making scheme at Margadon was more at risk.

It was Monday again. Akers had wired $2,000 to Petrov's account this morning as partial payment on his marker. Pollard didn't have any more cash to spare. With his credit cards maxed out and his 1986 Chrysler worth no more than a few hundred bucks, Akers had come up $3,000 short. He hoped that Petrov would appreciate his partial payment as a gesture of intent to make good on his debt. Perhaps the casino operator would see that it was profitable to lend money to someone like him, someone who might miss a payment here and there, but who always came up with the cash and the penalty. Not a bad return on your investment, he thought.

Chapter 24

Thomas Fennimore stepped off the Ratheon Beech turbo-prop onto the tarmac at Augusta Airport, his bulging briefcase in one hand, a garment bag in the other. He didn't expect to be here very long and didn't care if he didn't sleep tonight. This was going to be great fun.

The connecting flight from Boston had been delayed a bit, but not enough to crimp his plans. The auditors would meet him at five o'clock at the appliance store—a half hour before closing—where he would present a federal warrant to review the books. If they found what they were looking for, they would need one more warrant, and Elena was on standby tonight in D.C. to secure it.

Following the line of passengers into the small terminal, Thomas unknowingly passed his quarry. Roland Drummond, Sr. and his son Skip were ticketed for the next flight to Washington

National, where they would be met by the FBI and taken to confront Ruth Ferguson in jail. Then they would bring their little girl back home where she belonged.

Spencer stormed through the back door of the house, this time without bothering to knock.

"Viv?"

The landlady rushed to the kitchen for the news. The four-year-old was watching television in the den, already anxious about her mother being gone so long.

"They've got her. I think the feds picked her up about three hours ago."

"The ones she called?"

"No, the ones who are after me. We've got to get out of here right now!"

"But Karen won't tell them where we are."

"It doesn't matter. The address is on her driver's license."

The older woman grasped the gravity of the situation. Karen wasn't coming back, and it was time to honor the promise she had made only yesterday. "We have to hide Megan."

"We have to hurry, Viv. Is there someplace you and Jessie can go till this blows over?"

"We can go to Jerry's. He's from the church."

"Are you sure we can trust Jerry?"

"Of course. We've known each other for years. And he has a barn where we can hide the car."

"Great! How soon can you be ready?"

"Ten minutes," she answered, pitching the contents of her laundry basket onto the table on the back porch.

"I'll put Jessie's things in the car. Hurry!"

Spencer tore through the trailer, picking up all of the clues that she had been here—her clothes, the extra toothbrush, and all her notes and printouts. To that, she added a few things that

Jessie might need over the next couple of days. When she had loaded things into the Jeep, she ran back onto the back porch, nearly falling over a laundry basket full of puppies and a bewildered Maggie and Thor.

"Come on, you two. Let's go for a ride." She picked up the basket and slid it into the Jeep's cargo area. The older dogs followed, immediately nosing the puppies to make sure all of them were there.

Viv and Jessie appeared at the back door, the latter holding her pink blanket. Spencer helped the little one into the back seat and clipped her seat belt. Viv stowed the dog food and a few of her own things.

"Where's Mommy?"

"She's in the city, meeting some people."

"When is she going to come home?"

"I'm not sure, honey."

"Where are we going?"

"We're going to stay with a friend of Viv's for a little while."

"Why?"

"Because," she hesitated, "some people are coming over and we don't want to see them."

"Are we hiding?" This she understood.

"Yes, Jessie. We have to hide, but it's going to be okay," Spencer assured.

"How will Mommy know where to find us?"

"I'm going to tell her where we are."

"Are you going to see her?"

"No, but I'm going to tell my friend to go see her. And my friend will bring her to us." Spencer hoped like hell that she was telling the truth.

"I want to go see her too." The four-year-old could tell that Spencer and Viv were worried, and that made her worried too. "I want to be with her."

"You can't right now, sweetie. You have to stay with us," Viv soothed, sensing how confused the child must be.

"No!" she shouted, and started to cry.

"Jessie? Listen to me, okay?" Spencer said softly. "Your mommy will come as soon as she can. She wants you to stay with us, not to come where she is." The driver strained to make eye contact in the rear view mirror. "Please, honey? It'll be okay."

"Will you stay with me?"

"I'll stay until we get everything settled at . . ." she looked quickly to the landlady.

"Jerry's."

" . . . until we get settled at Jerry's. Then I need to go tell my friend where we are so your mommy can find us. While I'm gone, will you help Viv look after the puppies?"

The child's blubbering stopped as she stretched to look behind her at the dogs. "Okay," she finally answered.

"Thank you. I really appreciate you being such a big girl, Jessie."

"Well, look at it this way," Pollard said chuckling. "Diaz still looks like a fool."

"At least that's something," Akers agreed.

The two agents had stopped for a leisurely lunch after the excitement of their morning. Director Wilkinson would be pleased that they had nailed a fugitive, even if it wasn't the one they were looking for. A collar like that would keep the pressure off them on the Rollins case. The Bureau hated to spend resources and get nothing in return.

"Why don't you drop me back at the van so I can check in with the techies?" Pollard asked. "I'll walk over later to pick up my car."

Akers pulled over to the curb on Constitution Avenue. "I'm going to head back to the office and get this Ferguson woman processed. Call me if anything comes up—anything."

Pollard slammed the door and strode to the van.

"Anything happening here?" he asked casually.

"Didn't you get my call?"

"What call?"

"I left you a voice message about two hours ago. Rollins called in and wanted to know where the woman was. Diaz told her she never showed—"

Fuck! Pollard stormed back out of the van to see Akers disappear into the distance. The Ferguson bitch was working with Rollins all along, and they had just turned her over on a kidnapping warrant. Angrily, he pulled the phone from his pocket, the window indeed announcing a voice message. He placed the call to Akers, dreading the tirade he knew would come.

"Akers."

"Cal! The Ferguson woman—she's working with Rollins."

"What the hell? How do you know?"

"Rollins called Diaz about two hours ago to find out where she was."

"Why didn't that stupid fuck call and let us know?"

"He says he did, but the idiot must have dialed the wrong number or something." Pollard wasn't about to admit that he had forgotten to check his messages.

"Stay where you are in case she calls again. I'm going to go get some answers from that bitch if I have to break her arms," he growled.

"Hey, Elena, birthday cake in the break room," her fellow agent announced, jerking her head toward Chad's office.

For the last two days, Elena had fought the urge just to yank the bug off the bottom of her desk and crush it with her boot, but they had all agreed that it was better to work around it than to worry about it showing up somewhere else. Chad's office was swept several times a day and deemed secure, so all of their business with the Spencer Rollins case was conducted there.

"What is it?"

"We got the dirt on Stacy Eagleton," a female agent proclaimed with a grin. "She had a little trouble about eight years ago when she worked for Southern Health Supply in Atlanta. They started an investigation into some inventory problems, but they dropped it when she resigned."

"What kind of inventory problems?"

"Short shipments, it would appear, a lot like what we think is happening at Margadon. But at Southern, she was pulling the cash out of her own budget instead of spending it on her vendors. Southern let it go quietly because they didn't want to call attention to the shipments that went out under spec."

"Akers and Pollard must have found out about it when they were doing the background checks. So she set up another scheme and cut them in on it," Elena concluded. "Is that what you're thinking, Chad?"

Her boss nodded with satisfaction. "Makes sense to me. How are we going to prove it?"

"Why don't we pull her phone records and see if she has any calls to these agents?"

"That's a start. Have we heard from Rollins again?"

"No. But I did confirm that the FBI has Ruth Ferguson in custody and that's she's awaiting extradition back to Maine on a kidnapping warrant. Apparently, they haven't made the connection between her and Spencer, so we're good there. But . . ."

"But what?" Chad asked, knowing from the private briefing he had received on Ruth Ferguson what Diaz was about to request.

Elena looked sheepishly at the other agents in the room, prompting her boss to dismiss them so they could discuss this alone.

"We're moving on that case as well. Agent Fennimore is arriving in Madison, Maine, right about now to start going over the books at Drummond Appliances. If we have any leverage for keeping Ruth Ferguson here in D.C., I'd like to call that in."

"We're no match for a federal kidnapping warrant, Elena."

"Chad, this woman risked her freedom to help with this case. I'm not asking for a pardon here. I'm just asking that we hold her here until Fennimore completes his work."

"We can't use the IRS to strong-arm people into giving up their kids. You know that," he scolded.

"But there's something wrong with this case. This mother should never have lost her kid in the first place, and Thomas thinks maybe the judge was bought. That makes it our jurisdiction and our obligation to investigate."

"What kind of evidence are we looking at?"

"Drummond Appliances was her ex-husband's company and it had a huge write-off right about the time the case went to court. It wasn't carried over to the next quarter like their other bad debts, and it wasn't handed to their collection agency. It was like they just gave something away."

"That's all you've got?"

"For Christ's sake, Chad! Just give him twenty-four hours to look into it. You know how I—"

"I know, I know. You hate coincidences."

Chapter 25

Ruth leaned back against the concrete wall counting her blessings. Jessie would be safe. Spencer and Viv would see to that, and nothing else on earth mattered. In a few days, Elena would find a way to end the Margadon case and Spencer would be safe.

But by that time, it would be too late for anyone to help her. An agent had stopped by to explain that they had received her extradition papers and she was to be sent under escort of a U.S. Marshall to jail in Maine—with or without revealing her daughter's whereabouts. They had already begun the search.

But they wouldn't find her, she told herself again. They had no way to link her to the trailer. And even if they did, Spencer and Jessie were probably already gone. Jessie would be taken to a safe place. She was sure of it. Thank God Spencer had convinced her to come clean with Viv.

Startled from her ruminations by a creak of the door, Ruth looked up to see Akers. She could almost feel his wrath from across the room.

"Why, hello again, Calvin," she said sarcastically. "Did you miss me?"

"Miss Ferguson, I've just been apprised of your involvement in another federal case and I think it would be a good idea for us to discuss some options that might be available to you." Akers was so angry that he wanted just to grab her throat and squeeze, but the only way they were going catch Rollins was to cut a deal, or at least to appear as though they were cutting a deal. If Ruth Ferguson knew the details of the Rollins case—and it was apparent that she did—her fate was a foregone conclusion. He just had to figure out how it would happen.

"Don't waste your time. I'd rather rot in jail, thank you."

"Would you?" he sneered. "You know we're going to find your little girl eventually, Miss Ferguson. What's going to happen when she starts school next year and all the kids have her picture on their milk cartons? Or when we send out the flyers to the schools? You think she's going to stay hidden forever?" The woman's face showed both her fury and her fear. This was good. "Let me answer that. No, we're going to find her. And when we do, she goes back to that awful place you didn't want her to be, that place that was so bad, you risked everything just to get her away. And you're going to be in jail, unable to do a goddamn thing about it."

"Except you're not going to find her," she argued, her voice more hopeful than certain.

"Let me give you another scenario to think about. You and Jessie Drummond get a nice house somewhere in a small Midwestern town. You get a new job that pays good money, enough so that you and your daughter can have nice things. You both get new names and the trail for Ruth Ferguson and Jessie Drummond goes ice cold. Agents get pulled off the case and reassigned. You never have to worry again. How does all that sound?"

Those were just about the same plans Ruth had made for herself. She didn't need this dickhead's help for that. Except that she was in jail and Jessie was hiding out there with Spencer and Viv.

"And all you have to do is tell me where I can find Spencer Rollins." His offer was simple—and a bald-faced lie. But she was their best chance, their only real chance.

"Go to hell."

"I really appreciate this, Jerry, especially on such short notice." Viv stepped aside as her old friend deposited the basket of puppies onto the wide front porch of his farmhouse.

"I know you wouldn't be asking if it wasn't important. Besides, it's about time I got the chance to start paying you back for all you've done for me over the years." Jerry was an electrician, a widower in his late fifties. He kept a few horses on his land, including a couple that he boarded for the extra money he could earn.

"You don't owe me a thing and you know it. We settled that a long time ago," Viv said firmly, squeezing the big man's shoulder. Jerry fell on hard times a few years ago when doctors diagnosed a ruptured disc that required surgery. With no medical insurance, he had no way to pay, and he couldn't work because his back hurt too much. Viv heard about his troubles through the church and showed up at his house one day with a check.

Nobody in Manassas had any idea that Viv Walters was worth so much, and she wasn't about to tell. At one time, she had owned all the land that bordered the few acres that now held only her small house and the trailer. She sold it back when Sheila and Robby were little, her late husband's farms and rental properties too much to manage. For over twenty years, the profits sat in CDs at several banks around town, rolling over every couple of years while she drew the interest to live on.

Jerry had lots of room at his house, and just as Viv said, the Jeep was out of sight in the barn. Jessie was playing with the puppies. Viv and Jerry started fixing dinner for everyone. And Spencer was pacing on the front porch, trying to figure out what she would do next.

As long as she was free, the FBI would keep putting pressure on Ruth. They had probably offered her freedom—freedom to take Jessie and run—but there was no way they would ever let her go. She knew too much. If Spencer turned herself in, Ruth would lose her only value.

"Spencer?" Viv came onto the porch. "We have a problem."

"What is it?"

The landlady sighed. "Lisa."

"Goddamn it! How could we forget Lisa?" Spencer walked inside to find a sobbing Jessie.

"She's all by herself," the little girl wailed.

"I know. But she'll be all right, Jessie. She's been by herself before."

"Not this Lisa," she argued, hiccupping amidst her tears.

Spencer sighed. Lisa wasn't just a doll to Jessie. She was an anchor, a constant. And with her mother gone tonight, Jessie needed to have the doll in order to be okay.

Thomas Fennimore and the auditors found exactly what they were looking for in only two hours, following the theory they had developed back in Washington. Skip Drummond was even dumber than Thomas had predicted.

Drummond and Ruth Ferguson had appeared in court in October of the previous year for their final divorce hearing. That was when permanent custody of Jessie Riane Drummond was awarded to her father.

It was also the month that Drummond Appliances wrote up a

bill of sale for a state-of-the-art home entertainment system worth over eight thousand dollars. The purchaser was a William Johnson, no address, no phone. But the troubling part—at least if you were an IRS agent looking for wrongdoing—was that there was no record of payment, either partial or otherwise. And the debt was written off as uncollectible two months later, with no record of billing.

It appeared that Skip Drummond had been too cheap to pay for his own bribe. That was greedy. But it was the stupid part that excited Thomas so much—the delivery logs for that day showed the entertainment system going to the home of Judge Malcolm Howard.

Thomas was ready for the second warrant.

"So Diaz is still in her office?" Akers checked in with Pollard in the surveillance van for the third time after learning that Rollins had surfaced. It bothered him that Diaz was working so late tonight and that her supervisor and several others were still in the office too. That meant something was going down soon. And since all this Roscone shit was bogus, Chad Merke was probably calling the shots by now.

"Yeah, but she hasn't gotten any more calls."

"I don't like it, Mike. They're up to something. Hold on, I need to take this other call." He placed his partner on hold and punched the blinking line. "Akers."

"I found it," the intern said excitedly. "It was in the garage at Franconia-Springfield. An old Ford, just like you said." From the key he had taken from Ferguson's pocket, Akers was able to narrow the search for her vehicle. He had expected her to take the Metro as she had done on Saturday, and that's why they had been watching for her on the Memorial Bridge. The location of the car he guessed from the fact that Franconia-Springfield was the end of the Blue Line and the closest stop to Fairfax, where the call was placed.

"Was there anything in it?"

"Yeah, there was a wallet in the glove compartment with a driver's license for Karen Michelle Oliver, address 843 Old Richmond Road in Manassas."

"That's the jackpot, Andrew. Good work." Akers clicked back to the blinking light. "We have an address. I'll swing by and pick you up in about fifteen minutes. I've got a stop to make. Then we're going out to see Spencer Rollins."

Akers pulled open his file drawer and rummaged through the gadgets in the bottom. When he found what he needed, he grabbed his jacket and left.

The wall clock in the third floor conference room said eight o'clock and the small group had already started to gather. Elena and six of her IRS co-workers took seats around the long table to await the arrival of their boss.

Elena checked the battery in her phone for the fourth time to be sure it was fully charged. Missing a call from Spencer at this stage of the game would be disastrous.

Chad entered quietly with another gentleman, unknown to most of the staff, but not to Elena. This was the director of the FBI's District Field Office, Jeffrey Wilkinson. Like Chad, Jeff was in his early fifties, a few pounds slower than when he had worked cases, but not a man to be taken lightly. He had enjoyed a stellar career and was well respected by all of the local law enforcement agencies, including the IRS.

Chad made the introductions and turned the meeting over to Elena so that she could make her case.

Before she began, she disclosed her close friendship with Spencer. It was only fair that Wilkinson should have all the facts when he considered the evidence—though their sex life was none of his business.

Step by step, she laid out their case, beginning with Stacy Eagleton and her history at Southern Health Supply. The first evidence against the two FBI agents was that they missed—or more likely, turned a blind eye to—the reasons for her resignation from that company.

From there, Elena described the evidence against the four Margadon employees: the doctored program that diverted funds from the federal contract into a hidden account, the extravagant purchases, and a record of personal contact during the FBI's background checks with agents Akers and Pollard.

Next she produced tax returns for both agents, followed by a copy of the bill of sale for Pollard's vacation home and receipts for Akers's travel and expenses in gambling locations.

Finally, she showed a chart that outlined the significant events of the past ten days, from the murder of Henry Estes to the arrest—the abduction, in fact—of Ruth Ferguson.

"But Ruth Ferguson is wanted on federal kidnapping charges," Wilkinson pointed out. "Picking her up was under their jurisdiction."

"With all due respect, Agent Wilkinson, Akers and Pollard knew from their wiretap that Ms. Ferguson was en route to meet me when they picked her up, and she had not identified herself as Ruth Ferguson. It's my contention that they did so to prevent further contact with our office and to gain access to Spencer Rollins."

A staffer from their offices upstairs entered the room and quietly dropped several pages onto Elena's chair. The agent walked over to examine the contents, smiling wryly and nodding. "And here's another piece of evidence I'd like you to consider. In the past ten days alone, Stacy Eagleton has made six calls to Agent Akers. That strikes me as unusual."

"It's not unusual to me, Agent Diaz." Wilkinson remained calm and professional in the face of the mounting evidence against his agents. "Agents Akers and Pollard have been assigned to investigate the murder of a Margadon employee. It's perfectly understandable that they would maintain contact with company officials. As you know, the Bureau has a lot of resources dedicated to this case, including our surveillance of you in the event you are again approached. If Spencer Rollins is innocent, I'm sure that will all be sorted out when she comes forward. This . . . evidence, as you call it . . . should be considered as part of a bigger picture."

Elena couldn't decide if the man was being sincere or obstinate. She knew he wasn't stupid and that he had to be concerned with her litany of circumstances that linked his agents to a conspiracy at Margadon. While he might offer an alternate explanation for the individual elements of her evidence, he surely couldn't dismiss the suspicious nature of all of it taken together. She was about to challenge his reasoning when Chad interrupted and saved her from sending the field director into a more defensive posture.

"Jeff, we're aware of how serious these allegations are, and we also understand that you'd rather have more ironclad proof of wrongdoing before acting against two of your own agents. What we'd like to ask of you is that you pull Akers and Pollard off this case while we continue our investigation and that you place Ruth Ferguson in protective custody right away. On our end, we're fairly convinced that the parties we have named—including your agents—have acquired money illegally and are attempting to circumvent tax laws. We plan to proceed with this case as an official investigation of the Internal Revenue Service."

"Why does Ferguson need to be in protective custody?"

"We fear that she's in danger because she knows about these events," Elena answered.

"In danger from my agents?"

Merke merely nodded.

Wilkinson considered their plea. The financial data on his two agents was unsettling, but he needed to weigh it in light of the IRS agent's personal interest in the suspect. If he took action against Akers and Pollard and the IRS was wrong, it would cost him the support of his entire staff. On the other hand, if he ignored their theory and they were right, it would cost him his career.

The field director stood. "I'll take your recommendations under advisement and will personally guarantee the safety of the prisoner currently in our custody until she is handed over to the Maine authorities." Wilkinson put his hands in his pockets and wavered. "As for agents Akers and Pollard, I seriously doubt that their investigative activities warrant your suspicions. However, if you choose to involve them in your investigation, I'm confident you'll discover that for yourselves."

Wilkinson was certain that his agents could not possibly be mixed up in embezzlement and murder. But like all well-trained investigative agents, he hated coincidences like the ones Elena Diaz had raised. Professionally speaking, he had only one option: Trust, but verify.

Chapter 26

Spencer walked stealthily through the woods in the dark, approaching the house from behind the trailer. It was too big a risk just to drive back to the house so she got directions from Viv on how to get access from a neighboring road. If someone were at the house already, she would leave or hide in the woods until they left. Otherwise, she would go on in the back door, get the doll, and go back through the woods.

The house and trailer were totally dark when they finally came into view. According to Jessie, Lisa was still "taking a nap" at Viv's, so that meant the doll was on the bed in the guest room. Foregoing the lights, Spencer walked purposefully through the back door, banging her knee hard on a table in the hallway. Finding Lisa was the only way to bring even a thread of comfort to the little four-year-old, whose whole world seemed to be unraveling all at once.

Her eyes adjusting to the darkness, Spencer spotted the small figure on the bed and scooped it up, turning to go back out the way she came, this time more cognizant of the table. When she reached the kitchen, a ray of light swept through the whole house, like headlights moving down the drive.

Spencer froze as she picked up the sound of a car creeping along the gravel. Her heart pounded as her brain tried to force her feet to move.

"You take the trailer. I'll get the house," a male voice ordered.

There were two of them and they were in the back where Ruth usually parked. Quickly, she ran to the front door, banging her knee on that *goddamned* table again. In the dark, she fingered the thumb bolt and turned the knob. Viv seldom used this door, and the top corner stuck when she tried to open it. With a hard yank, it came free.

The storm door was locked and she worked her long fingers frantically in the dark to flip the latch. She could hear the back door squeak, and when she finally pushed the storm door open, it sent a stiff breeze through the whole house. Careful not to let it bang, she lost precious seconds waiting for the hydraulic closer to release its air.

Moments later, she was off the front porch and headed for the woods on the side of the house. She would have to circle wide to get behind the trailer without being seen or heard. With any luck, they—

"Mike!" It was the agent inside the house. The other one appeared in the doorway to the trailer. "Get the flashlight. I think somebody just went out the front door."

Damn it! Spencer pushed along in the dark woods, staying low to avoid the anticipated sweep of the flashlight. The recent rains had made the ground soggy, so at least she wasn't making a lot of noise rustling the leaves. Over her shoulder, she could see the men entering the woods where she had gone in. If they found her trail in the wet leaves, they would close quickly.

The woman was behind the trailer now, picking up speed. Only a hundred more yards through the woods and she would come out where the Jeep was parked.

"Go drive around. She's gotta be headed to a car."

Spencer had won this game last time at Margadon, but that was with her Kawasaki. This time, she was on equal footing. Now on a dead run, she cleared the woods and climbed into the Jeep, tossing the doll into the back seat just as the rear window exploded in an ear-splitting blast. The vehicle lurched forward, fishtailing and spraying the air with gravel and mud. As she reached the main road, the long black sedan turned to block her escape.

"Son of a bitch!" She jerked the gearshift into four-wheel drive and bounced across the culvert, the powerful SUV catching the front of the car with its bumper and pushing it to the ditch on the other side of the road.

Triumphant once again, she sped away, turning as soon as she could onto a secondary road that would take her back to Jerry's. She needed to get this Jeep stowed as soon as possible, and then it might be a good idea for all of them to move again.

The bespectacled agent in a rumpled suit stood on the doorstep of the yellow Cape Cod home, flanked on both sides by deputies from the Somerset County Sheriff's Office. The porch light suddenly came on and the tall door swung open.

"Can I help you gentlemen with something?" Deputies often came to Judge Howard's home in the evening to get warrants signed, but they usually called first.

"Uh, we have a warrant, Judge Howard," one of them stammered.

"Very well. But you should have called first," he scolded, taking the document as he held the screen door open. "Come on in. I need to get my glasses."

The deputies and the IRS agent stepped inside, the latter following the sound of a sitcom that emanated from the den off the main hall.

"That appears to be what we're looking for, deputies," Fennimore said, standing in the doorway and pointing to the sprawling entertainment system. "Would you verify the serial numbers for me?"

"I beg your pardon," the judge said indignantly. "Who are you, and who gave you the right to go wandering through my home?"

"My name is Thomas Fennimore. I'm a Special Agent with the Internal Revenue Service. That warrant you're holding was signed by a federal judge in Washington, D.C., and it gives me the authority to search these premises for a JVC home entertainment system, delivered to this address by Drummond Appliances on October sixteenth of last year. According to their records, the system in question was never paid for and it was written off as an uncollectible debt. While you are certainly allowed to receive such a generous gift, Drummond Appliances is not allowed to deduct its value as a business loss and is therefore in violation of the Federal Tax Code." Thomas observed with satisfaction the ghastly look on the judge's face and he dropped the other shoe. "I'll be returning for your statement once I've completed the other phases of my investigation. Of course, if you wished to be forthcoming about any unusual circumstances pertaining to how you came to acquire this gift, I would be most grateful to take that information and your cooperation into consideration as the Federal Government proceeds with this case. I assure you that all violations will be prosecuted to the fullest extent of the law."

"I'm really sorry about your car, Viv."

The gray-haired woman waved her hand flippantly. "It's just

a car. Thank goodness you weren't hurt."

"Okay, the truck's packed, puppies and all," Jerry announced. He had loaded up their things as soon as Spencer had gotten home. The whole group was headed out to stay with friends of his cousin. The underground network was coming to life tonight, all because Viv had helped Jerry out when he needed the surgery.

"Listen, Viv, when Jessie gets settled, I'm going to ask Jerry to borrow his truck so I can go find a phone. I need to call Elena again and see what's happened." Spencer hoisted the tired little girl into the front seat.

"You should take Jerry with you. He might be of some help."

Spencer steered them toward the back of the truck so Jessie wouldn't hear. "I don't want to put him in danger, Viv. It's bad enough that I've put all of you at risk. And now Ruth's been caught." The emotion overwhelmed her for a moment and her voice shook while her eyes filled with tears.

"Don't worry about us. We'll be okay. I promised Ruth I'd take care of this child and if it takes my last ounce of strength, that's what I'll do." Like Spencer, Viv had fallen into the habit of using her tenants' real names.

Spencer drew the older woman into a hug and then helped her up into the truck beside Jessie and her doll. On the way to the next house, Spencer asked Jerry about borrowing his vehicle.

"You don't need to go find no phone. You can just use my cell phone."

"It's not that simple. They'll trace the call back to you, and then you'll be part of all of this too."

"I'm already part of it. Besides, they ain't gonna trace my phone," he said cockily.

"What do you mean?"

"Mine don't broadcast," he said with a grin. "At least that's what my customers say."

"How'd you manage that?"

"It's one of those old analog phones. I took it apart once to see how it worked and I had a couple of pieces left over when I put it back together. Ever since then, it don't flash no caller ID, and if we drive around out in the boondocks, they won't even be able to triangulate the signal."

Spencer was skeptical, but Jerry was an electrician, which made him the closest thing to an expert they had. But there was a hell of lot at stake here. "Are you sure?"

"Positive."

Akers dumped another load of gravel from inside his folded jacket into the ditch beneath the rear wheel. If they could just get a little more traction, they could get back up onto the road.

"Okay, let's try again." They had been at this for over an hour. As Pollard gently applied the gas, Akers bounced on the rear fender, pushing it into contact with the ground, throwing rocks and mud against his shins as he cursed. Finally, the sedan jolted forward, catching the lip of the ditch as it sent one final spray of mud into the face of the frazzled agent.

"Where to?" Pollard asked.

"Downtown. We need to do something about Ferguson before she talks."

"What did you have in mind?"

"You should bring her back out to the trailer to identify some of her belongings. A desperate woman like that might escape."

Pollard didn't like that idea. It would reflect badly on his service record if he had to report that she got away under his watch. But Akers was the senior agent and had done the dirty work on Estes.

"And Rollins?"

"Let me worry about Rollins."

251

Elena was dead on her feet. Since Saturday morning, she had managed only a few hours of sleep, most of that coming early Sunday. But things were finally coming together.

Twenty-three critical warrants sat on her desk, all signed by a federal judge and awaiting execution. The IRS would freeze all accounts for the individuals suspected of involvement. Margadon's Kryfex operations would come to a halt and the company's network would be disabled. Suspects would be arrested. And Spencer, Ruth and Ruth's daughter would be transferred into protective custody. Ideally, the operation would be initiated when Spencer turned herself in, as she was the one person who could pull the whole case together.

"Agent Diaz?" Chad stood in her doorway, his tie loosened and his coat thrown over his arm.

"You calling it a night?"

"Yeah, for both of us. Come on, I'll walk you down." Elena got up and walked into the hallway, away from the listening devices.

"I don't know, Chad. I have a feeling Spencer's going to call again. I think I should wait here."

"You need some sleep, Elena. There's nothing you can do from here that you can't do from home."

Elena nodded in resignation, returning to her office to gather her things. As she and her boss started down the stairs, the phone in her pocket rang.

Glancing at the display, she shook her head in confusion. "Elena Diaz."

"Did you get to her? Is she okay?"

Relief rushed through the agent's veins. It was Spencer.

"She's in custody. She's due to be extradited tomorrow morning." The agent hated delivering the bad news, but this wasn't the time for sugar coating. "But we're on it, and things look pretty good for her. We have to deal with you now," she said firmly, knowing that the sons of bitches in the van were tuning

252

in.

"They know who she is, Elena. They know she's with me."

"I know, but they're sending her—"

"They came to look for me. That means she's in danger. You have to get her out of there now!"

Elena held up her hand to shush her boss, who was encouraging her to have Spencer come in.

"I can't, Spencer. But we talked to the chief over there. He knows we're worried about it and he isn't going to let anything happen to her. And you know as well as I do that the agents are listening to us right now, so they aren't going to take a chance on hurting her. People are watching."

"These guys are animals, Elena. Didn't you see what they did to Henry!"

"I know, I know. But we're not quite ready for all of this yet. I need for you to stay out of sight for at least another day. Can you do that?"

Elena's request was met by silence.

"Here's what I want you to do, Spence. Tomorrow, the pizza place, the usual time. Do you understand?"

"Tomorrow?"

"That's right, Tuesday, same time as before."

"I've got it."

"Stay out of sight until then. And take care of yourself, okay?"

"Take care of Ruth."

"Don't worry about her. She'll be safe."

The call ended and Elena cracked her first smile in nine days. The boys in the van would be scratching their heads about this one. She was a genius.

"What's happening?"

Elena looked at her watch. "We need to get rolling with the warrants, Chad. She's coming in two hours from now."

"What's the 'pizza place' all about?" Chad was totally out of the loop.

"It's kind of personal," she answered sheepishly. "But she's going to walk into an all-night grocery in Alexandria at one a.m. and we need to arrange for a black and white to bring her into custody and take her to their precinct. I can't risk having one of us followed."

"But you told her tomorrow."

"I said Tuesday, same time. She knows what that means."

"So we're rolling?"

"We're rolling. It's time to get everyone into place."

Chapter 27

FBI field technician Bob Bates pulled off the headphones and reached for his tablet to log the event. Akers was sitting outside in his car watching the IRS building at this very minute. The technician knew he expected to be informed of the call.

But Special Agent Bates had orders that superseded those of Calvin Akers. Before tonight, the technician had never met Field Office Director Wilkinson. He was embarrassed beyond belief that the top man in the District office walked into his van right out of the blue to find him chowing down on a box of donuts. Powdered sugar was all over everything, even his face, he realized with horror once the director had gone.

But Wilkinson hadn't seemed to mind the mess. His only concern was that he had been remiss in monitoring the Rollins case, and he had asked to be apprised of all new contacts and relevant information. He hadn't given a reason, but this last exchange between Diaz and Rollins offered a clue as to why the director suddenly wanted to be involved at the investigative level.

In her last call, Rollins alleged that the FBI was holding a suspect who was in danger at the hands of its own agents. Her implication was that it was Akers and Pollard who had killed Henry Estes, the victim at the center of this investigation. Akers had purported all along that Diaz was impeding the apprehension of the suspect, but this new accusation explained why he was almost obsessive in wanting to know the details of her activities.

The technician opened his cell phone and placed the call. "This is Special Agent Robert Bates. I need to speak with Director Wilkinson, please."

"The pizza place," Spencer chuckled. "Good call."

"What?"

"I've got good news and bad news, Jerry. The good news is that you get to get rid of me, and in a day or so, your life might be back to normal. The bad news is that I need you to drop me off in Alexandria at one o'clock in the morning."

"No problem." Jerry enjoyed the excitement, and if it helped Viv, he wanted to do it.

Spencer smiled to herself at her ex-lover's coded message. When their respective libidos had ignited on their first date, she and the IRS agent skipped the restaurant and went right to Elena's townhouse. At one a.m., they emerged from their carnal explorations, starving, but with nothing in the house to eat. Spencer insisted that she was owed a dinner, so they picked up a frozen pizza at an all-night grocery nearby, later feeding it to one another in bed. To this day, it was always their recommendation when someone suggested going for pizza.

"Why don't we go back so I can tell Viv what we're doing? We need a plan for knowing when it's safe for her to go home."

Akers sat on Constitution Avenue in the black sedan, its front and rear fenders conspicuously smashed and one headlight out. The condition of his car was the least of his worries.

After dropping Pollard at the FBI headquarters, he had checked his messages at home, only to learn that Petrov was unimpressed with the partial payment on his outstanding debt. Akers was advised to receive visitors at his home at eleven p.m. It was now ten after.

Even if he picked up Rollins tonight and guaranteed her silence, he would no doubt return to find two of the gaming kingpin's muscled associates at his home. He may be able to persuade them to accept an outrageously inflated sum later in the week, but even that wouldn't be possible to deliver unless Eagleton released their payments and resumed operations at Margadon. His only leverage now was to threaten her with exposure of their scheme.

If she balked—or if he failed to deal with Rollins tonight—he was probably a dead man. That was the risk he had taken when he became indebted to a man like Yuri Petrov.

The agent sat up and took notice as Diaz emerged in her Audi sedan from the parking garage and turned in front of the surveillance van toward the Capitol. Moments later, Merke followed. Akers activated the small laptop on the passenger seat and watched the two blips round the corner at 9th Street on their way to I-395. He pulled out from the curb and fell in behind, close enough to keep the two vehicles in visual range, but not so close as to be detected. Diaz took the exit toward Alexandria while Merke continued southwest toward the Beltway.

When they reached the townhouse in Alexandria, Akers killed his only working headlight and held up as he watched Diaz park and exit her car. When she gathered the mail on her front porch and disappeared into the townhouse, he drove closer to her door and parked across the street to continue his vigil. A surveillance van was already in place up the street, the agent inside monitoring phone calls and the listening device they had placed in Diaz's living room.

As Akers turned to shut down the GPS screen, he was startled to see that Merke's car had doubled back and was headed toward Alexandria. He watched in fascination as the blip moved through the neighborhood, stopping on a parallel street behind Diaz's townhouse. Adding the tracking device to Merke's car at the last minute had paid off.

"Gotcha," he chuckled as he started his engine. "You idiots forgot I was the FBI, didn't you?" With his lights still out, the agent drove around the block and watched as Diaz emerged from an alley and climbed into the car.

He sure hoped Pollard was taking care of things on his end. Tomorrow might turn out to be a really nice day after all.

Jeffrey Wilkinson pulled into the underground garage at eleven thirty, confirming for his own peace of mind that the parking spot belonging to Akers and Pollard was vacant. As long as they weren't in the building, the kidnapping suspect in custody was not in any danger.

When he had left the IRS building earlier this evening, he stopped at the surveillance van to instruct the technician. Next, he returned to his office and collected the personnel records for the two agents. As promised, he guaranteed Ruth Ferguson's safety with a quick call to the holding area on the sixth floor. The guard verified that she was resting in her cell.

In the last two hours at home, Wilkinson had found nothing out of the ordinary that might raise an alarm about illegal activity. Neither agent was overly decorated for job performance. Nor had they been disciplined by the Bureau for any reason. Agent Diaz's financial records for the two corresponded with the known personal facts, but there were plenty of possible explanations for their non-work behaviors that didn't involve illegal gains.

Assured that the IRS was mistaken, he set the files aside and readied for bed. Then he got the call from Bates. He could hear the nervousness in the technician's voice, and it was incumbent upon him as director of the field office to lay these worries to rest. He couldn't afford to dismiss these concerns and be wrong. He would have to rein these agents in.

As Wilkinson approached his office on the fifth floor, he was surprised to see Agent Pollard enter the stairwell at the far end of the hall. What was he doing here so late?

Wilkinson continued down the hallway, stopping at the darkened office that belonged to Pollard and Akers. Not really knowing what he was looking for, he turned on the lights and walked over to the desks, which were pushed together so that the agents would face one another. The only sign of recent activity was the day planner on Akers's desk, turned to today's date. Across the bottom, Wilkinson saw an address. A Manassas address. Manassas was the last known location of Spencer Rollins.

The field director marched hurriedly down the hallway, acknowledging the handful of agents who worked the late shift. They were unaccustomed to seeing their boss at this hour. Wilkinson charged through the door that Pollard had used and started up the stairs, where the prisoners were housed one flight up on the top floor. As he reached the landing, he was met by Pollard, who was escorting a petite blond woman wearing handcuffs. What the hell was going on?

"Agent Pollard?"

The young man froze as he came face to face with his boss. "Yes, sir?"

"Is that a prisoner?"

"Yes, sir, this woman is being held on a kidnapping warrant. I'm escorting her to Manassas so that she can recover her personal items."

"At a quarter to midnight?"

"Yes, sir. She's being returned to Maine first thing tomorrow."

Wilkinson nodded vaguely. "Agent Pollard, I need your input on a case. Would you mind bringing your prisoner in here for a moment?"

Pollard hesitated briefly, but with no way to avoid his boss's request, he complied. Wilkinson held the door while the agent pushed the woman through.

"Just go into that office right there and wait for me." He nodded toward an open door and turned to poke his head into an office where a female agent studied a case file. "Agent Burke? Can you step across the hall with me for a moment?"

Rookie Special Agent Jill Burke hurriedly stood and rounded the desk, astounded that the man even knew her name. Oh, it was on the nameplate on her desk.

"And bring your gun."

Burke's eyes grew wide as she processed the request. Her gun?

Wilkinson and Burke entered the office across the hall, the director immediately moving to position himself between Pollard and the prisoner. Removing his own gun from its shoulder holster, he took control of the situation.

"Agent Pollard, will you very carefully place your gun and your badge on the desk and step toward the window?"

Oh, fuck.

"Agent Burke, collect this agent's gun."

She did.

"Now, Agent Burke, I'd like for you to escort this prisoner back to her cell upstairs. And when you reach the sixth floor, would you ask two of the guards to come at once to Room 523?"

"Yes, sir."

Mike Pollard stared into the barrel of the director's gun. He was toast.

ۿ

Akers followed Merke and Diaz to an area schoolyard where they met two uniformed officers of the Alexandria Police Department. After a brief meeting, the IRS agents left, but the cruiser remained in place. That triggered the FBI agent's curiosity. Apparently, these two patrolmen had been given the assignment of bringing Rollins in. Why else would Merke and Diaz have met them?

He wouldn't have much of a window to take Rollins out. His best bet was to get to her before the officers did. *Attempt the arrest, stage a struggle, and shoot her dead.* He had envisioned the scene over and over since the day after the murder when they first located her at the convenience store.

If they picked her up before he had the chance, he would have only one option. He would assert his jurisdiction in the case and demand that she be transferred from the local police into federal custody. The link to the kidnapping was a perfect excuse for urgency, but he had to act before Diaz and Merke arrived on the scene. Once she was in his custody, all he needed was a few moments alone. *Stage a struggle, shoot her dead.*

He had watched from a distance as the cruiser continued to hold its position. The GPS showed the IRS car on its way back into the District, presumably to prepare the warrants they would execute once Rollins was in custody. At least, that's what Akers would be doing if it were his case. But the IRS was going to get quite a surprise.

The key ingredient in their case was going to fall out of the picture tonight. Without Rollins, the IRS couldn't prove the conspiracy. The computer program had been disabled and all of the evidence regarding the murder of Henry Estes pointed to Rollins. Without her around to say otherwise, he didn't imagine this investigation would be open much longer.

ۿ

Jessie was sleeping soundly with her Lisa doll in a room with twin beds, the other bed occupied by the nine-year-old girl who lived in the house. Spencer eased down to sit by Jessie, brushing the blond curls from the little girl's face. She had held up pretty well considering the excitement of the night and the separation from her mother. From what Ruth had said, the poor child was used to being with adults who treated her like she was a bother, so at least that wasn't the case here. They had all been welcomed by these friends of Jerry's cousin.

Leaning down, she gently kissed the child's forehead. "Be safe, Jessie. Your mommy loves you very much." Careful not to wake the girl, she stood and tiptoed out of the room to say goodbye to Viv.

"I think you should plan to wait at least two days before you call. And use Jerry's phone like I did. You can't let them know where you're staying." Spencer was outlining what Viv should do if she didn't return right away. She had written down Elena's number, knowing that her friend would be the best source for information and that Elena would take extra measures to ensure Jessie's safety.

"Do you think I can go to a cash machine? I'm going to need some money."

Spencer nodded. "Just be careful. If it hangs up even for a second, take off."

"Good luck to you." Viv pulled her into a motherly hug.

"And to you. Jessie couldn't be in better hands."

With that farewell, the programmer got into the truck and closed the door.

"So what's this about a pizza place?" Jerry asked.

Spencer gave him directions to the all-night grocery, anxious to have this part end. Once she was out of danger, she could at least get Ruth out of the hands of the agents who were tracking her. She would be of no use to them any more. She had to hope there was some way Elena could help Ruth avoid what awaited her in Maine. Maybe if she were a witness in this case, that would get her special consideration.

"Is this the place?" Jerry had pulled into the store's parking lot. Only a handful of cars were parked out front at this hour.

"Yeah," she sighed, directing him to a dark corner of the lot. "Thanks for everything, Jerry."

"Glad I could help."

"You should get out of here. Okay?"

The man gave her a friendly salute, which Spencer returned as he drove away.

Conditioned to watch for a black sedan, her eyes nervously scanned the lot as she walked toward the store. When the automatic door opened, she turned immediately to the produce aisle on the far right, anxious about finding a rear exit. For ten minutes, she paced nervously, her eyes on the tilted mirrors that lined the back wall of the store.

Finally, two uniformed officers strode through the front door and spoke to the cashier on duty. One of the officers followed her route through the produce section. The other headed directly to the back of the store. Gradually, she inched toward the corner, where a swinging door led to the storage area and loading dock.

Studying her options, she watched as they drew closer. Both of them were in her line of sight, a barrel-chested African-American approaching from the produce aisle, a wiry Hispanic man from along the meat display in the back. The closer they came, the more her heart pounded in her chest.

"Spencer Rollins?" the Hispanic officer asked.

Almost imperceptibly, she nodded, her eyes wide with apprehension.

"I'm placing you under arrest for the murder of Henry Estes. You have the right to remain silent . . ."

His instructions droned on as he cuffed her hands behind her and gave her a cursory pat-down. The store's few shoppers had congregated in the neighboring aisles to watch the arrest, seemingly disappointed at the ease with which the suspect was taken.

Spencer was escorted back through the store, out the front door, and into the back seat of a waiting cruiser. The African-American officer took the wheel and the Hispanic officer sat up front beside him, a metal screen separating them from their suspect.

The car pulled out of the lot and turned, parking almost immediately on a dark side street. The din of the police radio was the only sound, and Spencer grew increasingly panicked that she had just made a big mistake. Shouldn't these two be taking her somewhere?

The Hispanic officer turned around and opened a sliding window. "Can you turn around and put your hands up here? I'll unlock those cuffs."

Still fearful, Spencer twisted in the seat and raised her hands. The officer gently removed the metal links.

"There's a vest beside you on the seat. You should put it on."

"Why?"

"Agent Diaz's orders."

Spencer visibly relaxed at hearing her friend's name, slumping back against the seat. Elena had arranged the whole scenario. "What's next?"

"When you get that on, I'm going to call in that we have a suspect en route and she'll know to meet us at the station."

"This is kind of tight," she said, struggling to get the body armor pulled down over her sweatshirt."

"You should probably take off your sweatshirt and wear it underneath. That's what we do," he explained. "Having it on the outside is kind of like wearing as sign that says 'shoot me in the head.'"

Spencer could have gone all night without hearing that. "Are you expecting any trouble?"

"No, this is just a precaution. What Agent Diaz wants, she gets." He and his partner faced forward while she pulled her shirt off and slipped into the vest.

"Yeah, she's kind of forceful, all right."

"We're glad to help her out. Last year, she put a commendation in our file for some work we did for her. Most people don't take the time to do something like that, but it really meant a lot to both of us."

That sounded like Elena, Spencer thought, always looking to shore up the right allies. When she needed a cop, she wanted a good one.

"You all set?" he asked.

"Yeah."

"Okay, I need for you to get back up here so we can put the cuffs back on, but we won't make them too tight. They're just for show."

Spencer did as she was told, feeling more confident when they pulled away from the curb.

"This is unit 416. We have an unidentified female shoplifting suspect in custody and are en route to the precinct."

"Copy."

Akers was agitated. After ten days of pursuit, his quarry was now within his grasp. A few minutes ago, the two officers had rolled from the schoolyard, stopping at the front door of an all-night grocery. When they went inside, the agent had parked nearby to watch for Rollins, if indeed this was the meeting point. He would intercept her. *Attempt the arrest, stage the struggle, shoot her dead.* The mantra played nearly nonstop in his head.

Instead, the officers emerged from the store with Rollins already cuffed. The cruiser pulled away and was now parked on the street around the corner from the store. Apparently, they were planning to wait for Diaz here.

But the GPS showed Merke's car still in the District, still parked at the IRS building. "Slaves to paperwork," Akers grumbled. His call to Pollard's cell phone went unanswered, which he took to mean that his partner had wrapped up his business with

Ferguson and was home in bed. Now it was time for him to do his part, to take custody of Rollins.

Just as he reached for the door handle, the black and white pulled away from the curb and continued down the street. Akers followed, and after three more turns, he realized that their destination was the Alexandria Police Department headquarters on Mill Road.

It would all end there.

It's almost over. For Spencer, the relief was palpable. Elena had come through with finally bringing her in, ending the malicious manhunt that she had outrun for ten days. Ruth was in custody, but Spencer was sure she was safe.

The car pulled into an angled space in front of a red brick building bearing the sign Alexandria Police Department.

"What happens now?"

The Hispanic officer turned to face her. "No one else has been informed of your status—again, those are Agent Diaz's orders—so they believe we're bringing in a shoplifter. For now, we're going to take you inside and lock you in a cell until Agent Diaz arrives and gets you transferred into federal custody."

"I'll still be in custody?"

"I'm afraid so. You're named in a federal warrant."

Spencer groused inwardly, but she hadn't really expected to just go free. There was a lot to clear up, and the proof would have to be laid out and verified before she could be exonerated.

The officers escorted her into the main entrance, stopping only to have her empty her pockets of personal effects—her wallet, her wristwatch, and her belt. Her possessions were itemized and placed in an envelope for return upon release. A buzzer sounded and she was led through one door to another past an open conference room. They waited again for the buzzer that indicated the next door was unlocked, and she entered a row of cells, one of which was occupied by a sleeping prisoner.

"So how come Agent Diaz isn't here to meet me? She get a better offer?" Spencer turned and held out her wrists so the officer could remove her handcuffs.

The Hispanic officer chuckled. "No, she said she didn't want to tip off her tail until you were safe and in custody. She was waiting for us to call in the shoplifter."

The African-American officer spoke for the first time. "You'll be safe here until Agent Diaz arrives. Good luck to you."

"Thanks, guys. Thanks for everything. I'll make sure Elena knows what a good job you guys did."

"Appreciate it," he said. The officers tipped their caps and took their leave.

Through the front window of the building, Akers could see Rollins being escorted out of the receiving area, presumably to a holding cell. He entered and approached the officer at the desk, flashing his badge as he introduced himself.

"I'm Special Agent Calvin Akers of the FBI. There's a federal warrant for the person your officers just delivered, a Spencer Rollins. I'm here to take custody of the prisoner."

"I'm sorry, Agent . . ."

"Akers."

"Agent Akers. The suspect who was just delivered was not identified as Spencer Rollins."

"Look, Officer . . . Ellis. I don't know who that woman said she was, but I assure you, she's Spencer Rollins and she's wanted for a brutal murder in Maryland. More importantly, she has knowledge of the whereabouts of a four-year-old girl who is missing tonight and is probably alone and in grave danger. Now you can sit on your hands and fret about who she claims to be, or you can let me question her at once. If you choose right, we might just save that little girl's life tonight."

Spencer sat on the stiff cot, resting her back against the wall. Once again, she allowed herself to think that this ordeal might be over. As soon as she was free, she would take on Ruth's fight, wherever it was. She would spend her last dime making sure they hired the best lawyer in Maine to get the kidnapping charges dropped and the custody issue settled once and for all.

And maybe when they got things taken care of in Maine, Ruth could come back down to Virginia and really start over, free and clear. Spencer had tried not to think about it too much, but she really wanted Ruth and Jessie in her life.

God, was it just this morning they had kissed goodbye?

Spencer looked up to see the officer from the front desk unlocking her cell. *Elena's finally here!*

"Step this way, ma'am." He held the door open as she walked down the narrow hallway and waited for him to swipe a card that would open the exterior door. "First door on your left."

Spencer did as she was told, confused at seeing a table and four empty chairs. The door closed behind her and she whirled, finally spotting the figure in the corner of the room.

"Good evening, Ms. Rollins."

Recognition was instant as she stared into the cold face of Henry's murderer.

"Help! Officer! He's a murderer." she yelled. Frantically, she crossed the room to the other side of the table to put distance between herself and the menacing agent.

"This is an attorney conference room, Ms. Rollins. Soundproof. Besides, even if they could hear you, they won't be coming to help. I'm the FBI, Ms. Rollins. They all know how much trouble you're in now."

"You killed Henry."

"That's right. Nosy fellow." *Stage a struggle.* Akers stepped closer, hoping to provoke an attack. "You should have seen him die. Probably the first time he ever had any color."

Spencer stepped back, almost against the wall.

"Oh, and your little friend . . . Ferguson? On her way to jail. I'm going to personally see to it that she does hard time. By the time she gets out, that little girl of hers won't remember a thing about her.

In a fluid move, the surprisingly nimble agent vaulted the table, landing within arm's reach of his prey.

"Bastard."

Akers's arm raised as he aimed his service revolver directly at her chest. "You shouldn't have gone for my gun like that."

The next two seconds seemed to pass in slow motion. In terror for her life, Spencer lunged forward, both hands reaching out to push the revolver away. The sound of the sudden blast reverberated off the concrete walls as a hammer hit her chest and a fire erupted in her belly.

In the next heartbeat, Elena and Wilkinson stormed through the door, their weapons already drawn. On their heels were the duty officer and the two patrolmen who had brought her in.

"Spencer!"

"She went for my gun," Akers declared. "I had to shoot her."

"Put your gun on the table and step away, Agent Akers," Wilkinson commanded. "This is over."

Akers stared back at the two steel barrels, his face contorted in anger. He raised his right arm to take aim at the IRS agent he had come to hate and instantly took two bullets to the chest.

Before he hit the floor, Elena was rushing to her former lover's side.

"Bulletproof, my ass," Spencer hissed, the pain in her gut greater than any she had ever known.

Elena lifted the sweatshirt and saw the perforation. Even the highest grade of body armor couldn't handle a bullet from point blank range. She lifted the vest to see blood dribbling freely from a wound just above the pelvis.

"Get an ambulance!"

Chapter 28

The clunky sound of plastic dishes stirred the unfortunate occupants of the sixth floor of the FBI field office. Ruth pushed herself up on the rigid cot and swung her bare feet to the cold tile floor, angry at herself for being hungry enough to eat. To her thinking, if she refused to participate in this incarceration, she would be spared the memory when she was finally freed. It was bad enough that they had dressed her in this orange jumpsuit.

How frightened Jessie must have been at spending the night away from her. At least Spencer was there with her, and the bond she had seen growing between those two was her only real source of comfort. With help from Spencer and Viv, Jessie would be protected from her mother's probable fate, a return to the dismal place from which she had fled.

Sitting now in the stark eight by six concrete room Ruth turned her thoughts inward, though introspection at this juncture was moot. Going out on a limb to see Spencer to safety was not an action she would second guess, unless it meant that Jessie's new life had been compromised. She hoped that her efforts weren't in vain and that Elena was still working on bringing Spencer in. From the looks of things, Ruth Ferguson wasn't a priority for the IRS.

Two pairs of footsteps—one decidedly female—grew louder as they approached her cell, and before she ever saw the face, Ruth knew one would be the IRS agent. A tired-looking Elena waited while the guard opened the door and motioned her out.

"Good morning, Ruth." She held up her hand to silence the question on the prisoner's lips. "We're going to a conference room so we can talk privately about where everything stands."

Ruth nodded once and followed her down the hallway, the guard bringing up the rear. Once they were situated, he closed the door and took his leave.

"Is Jessie okay?"

"I honestly don't know the answer to that." Elena saw the frantic look and continued quickly. "We don't know where your daughter is, but I think it's safe to assume that Spencer left her in good hands."

"Spencer left her?"

"We brought Spencer in last night. She . . . we had some trouble at the station with one of the FBI agents—Akers—and she was shot."

"Oh my God!"

"Don't worry, she's going to be okay." The agent stretched out her hand to pat the arm of the woman across from her. It was clear that Ruth had come to care for her friend, and from what Elena could gather from Spencer's insistence that she come here first thing this morning, the feeling was mutual. "She was wearing a protective vest and the bullet struck her chest plate and ricocheted to her lower abdomen. She had surgery last night, but she's going to be fine. Really, I just left her not a half hour ago."

Ruth began crying as the horror of Spencer's close call overwhelmed her. "Is it over?"

In simple terms, Elena explained what had happened last night. The evidence in the case was frozen, and the suspects were in custody. All would be arraigned this morning, including Pollard, who now occupied a cell in the opposite corner of the sixth floor from her own. Akers had died instantly of his wounds.

"So what happens now?" Ruth asked.

"You mean with the case?"

Ruth shrugged. "And with me."

Elena sighed and leaned back, forcing herself to look the woman in the eye. "A U.S. Marshal is slated to take you back to Maine this morning. I can't stop that, Ruth. I wish I could."

The prisoner dropped her head, her lower lip quivering in frustration and worry. "And Jessie?"

"Things with Jessie are really complicated, but we have a few options to play with here. And I do have some good news for you."

Ruth looked up to see a glint of encouragement in the agent's brown eyes.

"My assistant, Special Agent Thomas Fennimore, has been up in Madison going over the books at Drummond Appliances. He found an interesting transaction—a rather expensive gift to a Judge Malcolm Howard—right about the time of your divorce and custody hearing. We're pretty sure it was a bribe, and I think we'll be able to force the facts out one way or another."

"A bribe!" Suddenly, it all made sense. No wonder the judge had simply accepted Skip's word for everything. It was all arranged.

"That's right. And the real fun is going to start in about half an hour. That's when your ex-husband and his father are due downstairs to meet with the agent in charge."

"Why would they come here? I'm supposed to be sent back today, right?"

"Right, but they came to collect Jessie. At least, that's what I heard they were ranting about yesterday. But when they show up today, they're both going to be arrested, and I get to do the honors," the agent grinned slyly.

Ruth would love to see that. But it wouldn't answer the question about her daughter's fate. "So you said there were options . . . with Jessie?"

"I did, and this is where you're going to have to make a tough choice, Ruth. Custody issues really aren't my area of expertise, but I know that you're going to be asked to produce your daughter to the court to show that she's okay. Until otherwise decided, she's supposed to be with her father. My guess is that the Drummonds will post bail, and she'll probably be sent back to Maine."

Ruth was already shaking her head at that scenario. No way was Jessie going back to that. She had promised.

"Another option is that you leave her where she is. If you do that, your chances of being released any time soon aren't very good, and the odds of you ever being given permanent custody are probably nil. But if you think she's safe where she is and that it isn't worth the risk to give her up, just don't tell anyone where she is."

"But then I might not ever see her again."

"You have to decide if keeping her out of your ex-husband's hands is worth that."

Ruth needed to reach deep inside to answer that question. Winning custody for the sake of winning was Skip's game. "He beats her, hard enough to leave bruises. She hates being there."

"I can make sure that social services understands your concerns. They might be able to place her in a temporary shelter until the charges are resolved. But then it's going to be up to the court to look at everything again."

"They don't care about her. Nobody loves her but me."

"Maybe that's your answer then," Elena said calmly.

"To keep her hidden?" The tears poured again as Ruth weighed the ramifications of that choice.

"I was actually thinking that you should fight for her. If you're really the only one who loves her, it seems like she needs for you to do that," she explained. "And the bribery thing might work in your favor."

"How?"

"I think at the very least, you'll get a different judge. I have to be honest, though. The kidnapping charge is going to work against you. But we can probably leverage what we have on Drummond Appliances to get some concessions from your ex. I like to see people like that do time, but we'll bend to get the best outcome for your daughter."

"Thank you."

"You're welcome."

"No, really, Elena. I appreciate all that you're doing here. I know that Jessie and I really aren't your concern."

The IRS agent chuckled. "That's where you're wrong. Spencer is my concern, and what you did for her makes you my concern too."

That's exactly what Spencer had said. As Ruth had noticed that day on the Mall, Elena softened at the mention of her ex-lover's name, and her brown eyes sparkled. "You really love Spencer, don't you?"

"She told you?"

"Yes."

"I love her more than I realized. I've been such an idiot. I can't believe I . . . well, at least now we have another chance."

Ruth drew a shallow breath as she fought the mounting pressure in her chest, an inevitable despair sinking deep into the pit of her stomach. *Spencer and Elena.* She opened her mouth to speak, but the words wouldn't come. Pushing back from the table, she stood.

"I need to fight for my little girl, Elena. Can you find out from Spencer where she is?"

"Of course."

"And, uh . . . tell Spencer I said thanks for everything and good luck."

Chapter 29

"Your lawyer's here, ma'am." Ruth looked up as the woman unlocked her cell and swung the door open. This deputy was one of the friendly ones, she remembered. She had found out right away that Skip had a number of friends in the sheriff's department, and they made certain that her stay in the Somerset County Jail was as miserable as it could be.

"Finally," she grumbled. She had been sitting in jail for six days after her arraignment awaiting a chance to go over the details of her case with her court-appointed attorney. He was backed up with other clients, he explained. But he guaranteed his full attention when her time came. He thought he might be able to negotiate a guilty plea in exchange for time served and probation. That would leave her with a felony record, but at least she would be free.

Once she got out of jail, she would have to hire a family

lawyer to help get Jessie back. For that, she had to get back on her feet with a job and a place to live. Luckily, she still had over seven thousand dollars stashed at the trailer in Manassas and had gotten word to Viv to collect it for safekeeping. It was unlikely that Ruth would be allowed to leave the state of Maine anytime soon.

In the meantime, she was grateful that Elena had come through for her on getting social services involved. Jessie was staying with Arlene, her friend from the bank, until custody was resolved. Over the weekend, Arlene had brought the little girl for a visit, but Ruth hoped she wouldn't have to come back to this place too many more times. Four-year-olds had no business being around a jail.

Ruth walked down the polished hallway with the deputy, stopping as the woman unlocked the door to a conference room and ushered her inside. Two men immediately stood to greet her—one, a familiar face; the other, a stranger.

"Thomas!" Ruth was glad to see the IRS agent again. He had visited three days ago to update her on what his agency was doing behind the scenes to build a case against Skip and Drummond Appliances. She credited Elena for the extra effort Thomas gave to keeping her informed. Technically, the IRS case didn't really concern her, but Elena had promised that they would work with prosecutors to get both the criminal and custody cases settled in Ruth's favor.

"Good morning, Ms. Ferguson. I have a lot of good news for you today."

"Good, I could use some." Ruth turned to face the stranger. He was a man of about forty, clean shaven with short brown hair that had been slicked and combed neatly. He was impeccably dressed and carried an expensive-looking briefcase.

"Ms. Ferguson, this is Will Cavanaugh. He's an attorney from Augusta and he wants to go over some of the details of your case with you."

"Pleased to meet you, Ms. Ferguson," the attorney said politely as the three took seats around the small conference table.

"Same here. I'll help you however I can." Ruth still wasn't clear on how Cavanaugh fit into the picture, but she figured it would come to light soon.

"Before we get started, I was asked to give you a message from Agent Diaz. She said to tell you that Spencer was released from the hospital yesterday afternoon and is recovering at Agent Diaz's home in Alexandria. I have a telephone number where you can reach her if you'd like to give her a call. And of course, you may reverse the charges."

Spencer. Ruth had spent way too many hours in her cell thinking about Spencer and how she was going to react to Elena's sudden epiphany about her feelings. That's what Spencer had said she wanted from Elena—a commitment. Ruth couldn't begrudge their happiness, but that didn't stop her from thinking that Elena's timing sucked. "How is she? Did Elena say?"

"I think she's doing well, but you should call her yourself if you really want to know."

"All right." Ruth doubted she would call. That would be awkward. "If you'll leave me the number . . ."

Agent Fennimore scribbled it on a pad and tore off the sheet for her. "Okay, I want to give you a little update on where we stand with the Drummonds. Judge Howard has resigned from the bench, but that's not going to save him from formal charges. There is a small window for leniency, provided he cooperates with our agency regarding the case against Drummond Appliances."

"I can't believe someone in his position would do something like that."

"Unfortunately, that sort of thing happens more than we like to think. This probably isn't his first bribe. People usually learn by word of mouth when judges are for sale."

Ruth shook her head in disgust. "What does it mean for me that he resigns?"

"Well, it guarantees a new hearing. In fact, once the attorney general starts looking into things, there may be a lot of other cases that get reopened too."

"So I get a new custody hearing and a new judge, right?"

"That's correct. But Mr. Cavanaugh and I have discussed a strategy for resolving both your criminal and custody issues, and perhaps the IRS charges against Drummond Appliances as well."

Ruth looked back at Cavanaugh, who was removing documents and forms from his briefcase. It seemed odd to her that the IRS would hire an attorney out of Augusta instead of bringing one of its own from Washington. Maybe that's because the IRS lawyers didn't know much about child custody law, she thought.

"Now, Drummond Appliances—or more specifically, your ex-husband—is admitting to the bribery charge, but he insists that he did so to ensure the well-being of his daughter. He cited the court's tendency to award custody to the mother except under the most extraordinary circumstances. We think he may be posturing for the papers. It seems to matter very much to Roland Drummond, Sr. how all of this is perceived by the community."

"No surprise there." Ruth thought Skip was a chip off the old block in that regard.

"Mr. Cavanaugh believes that with the right witnesses we could successfully counter any testimony that calls into question your fitness as a parent. I personally don't think it will ever come to that. Once we make our tax case, all of the officers of Drummond Appliances—that's Roland, Sr., Barbara, and Roland, Jr.—will probably be facing prison terms. I think it will be in their interest to pursue an alternative resolution, and that's where the issue of child custody comes in. We are prepared to make concessions in our case if it means you getting your daughter back."

"Thank you." Ruth leaned back in her chair and folded her arms across her chest. The idea of seeing all the Drummonds in jail brought a satisfied smirk to her face. She wondered how many people had made the mistake of underestimating the mild-mannered Thomas Fennimore. Beneath the unassuming bowtie and spectacles, this guy was a bulldog.

"So what happens now?"

"Now we need to get to work preparing your case. I want you to tell Mr. Cavanaugh your story."

The attorney pressed the button on his portable tape recorder and spoke for the first time since they began. "Start at the beginning, Ms. Ferguson—all the way back to the time when you and Roland Drummond, Jr. were married."

For the next three and a half hours, Ruth went through the story of her failed marriage; all the details she could recall about her ex-husband's physical and verbal abuse, the fear and hysteria Jessie experienced each time she was returned to her father, and the escape to Virginia. By the time she had gotten through the whole tale, her mood had soured, just as it did each time she dwelled too long on the dismal impact Skip Drummond had made on her life.

Cavanaugh put together a list of everyone Ruth could think of who could corroborate her claims that Jessie had been mistreated by her father or who might vouch for her parenting skills. His approach was thorough—almost excruciatingly so—Ruth thought when he finally turned off the recorder.

"Boy, I dread having to go through all this again when the public defender comes back."

Cavanaugh looked to the IRS agent in confusion.

Fennimore cleared his throat. "Uh, if Mr. Cavanaugh represents you, you won't require a public defender."

"I don't understand."

"I'll need to file a notice with the court regarding representation," Cavanaugh said. "The court will not appoint a public defender if you have hired another attorney."

"I see." Ruth was embarrassed by the circumstances, but obviously there had been a misunderstanding. "I'm afraid I'm not able to pay very much, Mr. Cavanaugh. I don't have a lot of money. When I explained my financial situation to the judge, he said I was eligible for a public defender."

Cavanaugh continued to wear a confused expression. "If there's been some sort of mistake . . ."

"No, not at all," Fennimore said. Turning to Ruth, he explained, "I was instructed by Agent Diaz to secure counsel who could work with our office on both the criminal charges and custody issues. That's why I chose Mr. Cavanaugh. I think he's our best bet for handling all of this. Of course, if you'd rather have a public defender . . ."

"It isn't that, Thomas. It's just that . . ." She turned to the attorney. "Would you be willing to have me pay some of your fee up front and maybe make payments on the rest? I don't even have a job right now."

"My fee has already been taken care of with a retainer."

"I don't understand." *Is the IRS footing the bill?* "Who's paying?"

"Spencer Rollins."

"How did she seem, Thomas?" Spencer kept her voice low so that Elena wouldn't hear the conversation from the kitchen downstairs. "Do you guys have any idea how long this is all going to take? I hate to think about her sitting in that jail all this time."

Spencer had been working on Ruth's behalf practically since the moment she came out of the anesthesia following her surgery. She had tried everything, from pressing Elena to intervene—*there was nothing more she could do*—to posting bail—*bail was denied because Ruth was a flight risk*—to hiring an attorney to work with Thomas to get the charges dropped and win back custody of Jessie. That's where things stood now.

"That better not be you talking to somebody, Spencer," Elena shouted from the stairs. When she entered the room, she spotted her friend on the phone. "Is that Thomas?"

Spencer nodded.

"Gimme." The agent held out her hand for the phone. "Thomas? How'd it go with Cavanaugh? Is this going to work out?" She grinned at her staffer's response and shot Spencer a thumbs-up. "That's what I like to hear. You'll keep us posted, right?" Elena motioned Spencer toward her king-sized bed. "All right, we'll catch you later. Good work."

Spencer grabbed at the phone in frustration, but the line was already dead.

"I sent you up here to rest, not to worry more about something you can't do anything else about. Thomas has it all under control." Elena pulled back the covers and fluffed the pillows.

"I know. I just feel awful for her. She did all this for me and then she ended up back in Maine in jail. And I can't do a thing to help her."

"You are helping her. Thomas says Cavanaugh's good. I know it's tough for her to be locked up right now, but this way's going to be better for Ruth in the long run. If things work out the way we've set it up, she gets the charges dropped, she gets her daughter back, and she isn't going to have to be looking over her shoulder every day for the rest of her life."

But is she ever going to forgive me?

"You promised me you'd rest, honey. Come on, get your clothes off and get in bed. You want me to rub your back awhile?"

"Sure." Spencer shrugged out of her jeans and T-shirt, tossing them onto the floor beside the bed. She added her bra to the pile and settled between the sheets on her stomach. Elena's slender hands went to work on her warm skin.

"How's this?"

"Mmmm . . . feels good."

The Latina woman's fingers worked the tight muscles near the spine and Spencer felt her whole body relax. Before long, the hands flattened and sensuously stroked the ripples and curves of her back.

"It's nice to have you here, Spence. I'd forgotten how easy it was to spend time with you . . . just the two of us."

"Mmm . . . nice."

"I've missed you."

Spencer stiffened as she felt Elena's soft lips on her shoulder. "Elena?"

"I was crazy to let you walk away from me."

"No, you weren't." Spencer rolled over, simultaneously pulling up the sheet to cover her breasts. "You were right about us. I wasn't ready for that and neither were you."

"But I'm ready now, sweetheart. I'll give you anything you want." Elena leaned down and buried her face in Spencer's neck. "I can't believe I almost lost you."

"Oh, Elena." Those were the words Spencer had wanted to hear seven years ago, but her heart had moved on. "I love you. I'm always going to love you . . ."

"Shhhh . . . get some sleep, baby. I'm so glad to have you back."

This time, it was Spencer who wasn't going to be able say yes. She had already lost her heart to someone else.

Ruth sat on her cot, her hands shaking as she looked at the phone number on the scrap of paper. This wasn't a call she could avoid. She needed to know for her own peace of mind that Spencer really was going to be all right. Also, she needed to say thanks for all the work Elena and Thomas were doing, and for

Will Cavanaugh.

Alone in the women's wing, she could hear the other inmates being escorted back to their cells after visiting hours. She had asked earlier to use the phone, and the deputy on duty tonight had offered to allow her in the day room once the others cleared out. He would come for her soon.

Today was the first day since Ruth had been arrested that she felt as though she was making headway. Her time with Thomas and Cavanaugh had been productive. They were both confident that she would walk out of jail without even going to trial, perhaps as early as next week. And the best news was Cavanaugh was almost positive he could get Jessie placed with her permanently, with only limited visitation for Skip. Ruth figured if that happened, Skip would probably just disappear from their lives altogether. She would even waive child support if it meant no more contact with Skip.

"Still want to make that call?"

Ruth's stomach dropped as she stood. She followed the deputy into the day room, heading for the pay phone as he took a seat at a table across the room. *So much for privacy.*

She placed the collect call and waited.

"Hello."

"Elena?"

"That's right. Is this Ruth?"

"Yeah, it's me."

"Hey! I got a good report from Thomas this afternoon. He says your new attorney is a real crackerjack."

"He seems to be. Listen, I want to thank you and Thomas for everything you're doing. I know it's a lot more than you guys are supposed to do, but I really appreciate it."

"Don't thank me. I'm just following Spencer's orders."

"Then maybe I should thank Spencer too. Is she there?"

"Yeah, she's in bed already but I don't think she's asleep."

"Don't wake her if she is." Ruth thought for a second she

might get a reprieve, but it wasn't to be.

"Hello."

"Hey, Spencer."

"Ruth . . . how are you?"

"I'm okay, but I should be asking you that. You're the one that got shot."

"I'm fine. That bullet was nothing compared to all the pain Viv put me through with her chores."

Ruth laughed softly, glad that Spencer had lightened things up. "I wanted to say thank you for all the help. I don't think I've ever had this many people in my corner before, and it really means a lot."

"I told you I'd do everything I could."

"And you were true to your word. That sort of thing looks good on a résumé."

Now it was Spencer's turn to laugh. "I'll put it up there with those other things."

"Look, I don't have much time. I just wanted to see how you were doing and to tell you how much I appreciate everything. If things work out with Jessie, I . . . think I'm going to try to get my job back at the bank."

Spencer was so quiet Ruth worried they'd gotten disconnected.

"You mean you don't think you'll come back to Manassas?"

"I don't think so. I think I should stay here. My family's here . . . maybe we can work things out."

"Ruth, are you sure about this?"

"Yeah. I've been thinking about it a lot." Spencer didn't answer at all this time. "So . . . I have to go. The guard's waiting for me. I really want to thank you for everything. I'm glad Jessie and I had the chance to know you."

"Ruth . . . please call me again when you get out."

"Okay, sure." Ruth knew she wouldn't. It would be too hard to go through this again.

Spencer rolled over to look at the digital clock—3:14. Elena lay beside her in the bed, nude, but on the far side with her back turned. Spencer had put on a pair of pajamas left over from her hospital stay.

She was sick about her conversation with Ruth. She hadn't been able to say how she really felt with Elena in the room. That situation was awkward enough without bringing Ruth into the picture.

But what did it matter anyway? Whatever feelings she and Ruth had shared at the trailer were gone. At least, they were gone for Ruth.

Chapter 30

Spencer turned the old Chevy Cavalier onto the dirt road and stopped to collect her mail from the row of boxes. A half mile ahead, the road ended at what used to be the Rollins property, a sprawling three acres with an expansive view of Jordan Lake.

Spencer had swapped the coveted vista where her parents' house had once stood for a wooded lot on a cove with a three-bedroom cabin. She had hired out the renovations to one of her neighbors, a contractor who remodeled the kitchen and baths, updated all the wiring and added insulation for year-round comfort. The finishing touches were a dock for the boat she didn't yet own and a gazebo for the parties she would probably never have.

But the cabin was now home. In February, she finished her first six weeks of training in Albany, Georgia, after which she started her new job as a criminal investigator with the IRS, applying her programming skills to the hunt for business fraud. That had been Chad's idea, one that her best friend had enthusiastically supported. The disappointment—at least for Elena—had been Spencer's request to be stationed permanently at the field office in Raleigh.

She needed a new start, and here she had it. Special Agent Spencer Rollins had a new career, a new home and a new Kawasaki. And if she ever decided that she wanted to try picking up chicks again . . . well, now she had a gun, too.

The programmer grinned as she turned into her dirt driveway, immediately recognizing Elena's Audi sedan. Her friend had been noncommittal about the invitation to spend the weekend at the lake, so she was pleasantly surprised. They had gone through a rough patch right after the shooting, when Elena had confessed that her romantic feelings for Spencer had reignited. She was ready to finally commit, she had said, to make all the promises her former lover needed to hear.

But Spencer knew for certain that her feelings for Elena had settled for good in the realm of friendship. The love she felt—that she would always feel for Elena—was not the romantic love she had once had. Nor was it desirous in the physical sense. The flame between them was gone.

"You made it!" Spencer entered through the sliding glass door by the carport to find Elena coming in from the screened-in back porch. In three quick steps, they were hugging fiercely.

"It's good to see you," Elena said.

"You too! How long can you stay?" Spencer had offered to take a couple of days off if Elena wanted to spend a few days at the lake.

"I'm actually not staying," her visitor replied sheepishly.

"What? What do you mean you're not staying? Are you here for work?"

"No, I just came down to talk to you about something important."

Spencer lost her smile. "Are you okay? Is everything all right?"

"Yeah, yeah, I'm fine. Nothing's wrong."

"Then what?" Spencer followed Elena to the leather sofa and sat close, wanting an explanation before her heart jumped out of her chest.

"I figured out something recently and I wanted to come share my revelation."

Spencer was intrigued, but she was growing impatient. "What?"

"See, when things chilled with us after you got shot, I kind of figured you were still under a lot of stress about having to hide and about Henry being killed." She patted her friend's hand. That was still very difficult for Spencer to talk about. "And then there was all the testimony and worrying about Ruth."

Spencer sighed. "It was tough, Elena. But being down here has helped." She caught the look of resignation on the agent's face. "It's been hard to be here without you, though. I miss seeing you and talking to you every day like we used to."

"I miss it too . . . but I'll live. Sure, you crushed my heart like a bug, but I'm a survivor."

The blue-eyed woman cracked a smile at her friend's jibe.

"Anyway, what finally occurred to me is that you were shooting me down because you were hung up on somebody else, and that's what I came all the way down here to talk about."

That her words lingered there unchallenged was all the confirmation she needed.

"Why didn't you tell me about Ruth?"

The programmer squirmed uncomfortably, unable to meet her friend's eyes. "It didn't make any difference. It turned out she didn't feel the same way. How did you know?"

"I ran into her a couple of weeks ago at the FBI building. I was over there to see a friend of mine, who happened to be collecting testimony on the agent that picked her up, the one they arrested."

"I was wondering if she'd have to come back to testify." Spencer had spent days with the FBI going over the details of the case. She was the star witness in the upcoming federal trial for the Margadon conspirators, all of whom faced charges ranging from embezzlement to murder.

"Not only did she come back, she's living in that trailer in Manassas again."

Spencer's face registered genuine surprise. "What happened? The last time I talked to her, she said she was going to try to get her job back at the bank in Maine."

"I guess that didn't work out. She said that her ex still had a lot of friends that were giving her a hard time. And I got the feeling things weren't too good with her folks either."

Just hearing Ruth's name again caused Spencer's spirits to drop. She had spent a lot of time thinking about how things had turned out, wondering why Ruth's feelings had changed so suddenly. There were lots of reasons for that, Spencer had told herself. Women didn't just wake up in the morning and decide to be lesbians. Or maybe she thought her association with Spencer would compromise her chances for winning permanent custody of Jessie. She didn't doubt that Ruth blamed her for bringing all of the problems to her doorstep in the first place. Add to that the fact that Spencer had promised her that Elena would help. Instead, she had been sent back to Maine in handcuffs.

In a deal with prosecutors, the kidnapping charges were dropped. The Drummonds pleaded guilty to tax fraud, avoiding prison in exchange for coming clean about Ruth's care of her daughter. They paid a heavy fine to the IRS, and in the end, Skip relinquished all claim to Jessie Riane Drummond, forever closing that unfortunate chapter of his life.

Spencer knew the details thanks to Thomas Fennimore, whom she had called every week until the case was resolved. She had bypassed Elena with her questions, thinking it best not to hurt her further by raising suspicions about her feelings for Ruth, since it looked like nothing was to come of it anyway.

Spencer shook her head. "I'm glad she got out of there. She deserves a lot better than that."

"Well, she asked about you, and I told her you'd gone to work with the IRS and that you moved down here. She seemed pretty surprised to hear that."

"Why would she be surprised?"

"Because I think she thought you were living with me."

"Why would—"

"Don't stop me now! I'm getting to the good part."

Spencer threw herself against the couch back in frustration. She thought she heard someone laughing outside but when she strained to listen, it stopped.

"You remember that morning in the hospital after you'd been shot? How you insisted I leave you and go see about Ruth?"

Spencer nodded.

"Well, I did. And we talked about her options with her daughter, and what our office would try to do to help, just like I said I would. Somewhere in the middle of that conversation, she asked me how I felt about you. I told her that I loved you and that I was glad I was going to get another chance to show you how much."

Did Ruth really think she would just go back with Elena? *She might have . . . since I was too chicken to tell her I was in love with her.*

"I didn't know you two had feelings for each other. You should have told me."

"It wasn't something either of us really had a handle on. It was just a really stressful time for both of us. I think she just let her emotions get carried away."

Out back, a dog began to bark and a child's voice got louder. "Go get it, Willy!"

"I think it was more than that, Spence." Elena held out her hand and led her friend to the back porch, Spencer hoping against hope that she would see what she wanted to see. There by the door were two large duffle bags, a plastic knapsack, and a Lisa doll. "She risked a lot for you. It had to mean something to her."

"I'll be damned!" Spencer whispered.

"As you can see, I brought you a couple of visitors. I don't think she's figured out what she wants yet, but I thought she ought to take a break from worrying for a while and look at all the possibilities." Elena saw the growing smile on her friend's face as she absorbed the scene in the back yard. "I told her I'd be back to pick her up in a week or two, or whenever you called. Her car's broken down so—"

"And if I don't call?"

"If you don't call, then I'll figure it out." Elena chuckled. "I'm going to head out of here now and give you guys some space. Is that okay?" She was still holding her former lover's hand and she gave it a squeeze.

"You don't have to go, you know."

"Yes, I do. I've gotten on with my life, Agent Rollins. I'll have you know I have a date tomorrow to do the Museum of Natural History."

"With who?" Spencer didn't believe her for a minute.

"Her name's Jill Burke. She's FBI."

"You like her?"

"Yeah. But she won't sleep with me and it's driving me crazy."

"Now that's a woman I'm going to have to meet."

"Good! You can tell her what she's missing." Elena gave her old friend a strong hug and took her leave out the sliding glass door, knowing from the look on Spencer's face that the part about getting on with her life needed to be true.

Spencer walked out on the porch to watch the laughing child play fetch with a chocolate Labrador.

∞

Ruth tapped her toe on the gazebo's wooden floor, rocking the swing in a steady rhythm. She had heard the car pull up and knew Spencer was now inside with Elena. She was anxious about seeing Spencer again, but Elena had been adamant that she and Jessie should come for a visit.

Ruth and her daughter had arrived back in Virginia three weeks ago after learning from Viv that the trailer was still vacant. Manassas felt more like home than Madison, and it was a good time to make a permanent change. Already, she had gone for a couple of job interviews at local banks, and Jessie was set to start kindergarten in the fall.

She was genuinely surprised to learn that Spencer and Elena hadn't gotten back together after all, especially since it was obvious they cared so much for each other. But when she learned about Spencer's career change and the move back to her home state, Ruth could have kicked herself. By cooling things with Spencer when she was in jail, she had probably missed her chance to see if their feelings for each other could have grown into something more. That's what they had both said they wanted that night back at the trailer.

But it was too late to just call her and say it was all a misunderstanding. Then Elena came by a few days later to say that she was driving down to North Carolina to see Spencer on Friday and thought she and Jessie should come along.

"She'll be glad to see you."

"I don't know about that. We sort of lost touch after I went back."

"Do you really not want to see her again, or are you worried about how she's going to feel?"

"I want to see her, but I should have called her when I got out and I didn't."

"Believe me, Spencer doesn't hold on to things like that. Tell you what—you and Jessie ride down with me on Friday. If you don't feel welcome, we'll turn around and come back. Nothing to lose."

Ruth considered the offer, but she was afraid to take a chance.

"Are you ever going to forgive yourself if you don't at least find out where things stand?"

That's when Ruth realized that Elena understood her feelings for Spencer. And if the woman who knew Spencer best thought it was a good idea for her to go, then maybe she should.

"Spencer!" Jessie saw her first and made a beeline to where she stood, the excited puppy nipping at her heels.

Spencer caught the little girl on the run and swung her high in the air. "I missed you!"

Ruth got up slowly from the swing, marveling at how lovely and relaxed the woman appeared here at her lakeside home. She walked over to join Spencer and Jessie, smiling nervously and secretly wishing for a similar reception.

Spencer balanced the child on her hip and held out an arm to bring the mother into the circle, hugging her tightly—very tightly. "I missed you, too," she said, her voice filled with emotion.

Ruth basked in the warm reception, very nearly crying when she felt Spencer's lips press hard to her temple. This was a whole lot more than she had hoped for, a whole lot more than she thought she deserved. Her arms went around Spencer's waist and she held on as if the woman was her lifeline.

The vibrant Labrador impatiently clawed at their legs, jealous and excited to meet the newcomer.

"And this is Willy?"

"Look how big he is!" Jessie boasted.

"He sure is. And so are you!"

Like they'd never missed a beat, Spencer took Ruth's hand and wove their fingers together, turning toward the boat dock. "I hear you've gone back to the trailer."

"Yeah, for now. We just . . . we didn't belong in Madison anymore."

"I'm sorry that didn't work out."

Ruth shrugged. "I'm not."

Okay, I'm not either. "How's Viv?"

"She's great. She and Jerry are getting married in July. Her house is up for sale, so I guess we won't be able to stay at the trailer much longer."

"Viv and Jerry are getting married?"

"Can you believe it? She said they really got to know each other last year when all that happened with you and Jessie while I was in jail."

"Tough times have a way of bringing people together."

"You mean like us?"

"Yeah, like us," Spencer agreed, squeezing the fingers.

Ruth wouldn't let herself read too much into that, but her heart wanted to cling to the hope that Spencer wanted her and Jessie around. Even in these few minutes since they'd been reunited, her feelings for the woman had rushed back full force.

"Elena said you hadn't found a job yet."

Ruth nodded. "I had a couple of interviews, but I haven't heard back."

"Maybe you ought to look around here. This is a nice area. It's beautiful and the schools are great." Spencer stopped and turned toward the young mother, still hugging Jessie close. "Try it out, Ruth. I've got plenty of room here for both of you if you'll stay."

"Can we stay with Spencer, Mommy?" Jessie already liked it, especially the lake. "I mean may we?"

That got a laugh from both women, though Ruth blushed at her daughter's forward request.

"We'll see, honey."

Spencer tossed an eyebrow, no more satisfied with that answer than Jessie had been.

"Spencer and I have to talk about it." They also had to answer a lot of complicated questions about where they might go from here. "Maybe we can stay and see if we like it."

"I think that's a good idea," Spencer said.

"But I don't want us to wear out our welcome."

"That isn't going to happen here, Ruth. You can take all the time you need to sort things out, to see what you and Jessie want. I think you'll like it here."

Jessie had had enough of this grownup talk. Willy wanted to play with the ball again and she squirmed in Spencer's arm to get down.

"And what about what you want?" Ruth asked seriously.

Spencer pulled her into an embrace and looked her right in the eye. "I want what I've wanted since that morning you left the trailer—I want you and Jessie back in my life. We don't have to make any big decisions right this minute. We can do exactly what we said . . . take it slow and see where it goes. All you have to do is ask yourself where you want to be right now."

Ruth stretched up and touched her lips gently to Spencer's. "I want to be with you."

COYOTE SKY by Gerri Hill. 248 pp. Sheriff Lee Foxx is trying to cope with the realization that she has fallen in love for the first time. And fallen for author Kate Winters, who is technically unavailable. Will Lee fight to keep Kate in Coyote?
1-59493-065-1 $13.95

VOICES OF THE HEART by Frankie J. Jones. 264 pp. A series of events force Erin to swear off love as she tries to break away from the woman of her dreams. Will Erin ever find the key to her future happiness?   1-59493-068-6 $13.95

SHELTER FROM THE STORM by Peggy J. Herring. 296 pp. A story about family and getting reacquainted with one's past that shows that sometimes you don't appreciate what you have until you almost lose it.   1-59493-064-3 $13.95

WRITING MY LOVE by Claire McNab. 192 pp. Romance writer Vonny Smith believes she will be able to woo her editor Diana through her writing.   1-59493-063-5 $13.95

PAID IN FULL by Ann Roberts. 200 pp. Ari Adams will need to choose between the debts of the past and the promise of a happy future.   1-59493-059-7 $13.95

ROMANCING THE ZONE by Kenna White. 272 pp. Liz's world begins to crumble when a secret from her past returns to Ashton.   1-59493-060-0 $13.95

SIGN ON THE LINE by Jaime Clevenger. 204 pp. Alexis Getty, a flirtatious delivery driver is committed to finding the rightful owner of a mysterious package.
1-59493-052-X $13.95

END OF WATCH by Clare Baxter. 256 pp. LAPD Lieutenant L.A Franco Frank follows the lone clue down the unlit steps of memory to a final, unthinkable resolution.
1-59493-064-4 $13.95

BEHIND THE PINE CURTAIN by Gerri Hill. 280 pp. Jacqueline returns home after her father's death and comes face-to-face with her first crush.
1-59493-057-0 $13.95

18TH & CASTRO by Karin Kallmaker. 200 pp. First-time couplings and couples who know how to mix lust and love make 18th & Castro the hottest address in the city by the bay.   1-59493-066-X $13.95

JUST THIS ONCE by KG MacGregor. 200 pp. Mindful of the obligations back home that she must honor, Wynne Connelly struggles to resist the fascination and allure that a particular woman she meets on her business trip represents.
1-59493-087-2 $13.95

ANTICIPATION by Terri Breneman. 240 pp. Two women struggle to remain professional as they work together to find a serial killer.   1-59493-055-4 $13.95

OBSESSION by Jackie Calhoun. 240 pp. Lindsey's life is turned upside down when Sarah comes into the family nursery in search of perennials.   1-59493-058-9 $13.95

BENEATH THE WILLOW by Kenna White. 240 pp. A torch that still burns brightly even after twenty-five years threatens to consume two childhood friends.
1-59493-053-8 $13.95

SISTER LOST, SISTER FOUND by Jeanne G'fellers. 224 pp. The highly anticipated sequel to *No Sister of Mine.*   1-59493-056-2 $13.95

THE WEEKEND VISITOR by Jessica Thomas. 240 pp. In this latest Alex Peres mystery, Alex is asked to investigate an assault on a local woman but finds that her client may have more secrets than she lets on.   1-59493-054-6 $13.95

THE KILLING ROOM by Gerri Hill. 392 pp. How can two women forget and go their separate ways?   1-59493-050-3 $12.95

PASSIONATE KISSES by Megan Carter. 240 pp. Will two old friends run from love?
1-59493-051-1 $12.95

ALWAYS AND FOREVER by Lyn Denison. 224 pp. The girl next door turns Shannon's world upside down.   1-59493-049-X $12.95

BACK TALK by Saxon Bennett. 200 pp. Can a talk show host find love after heartbreak?   1-59493-028-7 $12.95

THE PERFECT VALENTINE: EROTIC LESBIAN VALENTINE STORIES edited by Barbara Johnson and Therese Szymanski—from Bella After Dark. 328 pp. Stories from the hottest writers around.   1-59493-061-9 $14.95

MURDER AT RANDOM by Claire McNab. 200 pp. The Sixth Denise Cleever Thriller. Denise realizes the fate of thousands is in her hands.   1-59493-047-3 $12.95

THE TIDES OF PASSION by Diana Tremain Braund. 240 pp. Will Susan be able to hold it all together and find the one woman who touches her soul?
1-59493-048-1 $12.95

JUST LIKE THAT by Karin Kallmaker. 240 pp. Disliking each other—and everything they stand for—even before they meet, Toni and Syrah find feelings can change, just like that.   1-59493-025-2 $12.95

WHEN FIRST WE PRACTICE by Therese Szymanski. 200 pp. Brett and Allie are once again caught in the middle of murder and intrigue.   1-59493-045-7 $12.95

REUNION by Jane Frances. 240 pp. Cathy Braithwaite seems to have it all: good looks, money and a thriving accounting practice . . .   1-59493-046-5 $12.95

BELL, BOOK & DYKE: NEW EXPLOITS OF MAGICAL LESBIANS by Kallmaker, Watts, Johnson and Szymanski. 360 pp. Reluctant witches, tempting spells and skyclad beauties—delve into the mysteries of love, lust and power in this quartet of novellas.   1-59493-023-6 $14.95

ARTIST'S DREAM by Gerri Hill. 320 pp. When Cassie meets Luke Winston, she can no longer deny her attraction to women . . .   1-59493-042-2 $12.95

NO EVIDENCE by Nancy Sanra. 240 pp. Private investigator Tally McGinnis once again returns to the horror-filled world of a serial killer.   1-59493-043-04 $12.95

WHEN LOVE FINDS A HOME by Megan Carter. 280 pp. What will it take for Anna and Rona to find their way back to each other again?   1-59493-041-4 $12.95

MEMORIES TO DIE FOR by Adrian Gold. 240 pp. Rachel attempts to avoid her attraction to the charms of Anna Sigurdson . . .   1-59493-038-4 $12.95

SILENT HEART by Claire McNab. 280 pp. Exotic lesbian romance.
1-59493-044-9 $12.95